Harvest
of the
Heart

Also by May Mellinger

CLOAK OF LAUGHTER

SPLINT ROAD

Harvest of the Heart

A NOVEL BY

May Mellinger

DAVID McKAY COMPANY, INC.
New York

To *that very special little girl*
my daughter, Mara

1.

CORY COOPER laboriously traced the letters on the first check she ever had written. It was in the amount of five hundred dollars and would be a down payment on her first home. Concentrating on this extraordinary effort, her deeply tanned face was impassive; both upbringing and the trace of Indian blood within her demanded that. Nevertheless, she gave fleeting thought to the fact that she had picked enough cotton and dragged it down the long rows to bury that small house many times over. The potatoes that had passed through her roughened hands would overflow the street on which it faced. The water with which she had washed down the walls and ceilings of the more fortunate would wash it from its flimsy foundation and slake a large field. Fourteen years she had saved to have this secret hoard. Now the Coopers need not be evicted again. She handed the check to Perry Taylor, and he gave her several papers on which she carefully wrote her name.

Her husband, Bert, would sign later in the places marked with an X. He was not enthusiastic about the house. He wanted something with a barn and a place for chickens. "I ain't looked at nothing with barns," she had told him. "We can't afford it, and I can't say as I care. If I never see another

[3]

chicken or hog or cow any way but cut up for fryin', it suits me fine!" Bert would grow to like the place, in time.

The children would finally have a place to come home to. Beau, who was fifteen, was working in a war plant, claiming to be eighteen, because he was big and did not care to go to school. His father heartily approved of the change; he did not hold with a lot of bookishness. It was 1944, and good jobs were easy to come by. Bert himself was a welder and made good wages. For once, he had plenty of beer. His back had not bothered him in this job half so much as it had in previous years, when he had picked cotton and mowed lawns and done all the worrisome things a man must do when married to a driving woman. He still said he did not like it out here in California; but Cory knew he would never go back to Oklahoma alone. She had made it clear to him that if he did return to his folks, he would do so without her or the children.

Ann Marie, the pretty, fast-developing youngest of the family, was easygoing and neighborly. Even at eleven, she would fit almost anywhere one dropped her, like a kitten.

What Starr, the thirteen-year-old, would feel about the move, probably no one would discover. She had not talked much for years. She read books. These days she observed high-school girls gravely—what they wore, how they spoke. She would enter high school in the fall and had been so far a brilliant student. High school was a strange world to Cory, who had dropped out of grammar school early and married at sixteen. Starr definitely would not be married at sixteen, her mother was positive.

Cory's children had never slopped pigs or killed hogs or gone barefooted for lack of shoes. These things she had changed for her own family, with her own strong back, agile hands, and dauntless determination. It was a triumph.

Walking tall and proud, Cory left the real-estate office and set about moving immediately.

Home was Number 45—a small house, made mostly of chicken wire and plaster. It sat on a narrow lot on narrow Angello Street, among fifty of its twins. It was a war-housing house, in a development born of the avaricious dreams of Perry Taylor, a real-estate man who had hungered during the depression and fattened with war—all on money furnished by his wife.

It was said of Perry Taylor that he was a sharp operator. But he seemed a benevolent man, plump and old. "I'd give things away to the needy if I could afford it," he often said in his own defense, "but a man has to think of his family. He works for his family—not himself." It sounded better than saying that he worked with frantic urgency to repay all he owed to his wife. He would be repaying her all his life, no matter how wealthy he grew; he knew that. But he did have some other projects in mind.

Only on Angello Street could one buy a house for five hundred dollars down, and small payments and large interest until long after the house surely should have fallen to pieces of its own cheap construction. "I make the down payment low, so people with small incomes can have a roof over their heads," Perry Taylor said in a deep voice to anyone who would listen—for he had hopes of being a county supervisor some day.

He never added that if a family got behind in its payments, the account was handed to an attorney, and that family was promptly evicted—which was a very, very frequent happening. In such distressing circumstances, Perry Taylor always instructed his secretary to tell the evicted that he was out of town. He did not like to waste time with them in depressing, futile talk. That was work for his attorney. He had to repaint the house and resell it. With property costs rising, there was always a bit of profit in the change of title. And as for those families who paid on and on, he obtained interest at the maximum rate from them. Eventually his investment in Angello Street would net him several times the amount he had thoughtfully gambled on it. Moreover, he was praised for initiating the very low down payment. It added luster to his civic importance. In civic and financial matters he was forging ahead fast, and he needed to do so, for the very contemplation of his domestic life made a lump like a vast indigestion somewhere inside of him.

The low down payment was deeply appreciated by the denizens of Angello Street. The plaster was hardly dry on a house before it was furiously inhabited by the ignorant, violent poor—all well supplied with ferocious children, who fought and screamed in the street while their parents worked. By day the only adults home on Angello Street were a few old grandmothers and grandfathers, gap-toothed, slow, and vindictive, and a few night workers trying to sleep in the broiling heat and the screaming. Occasionally they would pull back their shades and shout curses and obscenities at the children.

As soon as the Coopers were settled in Number 45, Cory began gathering the discarded bulbs and slips that were to make that yard bloom like no other on the street. Her sister, Artie, had given her a small daphne plant in a pot the previous Christmas, and this Cory planted beneath the front window, where it flourished, its delicate pointed leaves edged in pale yellow. In the spring, the plant was a puffball of wildly fragrant small clusters of blossoms, and to Cory it was a symbol of home.

Now at last the Coopers could have a dog and a cat—indulgences that were never permitted in rented houses. Most families did have a dog or cat here, but they were as apt as not to be used for sport or torture. Mr. Chotter, the Cooper cat, came to them as a drag-tail handful of kitten bones, and he grew in a matter of weeks into a magnificent young cat with a ruff about his neck and a great flowing plume of proud tail. The food budget had to be stretched to include pets, but Cory managed it. The children were loving and considerate of them.

As Starr watched one evening toward dusk, Mr. Chotter crossed the street hastily, being chased by a strange dog. Starr rose to her feet to assist him if need be. As he crossed the street, a hot-rod car that always entered Angello Street on two screaming wheels was upon him before he saw it. He turned frantically, and he would have escaped except that the driver of the car deliberately swerved to run him down. The car screamed on its way, trailing guffaws, and Mr. Chotter was a pulp of entrails and pitiful fur and blood on Angello Street. Starr went into the street sickened and pale, and gathered the bloody remains into a shoe box. Cory found her beside the box, wild with grief and indignation, rocking back and forth.

Endearments did not come easy to Cory. She patted Starr. "We'll get another cat," she said. Her voice was rough with sorrow.

"It won't be the same," Starr said, standing with her feet apart and her fists doubled.

Cory's words were weighted. "It's never the same," she said. "But we loved Mr. Chotter. It has to go somewheres.

[7]

You can't just stopper it up and let it turn sour. We'll bury Mr. Chotter here by the daphne. It's a pretty place." She found a spade and quickly dug the hole in the loose sand, while Starr wept steadily. They buried Mr. Chotter, and Cory said, "Come with me."

The pound master was used to tragedy. His expression did not change as the woman in dirty jeans led the sobbing, spindle-legged young girl down between the rows of cages. Puppies came wagging to the bars to inquire if these might be their folks. Older, more beautiful dogs, lost and condemned, looked sadly and turned away. They *knew* their folks.

Cats sat proud and disdainful and asked nothing, like rows of jewel-eyed philosophers. One mother cat groomed her young with the thin pink file of her tongue, insensible to other matters. Cory stopped before these, and a small puff of tiger-striped tan and red straddled his clumsy way to the edge of the wire and looked up at them with the blank blue eyes of the very new. He put his tiny briars of claws into the wire and tried to climb toward them. Starr wept and turned her eyes away, holding her arms tight to her narrow chest. "No cat could ever be the same," she reiterated. "He had to die because somebody was plain mean."

"He's not the same, but this kitten must die, too, unless someone's willing to look after him. They'll all have to die here, unless somebody wants them."

Starr shuddered at this house of death. "All of them?" she whispered.

"Yes. They do it quick, and the animals don't suffer. It's better than starving to death. You want we should take this little feller home—not to take Mr. Chotter's place, but just to feed?"

Tiger Q. Catt never was Mr. Chotter, or anything like him—but he established himself in love and used his considerable authority. And he did fill somewhat the hole left by Mr. Chotter. "When something dies, you have to look around quick and find something to take the place," Cory said, stroking Tiger Q. "It takes up time and keeps your mind from going back. Cat, dog—even a baby—you can't bring 'em back. But you can offer the place to somebody that needs it. It ain't no disrespect to the dead—it's the good in them, living on and put to use."

It was the same when the beautiful daphne plant died in full bloom, and they found that a gopher had eaten all its roots, leaving only a white round bleeding knob underground. Cory apportioned a dollar and a half from the grocery money to replace it with a spindly new plant. It was almost the same, in time.

Gradually the law and the social workers learned to shake their heads at the mention of Angello Street, but to the Coopers it was an enormous step forward. They were now people of property, with a flower garden, and paying taxes.

That first year, during the war, wages for cotton picking were good, and workers scarce. It was a temptation to keep the children from school to pick a lot and earn a greater measure of security, but Cory did not yield to it. Very little cotton was ready to pick before school started. But Cory went early to the fields when it did foam from the bolls. One could gain the advantage of the weight of dew in the early morning.

[9]

Certainly Starr Cooper's life was deeply influenced by Angello Street, but she never was quite assimilated by it. At first, when she was only thirteen, she would sometimes play run sheep run with the other children in the cooler evening; but she learned to go inside before dark. Some of the larger players had other games in mind.

In a detached fashion, she knew all the residents of the street, though the population was a shifting one. She knew the women in their gaudy satin best dresses, with their cheap, frizzy permanents. She knew the Bedeau family, who screamed and threw things. Ann Marie was always bosom friend or mortal enemy of Teresa Bedeau, a pixie-like child as sleek and slithering as a young eel—as sly a thief as lived on the street. David Bedeau, her brother, was old beyond his years, with a world-weary acceptance of violence and evil. Ann Marie admired his dark good looks; even his catlike indifference to the fate of others did not offend her.

In the first, prosperous years, there were plenty of bicycles and sleepy dolls and many guns and knives on Angello Street—over which the children fought terrible screaming wars. They slashed each other with rocks and broken bottles and even knives. Starr stood aloof from the violence.

A special hazard existed for the very young. An irrigation canal lay half a mile to the east. It ran swiftly down its deep concrete course to water the rich crops, and babies drowned in it from time to time—not only from Angello Street, but from the better regions of the town, through which the arrogant canal ran without cover or fence. There were no fences on Angello Street to confine babies. The unthinkable expense of fencing the whole canal did not even suggest itself to anyone living within range of the deadly rushing cool waters. And there was no scarcity of babies on Angello

Street. One did not miss a baby so much as the occasional big brother or sister who drowned in a desperate effort to save the baby.

On Saturday nights there would be many parties on Angello Street. Most broke up in fights and loud voices, so that it was good to be in the comparative safety of one's bed, listening to the sounds of laughter or fighting. Once there was a knifing. At least one boy with a proud new .22 for his birthday accidentally shot another through the foot.

The Whitcomb family was the only one as stable as the Coopers. They lived at the far end, where the street faded into sagebrush and sand, and the land belonged to the horned toads and to the gophers, as it had done since time pushed this valley out of an ancient sea.

Mrs. Whitcomb was in one sense much better off than any of the wives of Angello Street. Her husband had been killed in an industrial accident, and she and her family received a small pension as a result. It was much steadier than the wages of her late husband had been. True, it was not adequate, and she worked to supplement it. Her eldest son, Jerry, had recently quit school and gone to work. She said it was a shame he wouldn't finish school, but he wanted to make some money, and she couldn't blame him, what with his younger brothers and sisters and all.

Jerry knew that his mother did not care whether he finished school or not. He was eighteen now, and being clever with machinery and having a steady hand, he was a cat skinner. His wages would have made his late father's eyes bulge in disbelief. His father had been a whimpering little man abroad and a mean, tyrannical one at home. Jerry knew they were well rid of him.

Jerry himself was handsome. He cut quite a swath on Angello Street. He also walked other and better streets, but he was aware of the invisible wall. He could play with the fringe of the Cadillac set because he had money in his pocket and was handsome; but he would not be quite welcome there until he had made a fortune. He believed it was entirely possible. But until that time, he cultivated everyone. He was of Angello Street, and he attended movies and picnics and parties with his neighbors. His mother was a friend of Cory, and sometimes worked with her.

Jerry had ample opportunity to observe Starr, and he did so at length. She was not an easy companion, in his opinion; she read too much. Still, she showed some slight preference for his company. From the time she was fourteen, it was assumed that she was Jerry's girl. He was patient with her, for she had class. It would be hard to live up to, but it was what you had to have in a wife when you married.

Jerry had learned that, working for Jack Renford. He had been sent to grade some of Renford's multitudinous acres for planting. Renford drove over the dusty job in a Cad, careless of the beating the beautiful car took. He could be careless if he chose; he was immensely wealthy. He had not bothered to alter his manners or his atrocious grammar. He had come to these dust-ridden acres with nothing but the labor of his hands, and he had taken some land in payment for labor during the depression, when his employer could not pay in money. The acres he accepted had yielded rich oil, which led to transport companies, construction interests—and a membership in whatever social set he chose to honor in Statsville. Even the Stats themselves referred to him as a rough jewel—though they certainly would have omitted the jewel part if he had not been a ruthlessly able businessman. He wore a diamond ring. He strode his acres with a red face and a bull-like bellow, and he could have bought and sold some of the Stats. Some feared he might do so.

But Renford had made one grave error. He had been shrewd enough to pension off his old wife, who dipped snuff and went barefooted. He gave her more money than she ever dreamed existed. But then he turned right around and married the first little nobody who had flipped a provocative hip at him. He could have done a thousand times better.

Linella Renford, the new wife, drove with Renford on many of his inspection trips, and Jerry wondered who watched who. When she left the car, her dress slid above her pretty knees, and she had a roll to her walk that struck some familiar memory—oh, the walk put on by Starr Cooper's sister, Ann Marie. No use to think about Ann Marie. She oozed excitement through her pores, but she had no class. And neither did Linella Renford. Jerry planned to do better.

He liked to fish and to eat—he was not a man of many words or great complexity. He enjoyed drinking, but knew it was rash. He worked steadily and enjoyed his own popularity. He teased Starr and occasionally escorted her to a movie. He never took her to rough places—no rougher than Angello Street, at any rate—or introduced her to young men who might try to jump his claim on her. Now and then he kissed her; but he was not one to talk a lot of mush. He was more ardent with girls he met on other streets.

Some of the women on Angello Street thought Jerry's small attentions to Starr romantic. Teresa Bedeau, though, who panted if you breathed down her little dark dirty neck, asked Jerry if he ever "got next" to Starr, and Jerry slapped her. Teresa backed away. "I bet you think you will, though," she mocked. Her curiosity was like a virus, intruding everywhere. "I bet you a dollar you can't," she said maliciously. "She thinks she's a princess!"

Starr herself scarcely ever heard of such things. She was not perturbed by her unfortunate address. It was a proud thing to have a home to come back to—theirs so long as they paid every month. Her studies took most of her evenings, for it was not easy being a brain in such a large school. Summers she worked at whatever she could find to do, to make money for clothes to wear to school. What spare time she had, she used for reading. The gap between the reality of Angello Street and the wide streets of which she read—the difference between her neighbors and the beautifully fortunate women of the magazine stories did not disturb her. These were separate things. Just as the life at school, where she held offices requiring a lot of work, was quite separate from life among her neighbors. At school the boys were at least usually respectful; on Angello Street they grabbed. She viewed the entirety of the boys on Angello Street as one composite octopus with arms beckoning and dragging the girls toward sex. It was a nuisance, but a fact, and one with which she had grown up. She simply avoided all the boys except Jerry, whom she could trust. Someday she might marry him. She could think of no one else who might be inoffensive enough to have around the house.

Not that he was entirely satisfactory. Like her father, he did not enjoy talk; and Starr wanted to talk and to listen. It seemed to her that sometimes she would simply burst with ideas and questions never expressed. Sometimes when she was coming home from a movie with Jerry, she would begin, "Jerry, don't you think—"

But Jerry would say, "Baby, I don't think much, and I don't talk about it." He would put his arm about her and kiss her, which was interesting, and even sometimes thrilling. But just the same, she went on thinking. Once she wrote some of the thoughts in a composition book, and Teresa Bedeau and Ann Marie found it and read it aloud. She had written: "A person ought to be allowed to live in peace as long as he doesn't hurt anyone. Fighting and howling hurt inside more than ever shows outside, and make you quiver a long time. It's like being burned."

"My God!" Teresa said in loud wonderment, "I thought this was a diary, and we'd find out what *happens* to Starr. They ain't a word in it about boys—not even Jerry!"

Starr took the book and tore it in two, and dropped it into the wastebasket. "In case nobody told you, Teresa—and I *know* somebody's told you, Ann Marie—it isn't nice to prowl through other people's things. Now you both keep your hands out of the one drawer I can call my own."

"But we didn't find out nothin'," Teresa said, wide-eyed.

"Not because you didn't try," Starr said. But she was not so much angry at the invasion of her privacy, as she was sad that she might as well have written in a foreign tongue. But thoughts were wayward things, and maybe each person suffered his own in his separate loneliness.

Once Starr paid a hard-earned dollar for a picture of an ocean wave breaking on a beach. She had never seen the ocean, but just to look at the picture made her feel cooler on a hot day. Bert said it was a waste of money. "Waste not, want not," he quoted, as he very often did, in spite of being the only wasteful member of the family.

[15]

Starr let the sentence flow past. She imagined herself curled on the clean sand by the cool wave forever about to break and never breaking. She hung it near her bed in the living room—or what would have been the living room if she and Ann Marie had not used it for a bedroom. Beau slept in the dining room on a couch; Cory and Bert had the one bedroom. The picture of the wave was very personally Starr's own property. Other members of the family seemed hardly to notice it.

When Starr studied at home, she sat where she could look up to rest her eyes on the wave, and every year it seemed more a friend. When she was a senior in high school, it was part of her life.

Christmas in 1947 was not so rich a time as previous ones. Bert's back had suffered greatly since the end of his welding job, and Cory carried most of the financial load. Beau now worked as a roughneck in the oil fields, and he made good wages, but only a trickle of his money found its way into the household. Bert said he should pay more for board and room.

Cory said she thought Beau paid plenty. She could not bear the thought of his going away and living among strangers. Who would wash and starch and iron his shirts and work pants until they looked brand new every day? No. Cory and her telephone could always find work. But she was not smiling very much that Christmas. She had circles beneath her eyes.

On Christmas Eve Beau disappeared into festivities of which his family knew nothing, and Bert went out with some of his Angello Street cronies and got drunk. Starr was asleep beneath the picture of the wave when her father returned, but his falling about awakened her. Cory was

[16]

trying to get his shoes off and get him quietly into bed. He was singing and resisting Cory's aid, tilted on the edgy difference between being singing drunk and sullen drunk. Starr went to see if she might help.

Her father was pushing a hand into Cory's face, and Cory caught off balance trying to help him, fell awkwardly, striking a chair as she fell. It was not the first time Starr had seen Bert slap Cory about, but somehow this time her anger rose and made a hurting lump in her throat. She ran to her mother.

Cory's face was crumpled with repressed tears. She raised herself to her knees, and Starr helped her to her feet. One eye was puffing with a blue bruise. "He didn't know what he was doin'," Cory said quickly. "It was an accident, like. He ain't hisself right now." She steadied herself against Starr's arm, and Starr looked at her father. She hated him.

"If he's not himself, what's he doing here?" she asked. "Whoever he is, why doesn't he go somewhere else?"

"Starr!" Cory said, shocked. "He's your father!" She put a hand to her discolored eye. "He'll be sorry tomorrow. Sorry as can be!"

Bert stared back at her with glazed animal eyes. "Interferin' womenfolks," he said thickly. "Man can't have a lil. . . ." He slid to the floor asleep. Starr continued to look at him—his mouth open, his beard dark on his face. He looked like any tramp.

Cory tugged at her arm. "Don't think ill of him," she said. "He don't mean me no harm."

"I hate him," Starr said, almost dispassionately. "I hate him for every time he ever hurt you. I hate his nothingness; I hate everything he is, was, or ever will be! I'm sorry he's my father!"

Cory stood tall, and her glance was intimidating. "Don't let me hear you say such things!" she said. Starr looked steadily at her, and she burst into tears. Starr led her to the kitchen and they bathed the eye to no avail.

"I do feel a mite low in my own mind," Cory said finally. "I been elected to have another baby, come June. Your pa don't know."

"Nor care," Starr said, holding one hand tight in another against her old flannel nightgown.

"A baby's mighty important, but it thins down a woman's work. I'd hate to get down, with you finishing school and all. And it costs, of course." Cory was apologizing to Starr!

It embarrassed her. "Make no mind," she said to Cory, in her own words. She could do more housework and study later; she didn't really need to buy anything else this year; she still had fifteen dollars left from last summer's work.

When Cory was in bed, and the lights all out once more, Starr lifted the shade and looked at the night sky. The sounds of revelry on Angello Street had thinned away, and a wind tossed the sea of bare branches on the trees that grew near the river bed. What was once a river was now a long narrow desert of white sand, bordered by woods. These woods rested the eyes and the spirit in a land of few trees. "Dear God," Starr said in the general direction of the tossing treetops, "help us to help each other! It's liable to be so hard." She did not know much about praying, but surely a prayer ought to find its way better on Christmas Eve.

Starr had only a few more months to go to high school. She knew her way about the campus. She was always on the honor roll, and sometimes on committees. She never went to the dances and parties of the Cad set, of course.

One of the pleasantest things in all high school was her occasional work with Dashell Taylor, who was president of the student body. She was not fool enough to have a crush on him. He was the most popular, most handsome boy in school. He was the son of Perry Taylor, who owned their house. He managed the football team and was a pole vaulter of local renown. But his most endearing feature was his smile. It was always personal—especially for the recipient, whether teacher or schoolmate or friend—and it warmed each one who received it. Watching Dash in study periods, Starr recognized that actually his face was sad—almost sullen—in repose, and perhaps it was the contrast that made the difference. When someone touched his shoulder, in the flick of an eyelash he came up from a dream of sorrow with that special smile.

Where Dash passed through a crowd of students, an almost inaudible wake of sighs ran after, like a breeze whispering through a forest. Prince Charming passed this way, it said; there is no Prince Charming, of course—but it looked like him.

And Dash never seemed to notice.

Whenever Starr had business to discuss with him, he gave her his full, courtly attention and helped as if it were always a particular delight to work with her. She was quick enough to agree with Ann Marie's adoring comment on Dash: "Don't you think he's simply too *dreamy?*"

"Of course," Starr said. "But *everyone* thinks he's wonderful. He is!"

"Are you sweet on him?"

"Silly! He belongs to Priss Walker—he always has, I guess. But I'm glad we're in the same class. He's nice to work with; he's nice to know." There was no use trying to explain to Ann Marie that the world was full of things one might admire and enjoy, and yet never have to keep. It was wonderful that larks sat on the barbed-wire fences and sang; the black lace frameworks above oil wells were beautiful against a sunset sky; it was also a joyous thing that Dashell Taylor lived in the world. It added to the pleasure of living; that was all.

For that matter, Priscilla Walker was something to see. Dash couldn't have happened to a prettier girl. Her father owned sleek herds of expensive cattle and great frothing acres of cotton. Starr had picked cotton in the long rows of his fields. Priss was small and golden and beautiful. She wore sweaters softer than a rabbit's ears, and skirts that cost a whole semester's wardrobe for Starr. She had a cascade of golden hair worn in a perky horsetail, and she was a study in motion. Her eyes danced, her feet danced, her hands forever anticipated her speech. She mourned that her selfish father let her have only a two-year-old Buick instead of a Cad. It held a laughing array of classmates as she zoomed from place to place.

Priss was as popular as Dash. They were an envied twosome. She was not above trying her power on Dash, however. When he assumed that he was taking her to the Senior Prom, she was coy and said she had not decided yet.

"Then I'll get another date," Dash said in quick, almost thoughtless retaliation. Starr was passing, between classes. He smiled and fell into step beside her.

Starr supposed this was something to do with the seating of parents at graduation. That was part of her job. She had casually noted Priss, pouting and pretty, but it meant nothing to her. Priss pouted so attractively, she often did it for effect.

"Are you going to the prom, Starr?" Dashell asked.

Starr had never been to any of the dances or parties; to her the dances offered only a fleeting wistfulness. "I hadn't thought of it," she said cautiously.

"Why don't you think of it, and let me pick you up for it?" he asked. He smiled and stood waiting.

Involuntarily Starr glanced back at Priss, still watching them. Priss turned on her heel and walked away. "But I thought you and Priss always ..." she began, overcome with shyness.

"Couldn't I call for you about eight—if you haven't made a date already, of course?"

"Oh, no! I mean I haven't any date," Starr said confusedly. "I'd love to go, of course. I never went to a prom before."

"Then it's high time you did," Dash said. "See you then?"

Starr nodded, almost beyond speech, and Dash raised one hand in salute before they went into separate classrooms. Immediately the difficulties of her situation enveloped her pleasure in panic. This would be Cad crowd. When the Cad crowd went formal, they left no glitter unturned. It was three days away, and Starr had neither a dress nor the money with which to buy one. Of course she could always telephone Dash and claim she was sick.

She *would* be sick if she didn't get to go with Dash! There must be some way to improvise something to wear; there *must* be some way, this once! She clasped one hand tightly in the other, as she had always done in times of great stress. She would go and see Aunt Artie. She was a great hand for improvising.

Aunt Artie was cashier in a sort of semi-restaurant, semi-night-club. She sat there behind the cash register fiddling with figures, her two inches of hair fashionably on end. She wore black, of course, that being the color of servitude; but there was nothing to forbid junk jewelry, and that she wore in ropes and strings and bracelets. Her bare ears were all but concealed beneath a delicate branching of wires supporting further dubious gems, but her eyes were warm with interest and concern.

"Kid," she said, after listening to Starr's predicament, "most of a girl's troubles are men, but a lot of 'em are clothes."

After work she took Starr to her room to look over her wardrobe for possibilities. There was little to make Starr hopeful. Then suddenly she noticed the bedspread. It was of raw silk, very heavy and taffetalike, with a border of small pale blue figures. It had been made of two lengths of material sewed together. Aunt Artie's glance followed Starr's in amazement.

"I could rip it down the middle, make a skirt of it, and then put it back together for you later," Starr said. "But I still would need a blouse, a cinch belt, and a pair of slippers."

"A boy friend of mine sent it from Japan," Aunt Artie said. "I didn't know what else to do with it but make a bedspread out of it."

But Starr had taken it from the bed, folded it, and was trying it for length. The heavy material stood out; it rustled. Starr's eyes shone over it to Aunt Artie. "With a yard of that gold-flecked material at Hartell's I could make a blouse," she said. "But it costs five dollars."

Aunt Artie found the five dollars, and the cinch belt, and the white sandals that could be glamorized with gold paint for a dollar ninety-eight. "I'll pay you back when I get a job," Starr said. "Oh, what would I do without you?"

"Kid, it's a graduation present," Aunt Artie said. "I'll pay for it with tips. See, I smile at 'em like this." She made a horrible leering face, and Starr kissed it. It was a tired face, lightly eroded by tears and crosshatched by laughter, and perhaps it had looked with favor upon too many no-account men. But there was warmth and wit and compassion in it. "Forget it, kid," she said to Starr.

Aunt Artie had said, "Forget it," to a multitude of relatives of varying degrees for decades. Several husbands had appeared and disappeared from her life. She lived from payday to payday. One of the reasons she always chose to work in restaurants was that food was a certainty there. Some food—enough to support life if one could find no other. Like most restaurant workers, she hated all cooks with consistent venom; but to everyone else in the world she turned a hopeful, friendly face. She was lonely most of the time, and Starr was both diversion and a great pride to her.

Starr rarely dated any boy except Jerry. He understood that school took some part of her life and set it apart. It might have troubled him if all the other girls living on Angello Street had not affirmed that his charm was equal to any opposition. In fact, her cool separateness from the teeming life of Angello Street interested him. Not that she was not a cold little number! But likely all the classy ones

[23]

were hard to get. It sometimes irked him, but still he would walk softly where Starr was concerned. After all, it was easy to find an easy girl. Starr's lush young sister, Ann Marie, for that matter. Probably. He would rather not know.

Starr's date with Dash nettled Jerry. This Dash was an unknown and probably more potent rival than most. A boy with class. "You know what *he* wants of a girl like you?" he asked darkly.

"He wants to put his girl in line," Starr said. "Priss will be furious, and it'll be good for her. Oh, Jerry, I haven't been to any of the dances, and this time I can go with the head man in the whole school! Like Cinderella! Only I know that the next day, that's all there is to that." She would make no further plea. Her cheeks were faintly hollowed, and the light brown hair blew about her face in the hot wind. "Are you jealous?" she asked, without coyness, somewhat surprised.

Jerry caught her by the shoulders, something of his violence in the strength of his fingers. "You're my girl!" he said. "Just remember that, and everything'll be all right. I'd marry you now if it wasn't for Mom and the kids—you know that."

Starr flushed, the color rushing up over her brown face. "Was that a proposal?" she asked.

Jerry was sometimes dumfounded at her literal-mindedness. He dropped his hands from her shoulders. There was a certain prestige in her going out with Dash. "I just don't want you to get messed up with that crowd," he said.

With a shy confidence, Starr reached up and turned his head toward her. "Couldn't you even say you loved me?" she asked.

"You know damned well, baby," he said. "Don't try to push me around!"

She always flinched at the word baby. He had said it lovingly enough, but . . . well, what was a word? It was his way. He had few endearments. She had almost none, herself. What would she call him? Just the name Jerry was endearment enough! She caught his hand and held it briefly to her cheek. "I won't go to the dance if you don't want me to," she said. And he was silent. She did want very much to go.

"Dash is an awfully nice boy," she said. "He knows that I understand that Priss is really his girl."

"I ain't afraid of him," Jerry said. "But just you watch yourself!"

They had to separate then. The hot wind was bringing up a sandstorm.

Cory, clumsy with advanced pregnancy, was excited by Starr's date. "You might marry into that crowd," she said. "You can do better than Jerry. He's good lookin', and the girls run after him, but it don't follow he'll be a good husband."

"It doesn't follow that a boy whose father owns a Cad will be a good husband, either," Starr said. "I thought you liked Jerry."

"Dash is the very keenest boy in school," Ann Marie said enviously. She was pinning her hair into wet snails; she wore a slip.

"Good heavens!" Starr cried, suddenly self-conscious. "One date, and I'm married off to money—we hope!"

"It's a plumb handy thing to have," Bert said. "When

you're young, you don't think how much work you'll have to do, to ever have anything you want."

Dusk came reluctantly. Starr bathed and dressed in a slow dream. The gold-flecked blouse and the rustling skirt were right. They brought out high lights in her hair. For the first time, she was glad to have that particular shade of blue-gray eyes. They were startlingly bright in her firm young angular face. But perhaps it was all a dream. Perhaps Priss would ask Dash, after all, to reconsider, and he would telephone to say he could not come. Hope and the lack of it fluctuated through Starr for hours beforehand, but she kept her own counsel. Only Cory noticed that often she stopped whatever she was doing and held one hand in the other, as if to quiet both of them.

Then the Cadillac arrived before the narrow lot, and out stepped Dash in the first evening clothes any of them ever had seen. He carried a spray of yellow-flecked orchids in a box that looked like a bubble, and his smile was radiant. He seemed strangely adult in his dark attire. Cory, Ann Marie, and Bert all were watching through the curtains. Starr went to the door to meet this stranger so different from the schoolmate she had known.

He handed her the plastic bubble with the orchids. "These were most like you," he said. "I hoped they would match your dress—and they do! I'll wait while you pin them on."

Starr's hand trembled with the flowers and the pin. Cory finally pinned them securely. "The *pretty* things!" Starr said, hugging Cory impulsively. "Did you ever *see* anything so pretty?"

"They match your dress," Cory said. "And flowers and

dress, they ain't either one pretty, really. But they do look like they belonged with him." She nodded toward the porch. She patted Starr's shoulder. "Have a good time!" she said, smiling.

She watched them go, her eyes softened with affection.

"Gee!" Ann Marie said gustily. "The luck of some people!"

Cory looked at her rounded, apple-petal daughter. "It's not all luck," she said. "How would you and Beau like to go to the movies?" She doled out the change from her purse, and knew that Bert would ask to be dropped in town near some tavern—which he did. Then she was alone, and could think back as she washed the dishes and straightened the house.

An orchid and a Cadillac and the most popular boy in school—even for an evening! It would be something pretty to remember always. It was a miracle to Cory that in a few weeks Starr would be graduated in a black gown and a square cap.

Seldom had the way been high-lighted by such special events as this evening, but it had been worth it. For all Starr talked so little and read so much, Cory was proud enough to strut at the very thought of her.

But these days she tired easily. When she finished the dishes she took a comfortable rocker outdoors and sat at ease. She rocked, and she remembered the hard, hard road that led to a prom and an orchid.

Sometimes the children had asked about Cory's childhood and early life, and she had answered them honestly; but they would never, never know how it had been. Cory remembered the flat farm and the hard chores. She had been

[27]

taken out of school in order to do more work. Bert also had dropped out of school as soon as his fine young body was strong enough to hold a plow steady in the furrow; and these two had married when most children their ages still were in high school.

In her husband's home, the bride continued the same sort of hard work she knew all too well. The women canning and sewing and making do, eking three hot meals a day somehow from soil and farmyard. "You either dig it up, cut it down, or go out and kill it every mealtime," Cory had told Starr, "and the menfolks never help, or think about the trouble. And they never give you no money at all."

Sometimes when they had sold a "critter" or two, they gave their womenfolk cheap material for dresses, or a clumsy pair of shoes. "But never nothin' pretty, and never nothin' really your own," Cory had said. "The money all belongs to the men, and they bury it. They never do tell you how much they got, either. Bert's pa, when he finally died, the old buzzard, had all his money in bed with him so's he could feel it—big old dollar bills, and little bitty gold pieces, and silver dollars. . . ."

"What became of it?" Starr asked.

"His ma divided it up in seven parts—one for each one of the children and one for her, because all of 'em had worked and gone without for it," Cory said. "They got more'n a hundred dollars apiece. 'Course Bert didn't give me none of his. Beau was a baby then, and I had a kind of itch to go somewhers and see if . . . Well, your Aunt Artie had come out here, and I heard from Ma how well she liked it and how much better women lived." Cory smiled. " 'Twasn't so hard to get your pa to buy a car with his money. He really thought he ought to buy some more heifers, but he was willin' to pleasure me sometimes then, when we was young. Besides, I threatened to leave him. So we started off to see California and visit Artie.

"But I knew I wasn't never goin' back. The dust was a-blowin' over everything already. Dust storms come here, and they go; but back there the dust blowed like it never aimed to stop—miles and miles and miles."

There was not eloquence enough in Cory to express her loathing for the land she had forsaken, or for the men who ruled it and ruled the women; it was communicated to Starr without words, and in bits and pieces of sentences now and then.

Bert and Cory drove into the great hot valley in late summer, with two-year-old Beau asleep in the back seat on a pile of dirty clothes. They had been a long time a-journeying. Sometimes she had asked to pitch their ragged tent so that she might sleep a whole night through. She and Bert had taken turns at driving, but sleeping in the car did not rest her. It was the coming baby that made her finicky. They had stopped now and then for repairs to the car, of course. Fortunately Bert knew a bit about the mechanism of it, so that they were not victimized as much as most by the mechanics along the way—sitting in a row thousands of miles long they were, like so many jackals awaiting the crippled cars. There already were quite a few migrants on the road, even in 1930.

When they came into the great valley, they had almost nothing but the car. Soon they were passing mile upon mile of cotton. "*Look* at it Bert! One boll has as much cotton as six bolls back home! Ain't it pretty?"

"Real pretty," Bert said warily, for he was afraid she

would want him to pick some with her. True, they needed money, but picking cotton was beneath the dignity of a man. The horrible fact was, that as many men as women were picking it here.

"If we picked until dark, we'd have money to pay for our meals with Artie when we got there," Cory said.

"I don't feel like pickin' no cotton, after so much ridin'," Bert said shortly.

"I feel like pickin' some. I'm a good picker—I could maybe make a couple of dollars before sundown. I'd just like to wrap my hands around some of them pretty bolls. Look how long the cotton is, Bert! It'd be so *easy* to pick!"

Of course it was never easy, but Bert picked along beside her. Together they earned three dollars before sundown. Cory was sunburned, but they did not come to Artie with entirely empty hands.

Aunt Artie was young then, and at the moment she was married. Through her husband they were able to locate a place where they could pitch their tent and obtain water and the use of an outdoor toilet.

"It sure ain't livin' high," Bert said fretfully. "I'll be glad when we get back home, and can live in a house. This here tent is hot as hell in the daytime."

"Most places you get a job, the place is air-cooled," Cory said innocently. "Then you don't have to stay in a hot tent. Matter of fact, I don't aim to go home till after this baby is born. I can pick cotton and feed us, if I can find places to pick it." She did not mention how very much she loved that faucet. She had always carried water from a spring before this.

Bert humored her. He often went and picked cotton with her. But she did not put the money she earned into his hands, as a wife was supposed to do. She tucked it away in her pocket, and although she paid for some things, Bert was never able to keep track of how much she had. It was this western way of doing things—the other women all did the same—that was unsettling. It took the authority out of a man's hands, some way. Often Cory claimed she had no money when Bert was almost sure she did, and he would have to pay for something like food or shoes, when she *knew* it was up to her to furnish these things. A man's money was for stock, or playing poker, or liquor, or swapping cars—or just to keep, back home. Cory may have had twenty-five dollars in only a few months, but Bert could not be sure.

He did not like it here; he often said so. Then Cory would say it was not long until the baby was due—maybe in November. She had not seen a doctor, of course; one did not think of such extravagance. They would telephone for one when her time came.

But her time came unexpectedly when she was picking cotton. Bert had not felt well enough to come along that day. As soon as she was sure, she called to a Negro man who was picking in the next row. He picked at enormous speed—even faster than she. "I need some help," she said. "Could you drive my car? I'm goin' to have a baby, and need to get home. I'd give you what cotton I have in the sack." It was a shame to ask him to take time out.

The man stopped. He looked at her in apology. "Lady, I can't stop—my children need the money," he said slowly. "But my Benjamin—he's pickin' over there—he don't pick so fast, and he can drive. I get him to take you to the hospital." Even as he called Benjie, his dark fingers were like vacuums sucking the cotton from the bolls; like a magic stream of white it flowed into his sack.

[31]

"Oh," Cory said firmly, "I don't need to go to a *hospital!* I'm healthy. Besides, we couldn't afford it. And anyway, I'm all dirty! I couldn't go to a hospital like this." Pride let her conceal the pain. Her high-cheekboned face was immobile, but lightly sweating.

"You're new out here," the man said. "You don't need money when you go to the County. They catch your baby for nothin'." His voice was kind, and his nimble fingers continued to draw the cotton.

Cory waited in the car while Benjie checked what cotton she had picked and what was in his sack into the check wagon. Hurry prompted her to try the County Hospital. How big and forbidding it was! It smelled sinister with strange medicines; people waited in lines.

"This baby's comin' real quick," Cory told the first clerk who asked so very many questions. "I got to find a place to lay down for a spell. I hate to bother you, but they ain't time to get home now."

So they took her out of the long line of those waiting, and washed the dirt of the cotton field from her young body. She was furnished an immodest rough nightgown. A woman doctor came and helped with the birthing. Dr. Starr, she was, and she was that kind and able, Cory could hardly believe this was so much easier than the birth of Beau had been. All the time Dr. Starr was working, you could see the pain and sorrow behind her eyes, even though she was still a young woman. Cory thought maybe she had birthed a baby, herself. But when she asked, Dr. Starr said she had no children, and just breathe in little pants, like a puppy.

From time to time Cory heard a loudspeaker calling for Dr. Starr. "Calling Dr. Starr" ran through her own drowsiness, for she had been given a pill that made her so sleepy she hardly knew which end was up—and a good thing, she thought to herself, so beholden to these strangers.

When the daughter had been born, Dr. Starr asked if someone should telephone the father. Cory admitted that they had no telephone. "I aim us to have one someday, though," Cory said. And being still drowsy, she thought more of the daughter newly born than about Bert, who would be alarmed when she did not return to cook supper.

Next morning she was herself once more and had someone phone Artie's husband at work, and so news finally percolated through to Bert, who came visiting in the afternoon. His shirt was not ironed, and Cory felt shame for it.

"I never thought about you bein' in no hospital," Bert said. "I fried some eggs for Beau and me, and Beau cried hisself to sleep. Don't seem right to have a woman leave her family and go away to a hospital to have a baby. It ain't friendly. Dr. Jones back home, he didn't need no hospitals."

Bert was annoyed; he knew she would take it to heart about Beau crying for her. Through the halls the disembodied voice called for Dr. Starr once more. Cory thought warmly of her; she was a smart woman and good. Certainly she was nothing like Dr. Jones, who didn't mind a woman suffering—and claimed it was the natural result of sin. The thought irritated her. "Old Doc Jones didn't know much fifty years ago," she said with unusual asperity, "and he's been losin' ground ever since. I never knowed how easy a baby could be birthed before. I aim to name this baby after the doc that helped with her. She's named Starr Cooper."

"I like Sadie," Bert said. It was his mother's name, and certainly honorable, but to Cory it sounded like faded kitchen aprons and stockings with runners in them. "I don't aim to have no Sadies," she said. Maybe she was getting above her raisin', but maybe this baby would grow up smart and very kind, like the woman doc—this solemn little Starr Cooper.

"Now we can go back home, anyway," Bert said with a sigh. "The baby's born."

Then Cory put her foot down. She hated to do it, for she loved Bert, and was used to him. She had borne him two babies. But she was nineteen years old, and it was time she took a stand, before she grew bent before her menfolks and afraid to risk her own judgment any more. "I ain't goin' back, ever," she said steadily. "You can go along now if you got your heart set on it. But I done slopped my last pig and milked my last cow. I can make out here somehow, even with the children—and I ain't goin' back. I never meant to, to tell the truth. Maybe I ought to've told you, but I was carryin' the baby, and it made me soft, like. I ain't ever goin' back, Bert."

"A wife has got to go where her husband goes; it says so in the Bible," Bert said, the anger rising in his face.

"Maybe I ain't no wife," Cory said. "Not if you go back, I ain't. I'm willin' to work. I'll pick cotton, I'll scrub floors— I'll do whatsoever I can to help. But I'll be *paid* for it; I can buy things—clothes and food, and maybe a little radio. Maybe even a home, in time. I ain't spendin' my life workin' for nothin', like my ma and her ma before her. I got me a taste of livin' out here, and I like it real well." A certain contrition made her falter, but she continued. "It ain't that I care less for you, Bert; I never wanted no other man, and I guess I never will. But I won't go back—not ever. I can taste the dust and smell the pigpens, and feel the awful low feelin'—hoein', hayin', renderin' lard—it's awful hard work, Bert, and it don't pay nothin' a'tall."

"A woman ought to be proud to work for her man," Bert said. "You just do women's work."

"I guess I ain't cut out for women's work," Cory said. "I like to get paid for it, and spend the money. I'll be here a week. You can study about what you want to do." She turned her back to him then, and said nothing else. He flung out of the room, stamping his heavy shoes hard on the floor.

But he came back a moment later. "You got any money?" he asked. "Beau and me got to eat, you know."

"No," Cory said, though she hated to lie to him. But sometimes you had to drive a man to work. Her own father had said she was a driving woman. Well, maybe it depended on the kind of man you got. Some men did not have to be driven. "My cotton sack's in the car," Cory said. "You can pick enough before sundown for a meal." Once more she turned her face to the wall. It was a gamble. Maybe Bert *would* go back. At the thought, easy tears rose to her eyes. She was tired, for a fact. But she never would go back—not even to join him.

In less than two weeks Cory was in the fields again, her hands as agile as a magician's. She could pick faster now that she was thin once more. At the end of the row, she would go to the car and give the baby a drink of water or would nurse her. Starr got a heat rash, lying there in the baking car with nothing on but an old feed sack for a diaper. Cory hurried with the picking. They would need money enough to see them through the time of no work, when the crops all were gathered and the new ones not yet ready. She squirreled away dollar by precious dollar. Bert complained that although they did make a living, they certainly were not getting rich.

Starr could not remember the tent. They lived in it for two years. Or perhaps it should be said that they slept in it, and stayed in it on rainy days. It was not new in the beginning, and they might have bought a secondhand one thriftily, but Cory had what Bert called another one of her spells. She walked right out and rented a house! It was a shabby, small house, costing sixteen dollars a month. The window sills were riddled with termites, so that if you poked a finger at one, the finger sank through old paint into nothingness. Not only did Cory rent this house and move them into it; she had a telephone installed!

Bert proclaimed that this was waste and folly. Never had there been such a luxury in a house belonging to his relatives. His father had warned that it was an instrument to waste women's time. He did not hold with it.

Cory did not argue that it was she who paid for it. She said that it was a help in locating jobs and saving shoe leather and tires, and certainly it was a handy way to call for the police or for a doctor. If it did not prove worth while, it could be removed.

Bert thought it was a vagary of her condition. She made an awful fuss about the third child—traipsing off to the hospital long before the baby was born, staying most of a day. It took her from her work, and equally deplorable, it left Bert to care for Beau and Starr—which was woman's work. If Cory had not been pregnant, he would have beaten her. The idea occurred to him more and more often. His was not the first wife that needed a beating or was a better wife for it. He drank a lot of beer these days, which Cory did not like. She wanted to manage the money. A man needed a little beer to keep his strength up. He needed to treat his friends. It was wearisome being married to a driving woman. Back home, things were managed better.

The County ushered Ann Marie into the world, and Cory was apologetic to Dr. Starr. "Before there's another one," she said, "I aim to be able to pay for it. It takes a while to get started, you know. We need so much."

"I know," Dr. Starr said. "Don't worry about it now."

"A woman has to worry," Cory said. "Who pays you?"

"The County. It comes from taxes. People pay taxes on land."

"I aim to own some land—enough for a house, anyway—then I'll be payin' part of your wages, won't I?" Cory asked.

Dr. Starr said yes, but not for long. She was going into private practice.

Bert hated the telephone; he always hated it. With it Cory found jobs. How she could nose out a lawn to be mowed or a kitchen to be scrubbed down! Even in the off season, she always found jobs. After the cotton was all picked, she found housework for herself and yard work for Bert, so that they need never ask for relief. Bert argued that they would eat better on relief, and save all that work. Did the law say you must break your back finding work? No. The employment agency had few jobs in the off season. But Cory *kept* finding jobs.

Gradually she acquired a list of people willing to work, and a list of households where domestic work—the very hard kind—was sometimes obtained. She stopped one day at the office of a public stenographer and had a sheet with four carbons typed:

[37]

For hard work, call Cora Cooper, 4138.

The words were written time after time, and Cory cut the sheets to small slips, and left one wherever she worked. The typing cost sixty-five cents, but like the telephone, it paid for itself.

From back home came news of hunger and dust and disaster; but Cory made a game of staying off relief. The babies were born on charity, but that was all. She had to earn more money as the children entered school, and she did. After the first year they spoke like California children, and no one called them Okies.

Cory could not divine when Starr had become uncommunicative. Always she had been a good student—better far than Beau or Ann Marie. When she was in the lower grades, she asked ten thousand questions. She was thin, and her questions had had such a sharp edge to them that sometimes Bert thought her sassy, and he would cuff her. He never did beat her hard, though, as Cory had been beaten as a child. After all, a man would sometimes beat a woman or his children—especially when he had been drinking. They had to know that.

"Some of the kids don't get beat up," Starr said, stubbornly factual, even at eight.

"Likely they just don't say anything about it," Cory said uneasily. "It's just your pa's way. He don't mean no harm."

Was it then that Starr started to grow away from her family? She asked her father no more questions after the time he bellowed that she should stick to her books. "I ain't got my head stuffed with all that bookish trash!" he yelled. He thought too much reading made a girl uppity. He did not hold with it.

Later Cory had said to Starr, "Ask the things to me—not your pa. If I know, I'll tell you straight out." But of course she didn't know the answers any more than Bert did. And besides, she was always, always working. All her life she had dropped into bed almost stunned with the day's hard labor and had slept exhausted, with no twilight time for confidences or questions.

Starr discovered that the teacher was almost always busy, too. She asked Beau things sometimes. He was so big and competent-appearing. But he was scornful. Looking at the plains stretching north as far as the eye could see, Starr would ask what was farther than that. Suppose you started walking and walking—would there always be more flat fields and tumbleweed and crops? Or was there a mountain so far you couldn't see it? What was on the top of the mountains on the eastern horizon? Snow in winter sometimes—that you could see. But did people live there? *Was* the air blue there? Did wild animals live there? Was it another country on the other side?

"What do you care?" Beau would ask in surprise and irritation. "We ain't goin' there."

Starr almost wrung her hands in frustration. "I'll go there someday," she said, "so I can see!"

Miss Shell was only a teacher's name to Cory; but she knew how much Starr had adored her. Surely Miss Shell had a head "stuffed with bookish trash." She taught Starr in her tenth year, and the lessons were sheer magic for Starr and, Cory sensed, much delight for the teacher. Christmas that year had found Starr feeling bad because she could buy Miss Shell no gift. But at Cory's suggestion she *found* a gift!

High in a tree formidable with thorny growth, there was

a great mistletoe plant with exquisite waxy berries. Starr climbed that tree—in some danger, and with considerable pain—and she brought the mistletoe down, preserving whole each leaf and delicate spray of berries. It took a long time. True, there was no pretty card—no shiny wrapping paper. Starr carried the plant in her arms clear across town to Miss Shell's house, then was seized with shyness as she went to the door and knocked, and ran away.

"The branch had some blood on it," Starr told her mother, "from the cut in my knee. But I wiped it with my dress." Cory was proud to wash that dress.

After Miss Shell, Starr gradually learned to turn her questions and thoughts entirely inward. She was quiet then, and lonely. The public library, Cory thought sometimes, was her dearest friend.

She was never lazy. When she was small, she washed the dishes standing on a box for height. When she was bigger, she had her own cotton sack and followed her mother into the fields to work. Her lean brown fingers grew more dexterous each year, as Cory had known they would. "You can always pick up at least a few dollars picking cotton in the fall," she explained. "I hope you don't have to, but there'll always be cotton, and you might as well pick it fast and earn more."

Cory began to have a reliable crew. A planter could call on her for a whole team, and she would bring them and see to it that they worked. All but Bert, that is. He never produced much volume, on account of his back. This prevented his mowing lawns in winter, too. Dr. Starr had examined it and found nothing wrong with it.

"They don't know what it is," Bert would say with a certain mournful pride. "You can't X-ray a pain."

Letters from back home were a long wail, year after year. The depression thickened, and the migrant workers were a ragged hungry tide. Cory worked longer, for lower wages, but she put aside a tiny sum each year in secret.

World War II caused jobs to blossom everywhere. A subsidiary of a war plant took over a shed in town, and Bert was taken on as a welder there. He belonged to a union and received magnificent wages. His back no longer bothered him. Cory could have worked there, too, but she stuck to her crew and the fields. That work she knew. She lost most of her crew to the war plants, and somehow she found others—the very dregs of the labor market, incompetent and lazy. She persisted, however, and the planters blessed her. She was still a young woman, but her tanned, lined face and her sturdy body were the symbols of earth itself.

Housing became a nightmare of effort. No more could they find a house to rent at a reasonable figure—if at all. Finally Cory used her long-hoarded emergency fund to make a down payment on 45 Angello Street.

The years had run past so quickly—how strange that Beau was nineteen and Starr seventeen—and even Ann Marie was in high school! Why, she, Cory, was thirty-six years old! In a way it would be nice to have another baby. But Cory hoped it would kindly wait until Starr had graduated!

She rocked back and forth in the shadows. It was cooler in the evenings. She wished she could stay awake until Starr returned from the dance—but she could not afford the luxury. She must get her sleep so that she could keep working as long as possible. If she bogged down, it would burden Starr in her last few weeks of school. Starr had asked for so little and had done so well—Cory wished she had been able to give her something real fine for a present. But she had nothing but the labor of her hands to give.

She arose and dragged the chair indoors once more, lest it be stolen. She thought of the orchid—what a curious-colored freckled thing it was, in its bubble box! But she knew that it cost as much as she earned by picking two hundred pounds of cotton. She wished that she might see into this dance without being seen. She would have liked to see a fine sight like that—all the flowers and pretty dresses and pretty youngsters ... and Starr. Slim-waisted, proud-stepping Starr at a ball.

2.

THE CAR was quiet; the seat was soft to the touch. Starr and Dashell breasted a stream of warm wind, and Starr's hair flew back from her face as if it were sculptured. Dash saw her from the corner of his eye. "You'll be the most beautiful girl at the dance," he said.

"That's silly!" Starr answered, but not caring. She would not have minded being a disembodied spirit at the dance. "Priss is much prettier. I thought you might call at any moment and say you were taking her, after all."

"Well, what vile manners!" Dash said severely. "But I didn't mean pretty. There are lots of pretty girls, but only a few beautiful ones. You're beautiful. It's a Viennese beauty—an international sort of thing. What will you do with it?"

Watching his face in the racing shadows, Starr clasped her hands loosely in her lap. He did not seem to be teasing. What an exciting idea! But it might be only a routine compliment. One could not be sure. "If it were true—and nobody has ever said so but you, Dash—I don't suppose it would make any difference. I can't choose what I'll do. I just do what I can and I must."

"What you can and you must do might prove very interesting," Dash said. "If nobody's told you you're beautiful, your whole family must be blind. And it's important to a girl, too. Now you watch, tonight, how I'll have to fight all the wolves in Statsville for dances with you. You'll know, then." His smile and warm voice were reassuringly matter-of-fact.

Starr smiled back at him. "I'll be watching," she said.

"Of course, the real test lies with the girls," he continued. "If they all hate you on sight, you'll never need more proof."

"I don't hate any of them," Starr said uncertainly.

"That has nothing to do with the matter," Dash answered. "Do you want a cocktail for Dutch courage, before we go face the pack?"

"I never had a cocktail. I'm not old enough."

One of Dash's hands briefly covered her own. "Good," he said. "The stuff only sobers you up. It's for the weak sisters."

The clubhouse was glittering with mirrors and fragrant with flowers, and Chinese lanterns made dim pools of light under the trees on the wide lawns. Starr forgot Jerry, forgot her family. She lived in one detached night and walked in her golden sandals through the fairyland of lanterns and tall trees. The dresses of the other girls flashed about, like so many flowers. All of them were part of the enchantment.

And did Dash's saying so make it so, of a sudden—was she beautiful? There was no time to consider. She was rushed. Every other dance, Dash claimed her again. True, between dances, she did not know the other girls well enough to join their small groups. But she had no time, any-

way. She glimpsed Priss now and then—not once with Dash
—always pouting, vivid, pretty, and surrounded by boys.

At intermission Starr caught one reflection of herself and
Dash in a long mirror. She was startled and pleased at the
picture they made. True, she did not look like the other
girls in their filmy party dresses. There was a sort of dignity
to her stiff skirt and gold-flecked blouse, and she saw it in
the unexpected mirror. Rather she looked like a distin-
guished young guest. With that knowledge, she knew poise
for the first time in her life. She welcomed all the delight
that the dance could offer. With certain grace she declined
the numerous requests for dates.

For even if this night were too beautiful to bear, and the
new confidence a gift more golden than the orchids on her
shoulder, she would not presume upon it. When she put
her hand on Dash's arm, it was always tentatively—just for
the evening—and tomorrow and all the future tomorrows
would not necessarily be one whit changed for her. Only
she would be changed, and that need not show.

When the dance was done, the couples formed into
groups and went to find scrambled eggs at the various small
diners that were open all night. Starr and Dash went also.
Though there were others present who had been at the
dance, none moved over to make a place for them, so that
they sat in a corner booth by themselves. "You see?" Dash
said. "You believe, now?" He was delighted.

"I see. And Dash, I'm glad they aren't all around us now.
This has been such a wonderful time, I couldn't bear any
more! It's enough; it's enough right now!"

"And would you like a cocktail now? Some of the others—"

"You just want to sober me up!" Starr said, smiling, teasing him with his own words. Then she put her hands flat on the clean table top and looked at Dash with her very serious gray eyes. "You've done a lovely thing for me," she said. "I thank you."

"You're so welcome, Miss Cooper!" he answered, mock-formal, reaching for a fork. "Eat your eggs before you die of exhaustion."

Cory decreed that Starr might sleep late the next morning, and the phone rang several times before she awoke. She finally aroused, but closed her eyes again to fix in memory the night before.

Ann Marie came into the room. "Are you ever wolf bait!" she said. "Calling up before breakfast—four of them already, with money, money, money! Listen who—"

"It makes no difference," Starr said, and she looked at her picture of the wave breaking. "That was last night, and last night's over—finished—all through."

"That was this morning," Ann Marie said. "Like I said, they telephoned like gosh they couldn't wait, and I told 'em you were asleep. . . ."

Ann Marie waited and listened, and was surprised that Dash never telephoned for Starr. Numerous friends of his did so, and Starr noted that there was a difference in their attitude from that of Dash. The places they proposed to take her on dates were never quite the right places—for girls of the Cad crowd. When Starr said no to them, she always felt—a shade wistful, perhaps.

But the dance did set a restlessness within her. There was the memory of beauty in the wide lawns and the Chinese lanterns—a spaciousness of living that she had met only in books was now a thing seen with the eyes. It made Angello

Street and its narrow houses shrink. It made the noise and
the obscenity more objectionable. Not that she wished to
leave her mother or her family. But if she should marry and
move away, it couldn't possibly hurt anyone's feelings. Perhaps she and Jerry would have only a furnished room at
first, but later a small house on a *quiet* street. Perhaps an
old house, that wouldn't cost too much.

Even Jerry may have shrunk in size and importance after
the dance; but this she would not consider. He was nicer
than most; he worked steadily and wanted to amount to
something. In his own way, he loved her, she was sure. And
all the girls on Angello Street would have been proud to
marry him. Yes, someday she would marry Jerry. Not right
away, but someday. One worked with what materials came
to hand. She declined no movie or picnic with Jerry after
that. But his invitations grew more widely spaced.

It was thoughtful of Jerry, she thought, for final examinations were at hand within a short time. Cory was hoping
that the baby would not arrive until after graduation. She
had missed a lot of work, and even part payment for the new
baby was a severe drain. Bert could not see why she should
pay anything.

"It's hard," Cory explained as well as she could, "but we
might be using up somebody's chance to have a baby free.
Somebody like we was before we got the house." She saw
that Bert did not agree. "Just because people make you welcome, it ain't no reason to wear that welcome out," she said,
still trying.

"Anybody that can get anything free, he's a fool not to
take it," Bert said. "We could use that money our own
selves."

Cory straightened her tired back. "A lot of folks these

days want something for nothing," she said. "They think it's smart to draw relief. But I remember, even if you've forgot, Bert, that our folks never took pride in sucking a government teat."

She had to go to the hospital in the middle of Starr's final examinations. Bert promptly went out to get drunk. It was Starr who waited at night in the outer room. Several prospective fathers waited with her. They had little to say. Starr held a textbook in her hand, and her mind balked at study while Cory was struggling with the miracle of birth. She wished Bert had come along; surely a father should welcome a baby into the world and tell its mother she did a good, hard job.

The hands of the big clock moved, groaning very slightly, and the lights in the halls were low. Nurses came and went, catfooted on the polished floors. The fathers strode about, smoking cigarettes and throwing them away. The night lengthened toward morning, and Starr tried desperately to read the book from which examinations would be given at eight thirty. A book was nothing beside a brand-new baby.

They wheeled Cory out on the high cart, and Starr ran to her. Cory was desperately white, but she smiled, scarcely moving one hand outside the covers. "Are you all right, Mom?" The tears were welling in Starr's weary eyes as she groped for Cory's hand. "Was it a boy or a girl?"

"It's a girl," Cory said. "We had a little trouble. I guess I got out of practice! Run see your little sister before they hide her away." Cory's voice was tired.

Starr ran after the nurse who was wheeling the baby down the hall. "Is it the Cooper baby? May I look at her?"

The tired nurse stopped for a moment, and Starr looked at the baby, already asleep, damp ringlets, petal fingers closed. When she raised her eyes to the nurse, the nurse stood straighter and smiled in the reflected radiance. "She's perfect!" the nurse said proudly, as if she had personally managed the matter.

Starr ran back to Cory and followed beside the cart. "She's the cutest, prettiest, most wonderful baby you ever saw! Oh, Mom!" Tears pooled again in Starr's eyes and spilled down her cheek. "When you first told me about her, I truly didn't want her. I'm sorry, now."

"Why," Cory said roughly, "it's a natural way to feel until you learn better! Each baby is the prettiest, smartest one of all! You come after school tomorrow, and we'll name her."

The examination in the morning slowly passed through a haze of sleepiness, and Starr came home unable to forgo a nap. The house was in disorder already; dishes cluttered the sink. In a few days she would have to have everything spic and span when Cory came home, and then there would be extra care of Cory and the baby. Meantime the laundry must be done, and the endless ironing of shirts and work pants for Beau and Bert. And every morning an examination. Where *was* Bert? Starr looked at the picture of the wave breaking, so cool and clean on the clean sand, so uncluttered by human beings and the work and disorder they entailed. Bert was probably sleeping it off somewhere, but Starr could not arouse herself to look for him. She sat on the edge of the bed for a moment, then put her hand down on the pillow—and suddenly she was asleep in her blouse and skirt, limp as the coverlet on which she lay. Sweat beaded her face.

In a few hours she arose, washed her face with tepid water, and prepared a meal. Afterward, she washed all the dishes and set Ann Marie to drying them. She aroused Bert from his stupor and pressed black coffee upon him. He said his back hurt, and his head hurt, and he wanted to sleep.

"Don't you even want to see the new baby?" Starr asked. "She's so pretty! And Mom'll feel terrible if you don't act like you wanted her!" A woman in a hospital liked to have folks know her family was interested. Besides, Starr was too young to get a driver's license, and she was loathe to spend taxi fare when Bert could just as well drive them.

Cory looked better. "You had a teacher with a real pretty name," she said to Starr. "I thought we might name the baby Caroline."

"She looks like Caroline," Starr said.

"I like Sadie," Bert began once more. But Ann Marie was for Caroline.

"She looks like ruffles and lace and baby bonnets," Starr said.

"Oh, go on!" Cory was half pleased and half reproving at this implied extravagance. "I'm sorry to leave so much work."

"We manage," Starr said cheerfully, knowing that the race of work and examinations was almost impossible. She had to run all the time to keep up—it wasn't as if she ever gained on it. If only Bert and Beau would do something to help! But of course they would not, and Ann Marie was so slow.

She asked Jerry to go with her to bring Cory and the baby home. Bert was away with the car—working, she hoped.

Jerry hesitated. He had to go out, he said, but, yes, he could spare time to go for Cory, if they might hurry. As he drove toward the hospital very fast, Starr thought that always they must hurry. "It's nice of you to help out," she said. "I always know I can count on you."

Jerry did not reply. He was rushing, too, and thinking of something else, probably. So often he did not answer. She would get used to it, of course. Someday he might be driving to the hospital to get their own baby. It was an idea as cold and remote as a dim star. But then one was always so busy with today that tomorrow could hardly be glimpsed. The thoughts slid through Starr's mind, flashing and gone. Two more examinations and she was done with high school. None of it had been easy, but the last of it was truly difficult, she thought. Then her thoughts turned to Cory, and her own problems were trivial, and her heart melted toward her mother. Starr had almost forgotten Jerry beside her, staring into the traffic ahead.

Abruptly he said, "I can't take you to the movie Saturday night. I have something to do."

Starr had looked forward to Saturday night movies. "That's all right," she said. "With the new baby home, and all the work . . . Maybe the *next* Saturday night we can celebrate graduation and a new sister, and so many things finally done. They work you late a lot these days, don't they?"

Again Jerry retreated into silence. When he spoke, there was a subtle uncertainty in his voice. "I'd better tell you before someone else does," he said. "You know I've been working for Ethan Hart. If he likes me enough, he can give me work almost the year around. And he does. He's always asking me to stay late for something, and then to eat with them. Sometimes they go to a restaurant, and sometimes the cook fixes something at home."

"They?" Starr said, warned by his voice.

"He has a daughter named Shirley. About twenty."

"Pretty?"

"Pretty, and a lot of fellows know it. She has a roadster."

Shirley Hart. She had gone to high school at some time, and had left for a private school. Her name was on the society pages of the paper—and probably her picture, too, Starr supposed, but try as she would she could not recall anything about her. Now she was a threat, tentatively. Probably she was only idly interested in Jerry, because he was so good looking. There were so many other opportunities for a girl like Shirley.

Starr let the subject slide through her mind, but it left a wake of doubt and confusion when she had dismissed it. She was alerted, in any event. And it had been honest and nice of Jerry to explain.

Jerry himself thought that he had been both honest and cautious. He had given warning, in case he finally must break with Starr; but he had also disarmed her suspicion in case this affair with Shirley should die in the very heat of its budding. Shirley had long legs, provocative eyes, and a dangerously venturesome nature. She knew what you thought before you knew it, yourself, and probably she had never been denied anything she wanted in her whole perfumed, explosive life. He was sure she deliberately provoked him, but when he had the opportunity to seize her in his arms, she slapped and scratched. But not for long—not very long! He had to laugh silently, knowing that it would be his job to hold out on *her*, if he wished to marry her. For she would not want to marry him—not at first, she wouldn't.

With all her fancy clothes and her red roadster and her father's properties, you might have supposed she had class.

She didn't, though. There was a brazenness about her that denied it. What she had would serve as well, however; she had the arrogance of a spoiled princess. Jerry's way might be paved with both gold and excitement if he played his cards correctly. But riding beside Starr, he was aware of the odds. Starr should be an ace in the hole.

And it wasn't as if he were deceiving her, or had not made a long investment in patience for her favors, small as they were, when lots of other girls on Angello Street would have. . . . He stole a glance at her profile. It was serene, and that was good. In a way she was like Cory Cooper—very hard to stir up about anything. Teresa's jibe came back to his mind. "I bet you couldn't!" He almost smiled. Shirley had him stirred up, and plenty! She was actually much easier to figure than Starr Cooper, and who would have believed it?

"After a week or so, I think things will be easier," Starr said unexpectedly. "I've been offered a job in the office at Overton's Stationery Store. The shorthand teacher told me about it. I'll have to say I'm eighteen to be hired."

"Think you can do the job?"

"I'll learn," Starr said. "The salary's low enough that they can afford it, and I learn quickly."

It was almost a month before Starr realized that Jerry had not offered to take her to a show, had not been around the place at all. She thought of it when Ann Marie came into the kitchen and reported that some girl in a red roadster had gone to the Whitcomb house and honked outside, and Jerry had come out all dressed up and gone away with her.

A streak of panic fled like sheet lightning through Starr's

mind, but she dismissed it. "It was only Shirley Hart," she said. "Jerry works for her father."

"In his best clothes he works for her father, I bet," Ann Marie said. "Teresa said she brought him home real late night before last, and she saw—"

"Never mind!" Starr said angrily. "Doesn't she ever stop spying to sleep some?" That hushed Ann Marie, but doubts grew like young thistles in Starr's mind, and there was a small aching within her, more like an illness than a wound.

The chief difficulty in Starr's first job was Hank Overton, the boss's son. He worked summers in the store and went to college other times. Starr would be thankful when college began, for every day it was harder to evade him—to pretend not to understand him—and above all, to keep his father from walking in on one of the hateful scenes that he produced with terrifying regularity. Starr did not particularly like Horace Overton, his father, who was very much a lodge member and every inch a backslapper. There was an effusiveness about him in his relations with customers—particularly those with the larger accounts—that embarrassed her. There was a clammy self-righteousness about him, particularly when he questioned her concerning her family and her moral viewpoints. He wiped his hands on his handkerchief during such discussions, and his eyes glistened moistly behind his glasses. But at least she did not have to hold him off with main strength.

She wore high-necked blouses now, although they were hot, because when she had worn an open-necked one, Hank had come from behind her typing chair, put his hands about her throat playfully, then slid them down the neck of the blouse. She could avoid this by standing each time he came into the room, but she did not wish to show him this much attention. Besides, she was making a serious effort to do fine work on this first job. She dared not go into the stock room when Hank was around, for he always followed to wrestle her. She would gladly have told his father, but some instinct warned her that the blame would fall on herself and not Hank.

She did not even believe that Hank hoped his buck-toothed charms would melt her. He only wanted to finger her, and nothing of her revulsion penetrated the thick hide of him, no matter what she said. He breathed on the back of her neck when she was working—if his father were out—and proposed rendezvous in auto courts.

"Let me alone," Starr said through her teeth, the noise of her typewriter covering her voice. "Go find yourself a female dog; go run with the pack, following through the alleys, where you belong. I'll tell your father on you!"

"He wouldn't believe you, honey chile," Hank said, his hand closing on her upper arm. Somehow she fought Hank off until school started.

Starr came from the air-conditioned store in the heat of the late afternoon and walked home sticky with sweat. She would lie for a few moments beneath the picture of the cool wave. When she and Jerry married, she would have enough money saved so that they might go somewhere to a beach for a day or two. She would walk on the wet sand, and let the wave break over her. She had hardly seen Jerry for months.

Impulsively she telephoned him at home. "We haven't been anywhere for the longest time," she said. "Could you spare time from the Harts to take me to a movie? Remember me—Starr Cooper?"

Jerry thought fast. He was pretty sure he had Shirley where he wanted her, now. A touch of jealousy ought to turn the trick. And he would further prepare Starr for the break. "Baby," he said, "let's go to a drive-in. It's been a long, hot summer, hasn't it?"

Jerry knew that Starr did not drink, but he stopped before the one really fashionable cocktail bar in town. "You can have a lemonade, you know," he said, looking very handsome and positive. She did not quarrel with him. Better to go along with a man's ideas if you possibly could. Fortunate that she had worn the taffeta skirt and gold-flecked blouse. They lingered in the bar for what seemed to her a long time. Groups of expensively dressed men and women came and went, and among one group there arrived a girl with cropped red curls. Starr heard the others call her Shirley. She did not ask Jerry if this were Shirley Hart. She knew. So Jerry had brought her here because this Shirley would come. They had been waiting for her arrival, because, soon after, they left. No words were spoken, but Starr's heart beat faster as she felt the tension tighten among them. Perhaps Jerry had wanted to show Shirley that he already had a girl. But without explanations, Starr moved among hostile forces.

It was good to be alone with Jerry at the movie. He put an arm about her, and she moved closer to him in the darkness. It was an easy, tender touching, familiar almost since childhood. When Jerry kissed her, she was grateful; it settled some of the turbulent, wordless doubts that had drifted like dust within her. But he continued to kiss her. A roughness and demand registered in his arms—he was like Hank

Overton, and for a moment repugnance rose within her. But this was only Jerry. She moved away slightly, to let the moment slide past. But he was of another mind, she finally realized. "Jerry," she said with difficulty, pushing at his chest, "you know better than this. You always did! Take it easy! I always trusted you not to—"

"And why should you, baby?" he asked, his voice rough. "Didn't you think I was human and male? Did you think you got everything for nothing? Didn't you ever talk to the other girls about what big girls know?"

It sounded like Hank, too. Finally she wept as she struggled. "Take me home," she said. "You didn't want to come to a movie! And you'll be sorry when you cool off. Please, Jerry! Maybe you shouldn't have taken the cocktails. Maybe you don't know what you're doing at all!"

"And maybe I do!" Jerry said with compressed violence. "Maybe *you* don't know! I waited and waited for you to grow up, and you just don't want to, ever!" The starter whined, and he jammed the car into gear. "I'll take you home, all right!" he said grimly. "For good!" They rode in silence for a time.

Starr wiped at her tear-stained face, then held one hand tight in the other in her lap. "I never thought this of you," she said, "and I wouldn't have come with you if I had."

"You asked for it, baby," Jerry said, still grim. "You asked me—remember?"

Bewildered and hurt, Starr said, "Whatever I thought was between us never was at all. You liked another kind of girl better than me all the time."

"Damned tootin'," Jerry said. "I'm going to marry Shirley Hart, so you might as well know it now. We're not engaged, but we will be."

[57]

Fury rose like a tide over Starr's hurt. "Congratulations!" she said. "Here we are home, already!" She opened the car door and left it almost before it had stopped. Then she reached back inside and slapped Jerry's face with all her strength. "That's for the sneaky wolf!" she said tersely. "And get this straight, for you might meet another girl like me in your life: I don't intend to 'pay' with sex for one little damned thing in my whole life! If ever I hear the term, the subject's closed, right then. There will be only one reason for me: because I want to! Clear?" She slammed the car door.

Jerry leaned toward her in the moonlight. "There's more to you than I thought," he said, half admiringly. "Almost makes me sorry I—Honestly, you can't blame a guy for *trying*, can you?"

Starr was already walking toward the house. "I can, but make no mind!" she said furiously. She went inside the house.

But after that, the weeks passed very slowly for her. It was not that her social life had been so gay with Jerry, but now she only shuttled dully between office and home, with once in a great while a family picnic in the cooler evening. The days were flavorless. Perhaps she had been hasty. Perhaps every man made his pass, sooner or later. On one picnic, Jerry was present, and she maneuvered until they were almost accidentally out of earshot of the others. Her heart beat with suffocating leaps. "I'm sorry I slapped you, Jerry," she said, and the color ran over her face furiously.

Jerry laughed. "Wasn't anything," he said easily. "I'm being married next month. Maybe Shirley'll slap my face, too!"

Feeling infinitely small and cheapened, Starr crept back

to the place where Beau and Ann Marie were roasting hot dogs. Ann Marie was happy. She had David Bedeau at her side, and his dark cynical face watched her round one for the moment. There was no place to run and hide.

She sat looking into the fire and thoughts ran through her mind like scalded things. Although she had paid many bills, and bought much food for her family, she now had fifty dollars saved. A few weeks ago she had called it linens and dishes and maybe an automatic toaster. It was now a mean fifty dollars cash. Well, next summer she would be entitled to a vacation, and she would take a trip. She would buy one beautiful piece of luggage, and she would go and look at the ocean somewhere. There must be some healing in the great impersonal expanse of it. Meantime, she could measure her way to that time dollar by careful dollar. It might be she could carry her lunch and walk to and from work and make it more. A vacation was something to look forward to—but not far enough.

Still the loneliness was gnawing within her. Every girl her age had a fellow, she was sure. Even Ann Marie had many dates, though she was only fifteen—and not setting the world afire in high school.

The worst times were the sound of the honk of the red roadster at the far end of Angello Street each evening. She was glad when it was gone. But often she was awake and heard it return late at night. Loneliness was a bog with no end.

For a couple of hectic months she accepted almost every invitation. She went out with cat skinners, truck drivers, and roughnecks, all of whom were normal to Angello Street. She went out with the highly polished young men of Dashell Taylor's set, who had never ceased to telephone occasionally.

She went to dimly lit dance halls, where the young men drank too much and sometimes fought, and the old ones pawed at the young girls whom they had brought. She went to the not-quite-correct but smarter cocktail bars and night clubs. And often when she had supposed she was going out to a show or a dance, she found herself at the edge of a cotton field instead, wrestling what she had supposed to be her escort, but what was actually a predatory animal. The grab-firsters, Starr called them to herself. She ceased to accept solitary dates, hoping that numbers might offer some protection, and it did help to some extent. But not always.

Finally she decided that she would make no more dates, seeing that all the men were divided into the suave-grab and the grab-firsters. It was too much trouble, and too dangerous. One conversation lingered in her mind half hysterically for years. She never decided whether to laugh or cry over it. The angry young man was driving her home, very fast. "You don't drink, you don't smoke, you don't pitch woo—my God, what *do* you do?" he asked, his weathered neck swelling over his collar.

"I read," Starr said. "Sometimes I sing. I like to sing with other people, and to discuss what I read—if I ever find anyone who reads without pictures, of course."

"A God-damned high-brow!" snarled the young man, whose reading was undoubtedly confined entirely to the fully illustrated field. "I can't get you home too fast! You don't *look* like a long hair."

For the first time that evening, Starr was genuinely interested. "Are they supposed to look some special way?" she asked.

But if he knew the answer, he would not dwell upon it.

[60]

"Take a girl out, waste gasoline, waste time—what does it get you?" he asked.

That curious thing about payment again! Starr waved a dollar bill under his nose. "You can have the whole investment back except the time," she said. But he knocked her hand down. She left the bill on the seat when she got out of the car.

And never again! she thought passionately. I doubt if I ever saw a decent man in my life, or ever will. And having determined that, she slept soundly for the first time in months, and awoke to realize that it was her birthday. She was eighteen.

In due time Cory noticed that Starr had no more dates, and asked why. Starr was casual. "I find I don't like men," she said. "I guess I'm going to be an old maid."

Cory's lips hardly quirked. "You have to make allowances for 'em," she said. "They're different from women."

"Not much different from dogs, though, are they?" Starr asked. "Want exactly the same things: food, shelter, sex, fighting, and someone to look after them and wait on them. A woman, usually."

Cory's face became serious. "When Mr. Right comes along, you'll change your tune," she said. "You're young. He'll come along; sure he will! And you'll be happy with him, and think he's the most wonderful thing in the world."

"Did you think that about Pop?"

Abruptly Cory's mind swung back to the young man she had loved, so straight and confident and sure of himself. And it swung again to the man who was now stooped as if he were truly old. A bit mean—just a little slippery with the truth, often pugnacious on the beer he bought with her own money. Where did the young love go? she thought. Dear

[61]

God, where did he go, and when? When I first stood up to him, when Starr was born?

"I thought the sun rose just to shine on him," Cory said, the long-ago remembrance making her voice soft. "I know you don't think well of him, but I married him. It's a funny thing, but no matter who loves you, all your life, the only ones that make a difference to you are the ones *you* love—real deep, no questions asked."

The cool hostility was still upon Starr. "You've fed and clothed him for years and years," she said, "and you know it. You could have done better." It was question and accusation all in one.

"I admit I studied about it sometimes," Cory said, obviously searching for words, which were not easy for her. "But even if I had found a better man—what would your pop have done? He was used to me. And supposin' I sent him away, and then didn't find a better man? He's not real vicious, like some. And when a woman's alone, it's hard to fix leaky roofs and busted pipes and crank a cold car. It's harder still to stand off the men that come around. Even a poor sort of man keeps the others all away, and that's something. He's handy to kill snakes and build fires, and nail things—" Her voice trailed off. She had done a bad job of explaining.

Starr's eyes were as wide as if she had just glimpsed hell. She backed wordlessly out of the room. She motioned to the dog and began walking away from the house. The tawdriness of Cory's and Bert's relationship made her ill. If she had learned the sum of the relationship between husbands and wives, then it was cowardly, ugly, degrading. And the books and magazines all lied, *they all lied,* when they should have been telling the truth! They had lied for hundreds of years! Could that be?

Blindly she walked toward the trees in the late afternoon. Ordinarily she would not have walked there. Tramps made their ugly hidey-holes there, dropping from trains into the sand of the dry river bed and then angling into the woods. There had been murders in those woods. But today Starr saw nothing but the cool green of the trees; she had never been closer to despair. The dog ran ahead of her and ran back, asking that she throw a stick. Starr did not notice him.

But presently when she was some distance into the woods, she heard him, and he was hurt. She ran toward the sound of his cries. He was caught in a rusty steel trap, whose jaws were fortunately weak. Set by some boy more vicious than an animal, she thought fiercely. She released the spring and massaged the toes that had been between the steel jaws. The dog was not seriously injured. He limped only slightly, and he headed for home.

"Hey!" said a voice behind her, and she turned, fright rising even as she turned. A large dirty tramp with the blue shadow of a heavy beard stood beneath a tree. And Lord, how far she had come into this wood! She could not return by the path she had followed in—the tramp blocked it. Quickly she turned and ran toward the river bed. At least it was clear of undergrowth, and someone passing on the highway a few blocks away might see her. The thing was, to get out into the open and stay there at all costs.

"Hey, wait! You lost something!" He was running after her, his heavy steps close behind. She took the most direct possible route, praying that she would not trip. Her heart pounded in her throat, leaving no breath for screaming.

She was too frightened to scream, even if there were anyone to hear her. Except for the double running footsteps
the wood was as still as if enchanted. There was no call, no
sound of any kind except the cars whooshing past on the
bridge over the river bed.

She broke from the cover of trees and very nearly ran
over a young man whose back was turned to her. He faced
the sand of the river bed with a paintbrush in his hand,
and before him was a half-finished painting on an easel.
Starr stumbled, trying to stop, and half fell toward him.
He caught her awkwardly, dropping his paintbrush. It
bled a blue stain on the white sand.

"Such a rush!" he said, but Starr interrupted.

"Please!" she said breathlessly. "Please, a dreadful
man—"

"Oh! I see." He was looking over her shoulder, and the
tramp was crashing nearer. "Sit down! I've been expecting
you for the longest time. What kept you?" He folded a
paint-smeared shirt wrong side out and made a seat for her
on the sand before he looked once more toward the tramp.

The tramp came on, more sedately. "The young lady
dropped her purse," he said, holding it before him. "I was
trying to give it back to her."

"It *is* mine," Starr said, still trembling violently.

She gave him what money the purse contained, which
was fifty cents, and he went back into the woods.

"I was scared," Starr said to the young man. "I knew
better than to walk alone in the woods, but they looked
so cool."

"I know. Rest awhile here, till you get your breath back,
then I'll take you home, if you like. My car's right up there
on the edge of the highway." He picked his brush from the

sand and began to clean it. Starr looked at him as frankly as he looked at her. He was a tall, rather thin man, about thirty, she would guess, with dark blue eyes and dark brown hair that waved slightly back from his face. The face was a pleasant one, quirked for a smile even when it was serious. Starr felt as if he must be a pool of calmness in a violent world.

"My name's Jeffrey Mayfield," he said. "I'm a geologist. I work in town for an oil company—and out on the desert sometimes. I've been here only a few weeks, but I've visited here several times before, because I had a classmate who grew up here. Any questions?"

"No. Only thank you. I'm Starr Cooper. I work in the stationery store as a stenographer, and this is my day off. It must have gone to my head, or I wouldn't be here interrupting you. I never saw anyone paint before." She arose and looked at the partially finished canvas. "You painted water in the river bed!"

"I like it better with water, don't you?"

"But there's no water there! If you were going to paint an imaginary river, you didn't need to come and look at this sand!"

"Yes I did! It's quiet here, and a bit cooler in the edge of the trees; and painting this gives me some excuse to sit here. It would just be odd to sit here without doing anything, wouldn't it?"

"I don't know. Why not?"

"I feel I need some excuse. I'm no artist, of course; but I always say if Winston Churchill can try, why can't I?" He had an impish sort of smile. "Are you interested in painting?"

"I don't know. How *can* I know? I never saw anyone

[65]

paint before. Once I bought a painting. It's a picture of a wave coming in to the beach. I never saw the ocean; I've never been out of this county."

"Anyway, you approve of water. Lots of water! And no wonder, growing up with the horned toads and the sagebrush and sand! Did it ever occur to you that the artist may have painted it without ever seeing such a wave?"

"No!" Starr was indignant. "I expect to see that very wave someday. I intend to go and find it next summer, when I have a vacation."

"You've quit trembling now," Jeffrey said. "Would you like to sit and watch me daub for a while, or would you like me to take you straight home? For the moment, there's this." He unfolded a paper bag and brought out a rather unattractive cheese sandwich and a small vacuum bottle. He broke the sandwich in two and gave half to Starr. He poured pop into the lid of the vacuum bottle and handed that to her also. "Breast of turkey and champagne," he declared.

They ate almost in silence. Starr watched him, but she was not afraid of him at all. After finishing the sandwich, Jeffrey looked once more at his canvas before folding it away. "Do you really think I should leave the river out?" he asked. "I could scrape it off."

"I don't see why," Starr answered. "You have one river more than most people around here, and you might as well keep it for your own."

"I might give it to you. That could be construed as a threat." He held out a hand to her and pulled her to her feet. Their shoes were filled with hot sand, walking to the car. They sat in the car and emptied the shoes.

"I like the whole thing," Jeffrey said, wriggling his toes

in his sock. "You're the very first girl I ever emptied shoes with, on first acquaintance, Starr-bright." He said it so easily, as if he had known her a long time, and liked her. "Maybe it's a good omen. You believe in omens, of course?" He was attractive, and he was trying to put her at ease, which was kind of him, but Starr would not forget that he was a man, and she was through with them. She would be courteous, and nothing more.

She showed him the way home, and he did not try to drive any long way around. They passed a miniature golf course, and he slowed. "I could beat you at that, I bet. Would you like to try?"

It was daylight, a public place, and close to home. Starr did not really want to go home—not ever. She hesitated, and Jeffrey pulled the car to a stop. "It won't keep you very long," he said. "I'll have you home in time for your date." He smiled and took her hand, and she went with him. Before they had played one round they were calling each other by given names, and even harsher names in the heat of competition.

He delivered her home before dusk. She had him drive on Angello Street, to see the disorder and the shabbiness and the cheapness of it. That ought to be enough to discourage any further attentions. He said nothing. As he stopped the motor at her front gate she said, "You see?" motioning vaguely, wondering if he would understand.

He looked straight into her eyes, and his own were disconcertingly kind. "I see," he said. Then with a certain shyness he added, "I wish we had some mutual friend to introduce us properly, but I'm so new here. I'd like to see you again, if you have time."

Suddenly she was deeply grateful to him for filling most

of an afternoon with fun and nonsense, and for a delicacy that she had never known in any man. "Make no mind," she said. "You can telephone me sometime if you want to."

"I will, then." He smiled again. "Next time, I'll come in and meet your folks. Thank you for the afternoon." And he was gone.

But there was a stillness within Starr where there had been only seething when she left the house. She looked at the picture of the wave with new affection. She washed her hair and ironed some blouses, then sat and read a book with real pleasure until it was time for sleep. And again she slept dreamlessly, to wake refreshed.

3.

$\mathcal{J}$T WAS two weeks before Jeffrey telephoned. He had found a swimming pool about five miles south of town, with a jukebox and small pavilion. Did Starr know whether it was a proper place for him to take her? She reassured him and accepted his invitation with a surprising lift of spirits. When he called for her, he came in to be introduced to the whole family. Cory liked him on sight, and Ann Marie was surprised into quietness. Even the baby crawled toward him as if he were no stranger, and Jeffrey picked her up.

One awkwardness never occurred between Starr and Jeff—he never offered her a drink. That first day he had to stop at his own place for his swimming trunks. He drove to an exclusive residence section and straight through the extensive shady grounds of a large and lovely home. Near a cottage by the garage, he turned the car around and said he wouldn't take a moment. "I live here in Dick's special quarters," he said. "He made this 'studio' when he was in college, and I used to visit him here. He doesn't live here any more, but his mother lets me use the place as my own, so long as I don't get loud and rowdy. Would you like to see it?"

Starr declined, and he was back in a moment with his trunks. "Mrs. Maple is the only wonderful landlady in the world," he said as they drove away. "She's a widow, but she has her own interests, and so doesn't butt in on people. Sometimes she goes on long trips, which is why she likes to have me about—to scare off burglars while she's away. She scares her own when she's home."

"She sounds terrifying."

"She's a deceitful small package of fluff," Jeff said, "completely lined with stainless steel. Lap dogs are the most dreaded of watchdogs, you know."

They swam that day and dried out on the grass. They ate the lunch Jeff had prepared—not very good, but thick of sandwich. "I should have brought the lunch, at least," Starr said idly.

"It's no trouble for me," Jeff said. "There's a refrigerator and a couple of burners on a little business where I can fry an egg for breakfast. And there are all of Dick's books and records and an easy chair. People with my kind of a job are apt to be transferred at the drop of a hat, and I haven't been so comfortable for years. You don't mind if I brag a little?"

"No. And it's a good lunch. Fills you up. I've been just a bit hungry most of my life, so I eat a lot when I can." It was easy to be frank with Jeff.

"A few square meals wouldn't fatten you unfashionably, for a fact," he said. "Not that I'm complaining, you understand!"

"You're not so overburdened with lard, yourself," Starr said critically, viewing his long, slim legs. Jeff replied that it was his great brain that took all the nourishment.

They danced to the jukebox, and he did not hold her

too closely. He liked to dance; his joy in it flowed easily to her. They were the only couple on the floor in the advancing dusk. When the lights suddenly went on—blue and green and red—they left.

All conversation was easy with Jeff. Their delight was mutual when they discovered that both read books. "I thought it was already a lost art!" Jeff said. "I didn't know they taught your generation to read at all without pictures and games to ease the frightful strain!"

"Maybe that was the trouble—I couldn't find anyone who liked to read. Not even my own family. It makes you lonely, doesn't it?"

"Lots of things make me lonely," Jeff said, with no smile. "I think maybe loneliness is the natural state of a human being—most of the time."

It was a new thought for Starr. If it were so, it made everything more understandable. She thought about it at length, in bed at home that night. If loneliness were the natural state, then no one ought to fuss about it. She had been lonely most of her life—why had she thought things would be changed? Only because she had made up her mind to marry Jerry, that was why. And if Shirley had not mercifully taken him instead, Starr would have been lonely all her life—all of it! Her narrow escape made her sweat to consider. For now she knew what companionship was.

Something rare and lovely—something to be enjoyed. A friend made all the days trip past with meaning that he was in the world, and that sometimes he telephoned. Not to go out and drink, not to wrestle in the obscure dark, but openly letting her enjoy some of the things he enjoyed. He loaned her books!

[71]

Finally she trusted him enough to go into his cottage with him to select the books, or even to listen to the absent owner's beautiful records.

Teresa Bedeau asked her if she were sweet on Jeff. There was no more reticence in her than in a little sniffing dog. Starr could answer with more pride than ever Teresa could guess, "Jeff's my friend." He made no move ever to touch or kiss her, and to herself she called him "the cool one," after all the wrestling and the bitterness she had known before she knew him. Sometimes she thought she detected a warmth in his glance, or a special smile when she amused him or turned a facet of thought new to his exploring mind.

Winter passed quickly, in a delicate sifting of rain. The mushrooms popped in the fields, and Starr taught Jeff to pick them, so that they walked miles in the filmy curtains of mist, with the dog running before them, hysterical at the smell of rabbits. Lone larks sat on the wire fences and proclaimed that it was spring.

"Why don't you paint a lark on a wire, with tumbleweed behind him? He's the happiest thing in the world." Starr watched the lark.

Jeff watched her. "Who paints a song?" he asked. "Who paints the sound of spring itself? Only color goes on my canvases." He pulled his old hat lower over his ears, still watching Starr's damp face framed by the bandanna she wore. "If I were a real artist, I'd paint you instead of the lark, and name it Spring."

Starr saved a few dollars each week, but it was no longer a matter of great interest to her. The lupine and the poppies were beginning to bloom in the foothills, and she was looking at the world through Jeff's eyes and finding it exciting. Sunday afternoons he always came to take her for a drive or for a walk. He was endlessly inventive to find new things to capture her interest and was often genuinely entertained by her comments, still flavored with her mother's colloquialisms.

When the wild flowers were at the peak of their blossom, Jeff drove Starr into the canyons on a Sunday afternoon, doubling back and back over narrow roads until he came to a sort of plateau in the foothills. He carried his painting equipment, and Starr carried food. They put a plastic tablecloth upon some of the flowers, so that the dampness would not come through where she sat and watched. He had selected late afternoon because of the light, and he showed her how it fell dark blue in the canyons and brighter blue on the lupine-covered hills in sunlight, and all the distances were misty blue with haze and golden with sun.

"When I was small I said I would come to these mountains and see what was here," Starr said. "Now I'm here, and they're much lovelier than I might have seen them if you hadn't shown me."

"I've been here before," Jeff said. "In the fall they're all tawny, like a lion asleep, and almost more beautiful than they are now—especially at dusk, when the sky turns that special cobalt."

"Did you come alone, Jeff?" It was the first time she had ventured a personal question to him. It was as if she held her breath.

He smiled, mixing colors from his tubes. "I came alone," he said very seriously. "I brought my paintbrush along, of course, to make it decent and endurable."

For a long time she thought of him here alone on the lion-colored hill at dusk. He was painting without words, very busy and fast, as if he had only this one day of all time to catch this blue and gold on canvas. He did not stop until the light grew too dim for accuracy. Then he folded away his materials, and she put out the food while the twilight sky glowed incandescent blue. There was such a peace in her whole being that she felt part of the sky and plains, still and complete.

"It wasn't good," he said finally, "but it was fun trying." The air was chill now, and he went downhill to the car and brought up coats. The first great stars appeared as they ate. The moon was a glow below the horizon, lighting the eastern rim of the mountains. Jeff said a fire would be fine, but it would also be conspicuous, and might bring fire wardens like a plague of locusts. They must eat quickly and go home.

"It's waiting," Starr said. "Something's waiting, holding its breath before the moon comes up. Can't you feel it?"

"Yes," Jeff said, very low, "I feel the waiting. But I had hoped you wouldn't, yet. Not for a while, anyway." There was a sadness in his voice.

Starr began hastily to put food and napkins back in a box, hunting them in the dusk. "We don't have to stay for the waiting," she said quickly. "The moon's rim is over the mountain, but we can go right now."

Jeff caught her hand and pulled her close beside him, and brightening moonlight made the planes of his face light, and his eyes all shadows. "We can't run away from the waiting in a car," he said quietly. "I can't run away from it ever."

Except in dancing, Starr had never touched him, and now she leaned against him, sympathetic with some trouble whose origin she could not even guess. She reached toward his shoulders with an instinctive comforting gesture—and was suddenly melted with shyness, her hands halfway. She looked at his face for guidance.

"Put them around my neck, this once," he said; and she did, quickly, laying her face against his coat. He tilted her face up and kissed her mouth, and it was the most perfect and natural and joyous thing that Starr had ever known. Nothing in the world was ever the same for her after that, nor would she ever truly wish it might be.

It was he who disentangled her arms and yet held her close, stroking her hair. "One kiss surely can't hurt you, and I wanted it such a long while," he said. "But now I have to spoil it—right now, while I have the courage. Put your head there on my shoulder so I can't see your face and you can't see mine." He held her there quietly. "There's no easy way to tell you. I never can say I love you, and I never can ask you to marry me. That's the sum of it. I had no right to kiss you—no right even to want to kiss you."

"You're married." Her voice was forlorn, but she was not evasive.

"Yes, Starr. In a way I've lied to you. At first I told myself maybe you were lonely, too. I said a bit of companionship never hurt anyone—especially if I left you lots of free time to see other men. I said if I evaded the subject, there would be no lie. I told myself a lot of things, but there really isn't any defense for me. I can't even say I'm sorry and mean it." His arms tightened about her.

Shock kept Starr steady in the yawning grief of the moment. She put her hands together and held them tight, as if they hurt—that was all. She did not look at his face. "Maybe I should have guessed. You don't any more suspect love than you suspect the coming of spring to hurt, do you? Where is . . . your wife?"

"Louise," Jeff said. "She's in Alabama, where her aunt looks after her. I can't take her around with me."

"She's . . . an invalid?" The painful words dragged on.

"You might say so," Jeff said. "She's—not responsible. She drinks and can't help it. Her aunt watches her for me, but Louise gets away. Sometimes she's in a sanitarium, and she improves temporarily, then. . . . And she hasn't anyone but me to pay for her. I send the money to her aunt—such a lot of money. . . . Starr, I can't talk about it. She writes to me, the letters of a good child. . . ."

"How long?" Starr asked. "I have to know. I have a right to know, even if it's hard for you."

"Seven years. It was while I was in training, right after Pearl Harbor, stuffed with romance and adventure. She was the prettiest thing I'd ever seen, and a bit tipsy—and so was I—at this beautiful old southern mansion. I knew simply nothing about her, but we married in a matter of days. Must I?"

Starr nodded against his chest.

"She was an only child, motherless since babyhood, and devoted to her father. The father had died suddenly a few months earlier, and she was still distracted with grief. She was eighteen then, and hadn't been entirely sober since her father's funeral. I learned later that I bore a slight resemblance to him. In fact, I learned a lot of things later, when we visited Aunt Nettie at 'home' for her blessing. Louise had nearly driven Aunt Nettie out of her wits, and Aunt Nettie was on the verge of proud starvation in her run-down old house, which she shared with Louise. She's a great lady—Aunt Nettie—without a snobbish or selfish bone in her body.

"I couldn't believe that Louise's drinking was serious. It took me six months to acknowledge it. There would have been a baby, but she fell down. When she lost the baby, she also lost most of her contact with reality. I had to take her back to Aunt Nettie, so she could be watched and treated." He was silent for a moment, as if mobilizing his courage.

"Sometimes she improves for a month or two, and I always try to get back to see her then. She remembers me, and is devoted to me, and full of plans for our future, now that she is well. But she never stays well for more than two or three weeks. That's all; that's all there is, please. . . ."

Starr could feel the restraint in his whole body. Then she did put her hands on his shoulders and held them tight and steady, and she laid her cheek against his face. "Make no mind," she said, out of the tearless blank of her shock. "It just hurts, that's all. You've nothing to be ashamed of— nor I. A person can't help being lonesome."

"Not yet," Jeff said. "But can we keep it this way? Nothing stands still. It grows or it dies. And I think you better say good-by to me tonight. You may not know the necessity for it, but I do. You're so very young and beautiful, Starr."

"I'll think about it," Starr said. She held up her face for a kiss, and thought for a moment he would refuse her, but he did not. Their very touch was promise and despair, confused and entreating. He pushed her away and frowned at her. "You see?" he said. "Even you can see, Starr!"

"Why wouldn't I? It's only that I have to lean on somebody sometimes, even if it's only for a minute!" She put her hands over her face, and the tears slid through her fingers. Jeff gave her his handkerchief and told her to blow. He picked up the tablecloth and loaded himself with the other things and started downhill, Starr stumbling after in the moonlight.

[77]

As he started the car she said, "I'm all right now. I'll be all right." But Jeff said nothing at all, threading through the deep canyons and over the round rims of hills until they were at 45 Angello Street. Then he said without touching her, "Good-by, Starr. I'll miss you all my life."

She tried to see his face, but it was in shadow. She did not trust her voice, but touched his hand on the wheel, then ran into the house.

For a while she was numb, of course. But most of her days were planned. They proceeded along their regular course. She worked five days a week; she washed and ironed on her day off; she helped with cooking and cleaning and minding of curly-headed Caroline. The baby was a sort of comfort, knowing no sorrow and few words, and she laughed almost all day long. Caro usually went to the fields with Cory, as Starr had done before her. "That's one thing my job has, that yours don't have," Cory said. "I can take my kids along."

The days slid beneath the broiler of the sun, each longer than an evil dream. But when Starr was finally in her hot, narrow bed, she slept poorly and dreamed often of Jeff. They would be touching fingers through a heavy wire fence stretching up to heaven itself, running endlessly in either direction. She would wake in tears. It's not fair, she would say in the night. It's not fair, the dreams!

There was still occasionally the suggestion that she date some new young man, but she was not interested. It was too much trouble. Probably just be another amorous ape masquerading in trousers. When Cory questioned her about what had become of Jeff, Starr said they had agreed to disagree—making it sound quite commonplace, though for the same effort she could have written it in tall letters in her own blood.

Cory would not pry, but Teresa Bedeau would. She marked Starr's every movement; her ferret eyes missed no movement by anyone on Angello Street. "Are you mad at him, or is he mad at you?" she asked Starr, cocking her head, dark curls bouncing.

"Neither of us is mad at the other," Starr said, her voice edged with irritation. "But I don't mean to give you the details, so you might as well go off and make up your own story about it."

"Well, jeez, what d'ya snap at *me* for?" Teresa asked in injured tones. "I sure like them earrings you're wearing."

"You can't have them."

The days and the weeks crept past, and Starr hated the silver-green sheen of the young cottonwood leaves and the blue-on-blue of blended hills and sky. Better I never had learned to look at color, she thought perversely; but being honest, she would then acknowledge her debt wryly. It was only that somewhere within her was an aching as if she had been beaten. Beaten much worse than Cory when she received a black eye from Bert. Nothing, nothing healed the inward wound. Every telephone was huge with temptation, but she did not succumb to any of them. Though once or twice she put a hand upon one and remembered Jeff's number with such yearning that she thought his phone must ring for the very wishing.

After four weeks, upon a sticky Sunday afternoon, she answered the phone, and Jeff said in a humble voice, "Hello, Starr," and nothing else.

"Oh, Jeff!" She put both hands to the receiver, aware

that her voice had betrayed all the dignity and denial she
had fostered in stillness.

"I . . . I'll be around to pick you up directly—is that all
right?" Still his voice was uncertain.

"Yes," she said, stricken dumb with hope. "Yes, Jeff."

She stood in the middle of the room and clasped her
hands to her head, trying to think of what to wear. Presently
she was running out to his car, and he was there—oh, the
friendly, comfortable remembered length of him! With his
face thinner, as was her own, and a bit more serious then
ever she had seen it. There were no words—simply happiness
restored from death. When they had traveled miles into
the baked countryside he said, "Where does a fellow take
his girl in this hostile land? It's all public, under the glare
of the sun. There isn't an inviting patch of grass—just dried
foxtails with horned spurs, for a person to sit upon, and no
shade except for jack rabbits and horned toads."

"It isn't the desert or the climate," Starr said. "I know
a worse desert."

"And I—I know it well enough," he said. He pulled the
car from the road, across the sand and into the doubtful
shade of a tree dying of its burden of mistletoe. He cut the
ignition and put his hands in his lap and looked straight
ahead.

"I got you into this, Starr, and I'll try to help you out,"
he said finally. "I couldn't any more leave it the way it was
than I could leave your baby sister floundering in a river."

"I didn't ask for help," Starr said, almost harshly. "I'm
a big girl now."

"I know you didn't." Jeff looked at her, and she blinked
back tears. "I can't undo what's done, but I can aim you

[80]

in another direction. At least I can try, and it would help my self-respect if you'd let me try."

"I'll listen," Starr said. "I've been wondering what to do—what to do with all the *time*. You can't read it all away, and it's a waste to go out with the kind of men I knew before."

Gently he took her hand. "I've thought an awful lot about you in the past few weeks," he said. "I've thought about what's to become of you."

"Well, what is?"

"It will only be second best," Jeff said. "But after all, God didn't give us brains just to fill out under our scalps. I know you don't belong on Angello Street. If you ever did, you've outgrown it, and it hasn't left a scar on you."

"It's the best I've known, and there's no place else for me," Starr said steadily. "I've thought about it, too. I could rent a hall bedroom on some other street, perhaps in another town, but it wouldn't be much better, and it wouldn't have Mom in it. Nor Caroline."

"I know. Your mother's a great lady, and Caroline is like your own child. But with them goes your brother and Ann Marie and your father—and all Angello Street. You have to get out, Starr, while you're still armored with beauty. You'll never escape if you don't go while you're young. I know."

"But, Jeff, don't you think that maybe things just happen to people—that things sometimes work out for them the way they ought to be?"

"Yes," Jeff said sternly, "things do just happen! Things that shouldn't happen to a dog! You have to see that they don't—that you make them happen the way you plan." He held the wheel of the car so tightly that his knuckles were white.

[81]

"I'm listening."

"I can't stay here always. Oil men move and move. When my boss says go, I go. So it's well that we send you out as soon as possible. The first idea is to find you a much better job, so you can acquire a wardrobe. Nothing can make you more beautiful, but you need expensive and beautiful suits and dresses—for which some firm will gladly pay."

"But how can I buy expensive clothes when Mom—"

He interrupted harshly. "I'm trying to separate you and me," he said. "I'm trying to separate you from your family. I have in mind to make you so exquisite that you can marry any unattached millionaire before he knows what fell on his head."

"I don't want to marry a millionaire," Starr said flatly.

"Might be a useful quality, though," Jeff said. "You might change your mind someday. It's something I can give you in return for . . . a wound, perhaps. And Starr, it would give me an excuse to see you sometimes! I would be so light of touch—oh, quite impersonal, if you'd only help me a little bit to keep steady! And afterward I would feel that I hadn't left you entirely without compensation and without weapons. Maybe someday you can look back and say, 'Jeff Mayfield was quite educational, in a way!' "

"I could already say that."

Noting her voice, he looked again at her, and tears had beaded her eyelashes and her lip was caught in her teeth. She turned quickly away. He put his hand over her two anguished ones. "Will you work with me, Starr, just to see if I might be right?"

She looked back at him with those honest eyes wet with tears. "I have no choice," she said. "I *have* to see you if I can, as you will. Now I know it. With summer coming on, and Hank coming back from college to work in the store again, I think I'd go mad fighting him five days a week whenever his father's back is turned. Except that sometimes I can see you, and for a few hours I think everything's all right in the world. Even when I know it isn't! It's like magic—I know it isn't true, but still. . . ."

She had to explain to Jeff about Hank. Then Jeff said she must find a job right away. He would begin to look.

"Thank you," Starr said.

"Dammit, don't thank me that way, as if you didn't know me."

"Then this way?" She put her arms quickly about his neck.

His own arms were tight about her for a moment, and his lips too swift on hers to question. But presently he put her on her own side of the seat, his breath short. "Not that way again—not that way ever," he said. "Help me to help us—don't let me destroy what I'm trying to do!"

"Yes, Jeff," Starr said quietly. "I do understand. But"—and one hand flew to her breast—"it heals a pain for a moment."

Jeff looked at her with hostility. "Just don't do it!" he said. "Never mind why." He started home. "I want to see you as soon as I look over the job situation. Is Starr Cooper your full name?"

"Yes."

"A cooper is a barrelmaker. You have a name like a barrel of stars—did you ever think of that?"

"I can think of better names."

"Maybe I can too. Now are you going to be a prickly mess to work with?"

"No, Jeffrey." Her face had settled to serenity. "I'm going

to let you groom me to be the wife of a millionaire. Will you find one for me then?"

He did not answer, and she realized that he was deeply troubled. She moved closer to him. "Stop being afraid for me, and stop being afraid for us," she said. "There are days and maybe weeks when we still can see each other. I won't pretend I don't love every one of them. If that's all there is, then I intend to enjoy what I have."

"I could take lessons from you in the matter of sheer guts."

"No. It's a feature of being thrifty. All my life I've seen old dresses made into aprons, and old aprons sewed together and boiled for dish towels. I've seen clothes mended and turned and remade; I've seen new handles put on old hoes, and old furniture nailed and glued again and again. I'm thrifty with what materials I have to work with—that's all."

"We have a little more time together." Jeff found it as precious as she did.

When she left the car, she smiled back at Jeff. He smiled uncertainly. As long as there was another meeting, she decided, they still could smile. Hope beyond reason flooded the whole world with beauty.

In this mood she used part of her next day off to visit Aunt Artie. Of all the people she knew, Starr could think of none better informed in the field of love and its disasters. She found her suffering a hang-over. "Ah, men!" Aunt Artie said with a grin that was imperishable. "I never should've had the third highball—never!"

"You have a lot of dates, don't you, Aunt Artie?"

"Seems like I never find enough to take up all the evenings," Aunt Artie said. "Still, it beats a steady husband *that* always costs you money, sooner or later." She sat up in her untidy bed and held her tousled head until Starr could prepare coffee on the hot plate.

"Yes," Aunt Artie said between sips, "I mortally can't afford a full-time husband. First one sold everything not tied down, and took off. Second one took the bank account, and a long-legged brunette took him. Last one powdered out without taking anything—nothing to take! But I had to pay his income taxes. Never make out an income tax form jointly, Starr. It leaves you liable for your husband's income tax. Oh, yes, they cost you if you marry them! On the other hand, they're no expense, and sometimes even buy your dinner if you *don't* marry 'em. It's simpler that way. Lonesomer, but simpler." Aunt Artie put a hand to her brow and emitted a heartfelt moan.

"It's a wonder you didn't have children," Starr said. "Didn't you want any?"

"Once I did—real bad—more than anything," Aunt Artie said quietly. "But seein' how things panned out, I guess it wouldn't have been right for a kid. I like 'em all right! Look at that Caroline—gee, that's a sweet baby!"

"Aunt Artie," Starr asked, "is it too personal to ask if you loved all your husbands?"

"You can't look back and be sure," Aunt Artie said gravely. "The first one, for sure. The second one—maybe I fooled myself. The third one—it was a relief to be shut of him. I knew better than to marry him. But, Starr"—and her eyes were very sad and vulnerable—"sometimes a woman gets desperate just to have something alive around the house."

Starr turned her eyes from Aunt Artie with a suddenly mature appreciation of her gallantry. Aunt Artie deserved better. And maybe she would have fared better if *she* had

[85]

married a millionaire when her first young love failed her. You had to acknowledge that. Once Aunt Artie had been a real beauty. The traces of it still sat behind her eyes, like some shimmering force lightly caged with years and netted with delicate alien lines and wrinkles. Starr could have wept for her helplessness and ultimate defeat.

Thursday Jeff took Starr to a movie, and on the way told her that he had found a vacancy in a position as private secretary to an oil tycoon. It would pay fifty dollars more per month than she earned now, and work and surroundings would be pleasant. But she would need a wardrobe and a manner. This man wanted something between a model and a debutante for a secretary.

"I have a hundred dollars," Starr said. "I suppose I could—"

"You couldn't find a thing suitable here, and it'll take at least three hundred. I'll advance you a couple, and you can pay me back from your increased wages. Just don't tell your folks that you get more salary on the new job."

"But three hundred dollars for *clothes!*" Starr was appalled. Cory had never had more than one "good" dress; she needed shoes.

"In a few months, you'll have paid for them, and they'll last a long time," Jeff said. "Then you can enjoy the extra income."

"But where do I go for them?"

Thoughtfully Jeff said, "Probably Westwood. It's near a college, and so, apt to have things to fit you. Yes, of course! The mother of a friend of mine is a shopper. I can get in touch with her, to make it quicker for you. I have to run down to Long Beach anyway, on business. You could ride down with me Friday night, and I could pick you up and bring you home on Sunday night. I might even get through on Saturday, and we could see a show or go dancing on Saturday night."

"My vacation begins Saturday," Starr said, already thinking of the new job.

"I always stay at the same motel, and I know it's clean and neat and not too expensive. It's near a shopping area. I'll pick you up—no, for appearances' sake, you'd better take the bus, and get off at the first stop. I'll be there, waiting."

The little subterfuge shocked her for a moment. But she realized almost simultaneously that it was Jeff's way of protecting her from possible gossip. It was hard to remember that he was married. She bought her bus ticket to the next town on the way home.

But the next day, her decision was not so clear. Perhaps she had better stay home. On the other hand, Jeff would be waiting. . . .

Perhaps she would have stayed if she had not heard a row through the door before she opened it. Ann Marie was almost shrieking at her erstwhile friend Teresa Bedeau. "I don't mind you lying and stealing and sleeping with everything in pants," Ann Marie was saying furiously, "but remember this: Don't try to steal from *me!* Now give me back my lipstick and my slip—and don't you ever take a thing of mine again!"

"All right, all *right!* I just borrowed 'em; take 'em back! But if you ever tattle on me, just remember I've been on many a cotton-patch date with you and *your* boy friends! Just remember that! And what's more, if you're thinkin' about marryin' David, you better play harder to get, fast! I tell you that to show I'm friendly. I—"

[87]

Starr knocked at the door, which had opened without a knock all these years. Not that she was surprised—Ann Marie had never been fastidious. Still, as long as she didn't know, she could pretend better. Ann Marie turned a round, guilty face to the mirror, and in the mirror her eyes were apprehensive. Starr went through the room and began packing a cheap suitcase. Cory came home from work and went straight to the kitchen.

"Goin' somewhere?" Teresa asked avidly. Ah, she sniffed and tracked and hunted scandal as a dog hunts a buried bone!

"Yes."

"Where?"

"Los Angeles."

"Tonight? Who with?"

"Alone, on the bus. Going shopping tomorrow."

"Gee, couldn't I go with you?" Ann Marie asked suddenly.

"No."

"Why not?"

"Because I want to shop alone."

"I wouldn't be any trouble, sis. I'd just go along and see the shops. What you going to buy that has to be bought in Los Angeles?"

"A suit. Maybe some shoes—several things. I just want to go shopping."

Cory came in from the kitchen. "If you see a real nice blouse for about two dollars," she said, "I wish you'd pick it up for me. Both of mine tore out under the arms."

A two-dollar blouse. Yes, that was Cory's speed, financially. Decades of hauling heavy cotton sacks, of stooping, bending, using the endless energy of her fine body—and she

[88]

could perhaps afford a two-dollar blouse. "I'll bring you a blouse," Starr said.

"Make Starr take me along," Ann Marie said to Cory.

"Wouldn't it be nicer for you if you did?" Cory asked. "Where will you stay?"

"With Sarah if she has room; at a hotel if she hasn't. I want to shop alone." Sarah was an acquaintance who had moved to Los Angeles. Starr had to think fast to remember her at all.

"Well, you was always the separate one," Cory said. "I ain't got the right to say take Ann Marie."

"I shan't take her."

"We can take her to the bus depot," Teresa said. Starr knew she simply wanted to see if she *were* going on the bus.

"Very well. I want to make the six o'clock, so I'll get there before dark."

"I'll fix you a snack," Cory said. "You won't have time for a meal tonight." Over Starr's protests she deftly scrambled eggs and made sandwiches and put them into a bag. "That'll have to do. When you coming home?"

"Maybe tomorrow night—maybe Sunday night. I'll get home before Monday. Don't worry."

"I don't worry about you," Cory said. "I never did. You don't do things just like I did, but you do show judgment. Just remember that they's wicked people in big cities."

And wicked people everywhere, Starr thought. Be hard to live in a place of greater wickedness than Angello Street, with its brawls and knifings and its drunks and has-beens. But one is not afraid of the familiar, no matter how ugly the face of it.

Luckily she already had her ticket to the next town. Teresa and Ann Marie stood around and watched until

Starr was seated and the bus moved away. "You know," Teresa said thoughtfully to Ann Marie, "I had a notion she had a man—just like anybody else."

"Starr with a man?" Ann Marie said incredulously. "No. Starr's all brain. She just uses the rest of her to hang clothes on."

Jeff established Starr at his favorite motel in a pleasant detached cottage, took her out to dinner, then followed this with a stage show as a special treat. It was her first, and she loved it. There was a certain constraint between them as he drove her back to her motel, but Jeff dispersed it with talk of the next day's shopping. He gave her the name and telephone number of the shopper he knew. He gave her one chaste good-night kiss, left her at her door, and started for Long Beach. "I'll telephone you when I'll be back," he said, and was gone.

In her strange soft bed that night, Starr dreamed upon his kiss, and wished she might have kissed him again—he was so sparing of personal contact. But that would be silly, of course; maybe even dangerous.

The shopper was available. Starr arranged to meet her when the stores opened. She was preparing to leave when Jeff telephoned from Long Beach. His work would be concluded in the early afternoon, he said, and if Starr liked, he would pick her up somewhere . . . he had a surprise in mind for her. Instantly Starr's joy rose like a barometer reading on a summer day.

Mrs. Romaine, the shopper, had a faintly French accent. She had a marvelous figure, blue-white hair cleverly cut to the curves of her pert head, and a wide, wise mouth, which opened in a laugh the moment she met Starr. "There is a

God, after all!" she said happily. "I get too terribly tired trying to make size forties look like size elevens. Oh, look at the figure!" She pushed Starr's coat back and ran an inquisitive light hand from ribs to hip line. "Natural!" she murmured ecstatically. "If some like you didn't come along occasionally, I'd cut my own throat. How much have you to spend, and what do you want to look like?"

"I want to look like a smart debutante turned secretary," Starr said directly. She gave Mrs. Romaine all the details as they hurried into a department store.

"A few of the basics here, and suits at a special place for your size—sale going on right now. . . ." Her sentences often trailed away. "A face to wear hats, too," she added, gloating. "Hats aren't made for faces any more, and few have a face to wear hats."

Mrs. Romaine had a pure zest for shopping, and a talent for talking prices down. Starr was excited and enthused before they had galloped about for an hour. And as her wardrobe took shape, something new crept unnoticed into her manner.

Actually, they did not buy a great deal, though they spent what seemed to Starr shocking sums on accessories—purses, belts, pins, shoes. They even briefly visited a hairdresser, who cut Starr's hair short and showed her how to dampen and dry it so that the gentle wave was careless short curls. And looking into the mirror, above the hairdresser's white bib, Starr saw her grave new beauty for an instant. It's really because of Jeff, though, she thought. It's not just new clothes and a new hair style—but, oh, how glad I am to have it!

Mrs. Romaine left, and Jeff came to take charge of her and all her bundles and boxes. She saw him before he saw

[91]

her, and watched the swing of his walk and the set of his head—so special to himself, so particularly dear and familiar. Then he saw her, and his whole face changed, filled with surprise and tenderness, so that Starr was deeply touched. Quickly she filled the moment with nonsense, putting out her gloved hand as if she expected him to take it. "You may kiss us," she said regally, holding the hand high as he approached.

He came closer, ignoring the hand. "I may kiss the ground you walk on!" he said, completely off guard for once. "I thought I'd know exactly how you'd look, but I didn't— I didn't at all!"

Starr piled his arms with bundles and stacked her own arms full. "I look expensive and correct," she said, "and I've had such fun—I wish you could have been along! Mrs. Romaine was wonderful. She must know everything there is about style and color and line. Did you know that the more expensive the shoppe, the Frencher the accents? Now this suit, for instance, was sold by a woman who said, 'Ees chic! Madame ees petite, ees chic! Eef I wore the suits like Madame, I would be more broker than I am!' " She peered around her packages at Jeff, and still he looked at her in that half-helpless, wholly dazed way, so that she lapsed into quiet walking beside him to the car. She could have danced in her sleek slippers and lovely suit, there on the street.

Jeff stored her packages in the back of the car and took her to the Farmer's Market for lunch. She had a wonderful time, watching the frosting of cakes in a window and throwing her pennies into the Wishing Well ("I'll probably be wishing I had them back," she noted thriftily). They lingered over lunch, neither quite conscious of what was being served. Starr smiled across the table at him. She would rather be here than anywhere in the world. This might be a temporary relationship, but it was the most rewarding one she ever had known. How tasteful were his clothes, how clean he was, how assured and happy! She reached out and touched his hand on the table.

"Darling Starr—be careful!" He smiled slightly, but his voice was so charged with emotion that she froze for a moment. Where their hands touched, some exquisite current crackled to life. It set the blood racing to her face, and she removed her hand quickly.

"I forgot," she said. "Forgive me."

He said nothing, but his glance was more intimate than his few kisses ever had been. She could not wish to evade it; she tried. His hand still rested palm up, on the table. If she put her hand confidently into his—oh, she wanted to, very much!

He broke the taut moment by standing. "We have far to go," he said. "Ask me no questions." They returned to the car, and Jeff devoted his whole attention to the afternoon traffic for more than an hour.

"Now I want you to shut your eyes, and keep them shut, no matter what, until I tell you to open them," he said.

Starr laid her head back on the seat and shut her eyes. She wished that the car never need stop, so that they never would be separated. The car did stop, however, and Jeff said, "You can open your eyes now."

An enormous green wave was breaking on a beach not fifty feet away. "Oh, Jeff!" She squeezed his arm, her eyes on the surf. "Let's go to it; let's go—" She was climbing from the car.

"Hey! You'll need this. Present!" He handed her a paper

bag, and a simple blue wool bathing suit slid out of it. Starr held it in one hand, speechless with excitement.

"Where's yours? We can get right in that wave! You *did* bring trunks? I almost can't wait! Hurry—oh, hurry!"

Running down the beach to the ocean, Starr shouted through the crash of breakers, "Jeff, this is the loveliest present in the whole world! Nobody but you would know how thrilled I would be!" She caught his hand, and they ran into the surf. Jeff held her when the slam of the wave took her breath away, and he kissed her there in the surf, holding her with hard wet arms—a kiss wild and tangy with salt.

Later as they warmed on the sand, Starr said, "The bathing suit fits exactly right. How did you know it would?"

"I know the shape of you, and even the shape of your thoughts," Jeff said without stirring. "I know exactly how high your heart with the adventure of sand and sea."

"And you're so calm and superior! As soon as I get through being stunned, I'll be annoyed with you." Starr cast herself back on the sand and blissfully closed her eyes. "And people talk about golden streets and harps and wings and mansions," she said. "Certainly things thought up far from a beach, or they could have done better!"

After early dinner they returned to the motel. Better to return to Statsville tomorrow, they had agreed. Jeff would find a room at the motel for the night.

The exquisite tension developed between them again on the way back. Jeff was wary as a stranger with Starr. To her it seemed the most natural thing in the world that they should be going home together. It was as natural as the sound of surf still in her mind—always known, never heard before. But she made an effort to put Jeff more at ease. "I'll take out every dress and open every package tonight," she said. "I can't wait to look at all the lovely things again."

Jeff tried, too. "May I look? I'm as interested as you are." He spoke very matter-of-factly.

They took the boxes and packages into Starr's cabin, and she began opening them with mounting excitement. Jeff sat and watched, and commented approvingly from time to time on colors and styles. Then Starr opened a box containing a robe of Oriental style and fabric, tan and gold and blue. It was plain. "I guess I got some other woman's package," she said regretfully. "Surely a pretty thing, isn't it?" She held it up, then slipped her arms into the sleeves.

"It's yours if you want it," Jeff said, his voice uneven.

She ran toward him, smiling, reaching for his hands. But when she clasped one she found herself unable to remove her own. It wanted to stay there in his, as if it had a stubborn life of its own. A flame of terrible excitement danced in it, too. Very slowly she raised her eyes to look at Jeff, to see if he were so afflicted. He had risen to his feet, and now wordlessly he set his hands on her shoulders, pulling her roughly close. His hands skimmed to her elbows, to her waist, pulling her closer, closer. He bent his head above her own, and the excitement was bursting like a star shell in the night sky. She crept as close to him as she could.

His endearments were a torrent, and his kisses all demand. And she was suddenly exultant that it was so. She could have sent him away with one word—but she could not and would not say it. And he did not demand it of her. She had thought he might.

Afterward, unsleeping beside him in the dark, she was frightened a little, but she put out a hand, and he held it. She knew again the exquisite peace of having him near.

[95]

"I'm not a bit sorry," she said. "If you never lie beside me again, then this once I love having you here."

Very seriously he said into the dark, "You know I love you; and I know I shouldn't have let this happen. I really thought I could prevent it, and I meant to. You know that, don't you, dear?"

"Yes. I know it. The trouble is, I love you, too! I love you all the time, every which way. I can live on the bits and pieces of just seeing you sometimes. But it's like starving to death in sight of food in a window. I could have prevented this, myself, but I didn't want to! Don't be sorry, darling!" She was quiet for a moment, then with almost a chuckle she said, "You know what I used to call you, to myself? The Cool One!"

But he would not be diverted into frivolity. "This makes such a difference, Starr," he said. "I don't see how it can be done, but somehow I have to get a divorce. Somehow I must. Then we can marry. There's no other answer for us—I don't even want any other."

"Yes, Jeff," Starr said, suddenly very drowsy. She put her face against his hand and went abruptly to sleep, and when she awoke, he was gone. The great surge of tenderness in the night might have been another dream.

She arose quickly and began to dress. Still in her slip, she hurried to the mirror to see what marks experience had left tattling in her eyes. Strange, strange! There was no difference there except a silken happiness! She would go and wake Jeff, she decided; and the joy within her was like bird songs in the morning. She was dressed and at the door when he knocked.

"Where have you been? I missed you," she said. Then

he was abruptly inside, and there was no strangeness between them, and never could be again.

"Not sleeping, for a fact!" Jeff said with a laugh. "And
consider how noble I was to leave—even for a little while!
I wanted to see you open your eyes this morning. I want
to see you open your eyes every morning, as long as we
both live." He scooped her into his arms and sat in a chair
and kissed her. "Now that you've seen your wave, do you
want to go back and visit it again today?"

"Yes. Oh, yes! I wish I lived within sound of it! Do you
suppose something told me when I first looked at its picture, that it was all tied up with everything that mattered
for me?"

"Pure superstition and coincidence!" Jeff said. "What you
need is breakfast and some sun-tan lotion. How can you
explain a sunburn acquired on a shopping trip?"

They both laughed and made up big lies to account for
it. "But I'm already brown," Starr said finally. "I won't
burn any more." She leaned her head against his shoulder.
"I'm happy!" she said. "I'm drunk with happiness—I've
never been so happy in the world!"

"Don't be," he said, holding her closer. "Don't be quite
so happy. It might be unlucky."

"Who's superstitious now? There'll be plenty of time to
be sad, if things go wrong."

She had a difficult time cramming things into her suitcase and packing them so that she might conceivably carry
all of them on a bus. They had to stop on the way home
and find out when a bus arrived in Statsville, and time their
arrival to it. "It's this shabby sort of little thing that makes
me squirm," Jeff said moodily. "I simply hate the covering

[97]

up! We'll both have to be careful from now on. I must write to Aunt Nettie right away, and tell her about the divorce. But the financial burden of the two of them still rests on me, even when I get the divorce. I hardly make enough for the two of us to live on, when I've paid their expenses."

"Why should you pay for them forever?" she asked. "For a mistake made years ago? How would they have managed without you?"

"I don't know," Jeff said quietly. "I only know there's nobody else to pay."

"Well, I can work," Starr said more cheerfully. "Mother has worked all her life."

"I would hate for you to." He looked straight ahead. "If we hadn't fallen in love, things might have been neater for both of us."

"I guess love isn't very neat or easy ever," she said, leaning her head briefly against his shoulder. "But surely it's a glory, and worth working for."

He kept his hands on the wheel and his eyes on traffic, but he leaned his cheek against her hair, and his voice was ragged. "I'll never forget it, my darling," he said.

The lies began when she arrived home. Teresa was there again, and she and Ann Marie were friends once more. They had just passed the bus station on their way home. "Why, you didn't get off the bus!" Teresa said, her eyes lighting with interest, her curls bouncing back from her face.

"There were two busses," Starr said, thinking fast. "I had so many bundles I called Jeff to bring me home. Want to see what I bought?" That distracted them for a moment. She had to tell what she paid for everything, dividing the

[98]

cost rapidly by three, so that she would not appear to have spent so much. She began to feel a bit more secure. Then her bathing suit came out, still damp.

Ann Marie held it in her hand, exclaiming at its beauty. "You went swimming!" she said. It was almost an accusation.

"I went swimming," Starr said. "I always did want to see the ocean. This afternoon I did. I loved it."

Ann Marie and Teresa Bedeau looked at each other thoughtfully.

Being watchful and wary took some of the exaltation out of Starr. As Jeff had said, the little lies were a great burden—more than one would have imagined.

4.

*W*HEN SHE appeared for her interview for employment the next day, it was as if Starr had taken from Jeff some actual poise and certainty, and nothing she sought could escape her. She had a serenity such as she never had known. She knew the job would be hers before she was interviewed; and it was.

She went directly from there to tell Horace Overton that she was resigning. Young Hank was in the store; his father was out to lunch.

"Well, *well!*" Hank said. "If it isn't the poor little rich girl herself! Dressed like Mrs. Astor out for shopping! How you must have missed me, baby!"

"Not enough to notice," Starr said. "Where's your father?"

"Out," Hank said. He looked not a whit less revolting than he had at the end of last summer. "Couldn't stay away from your desk, even on vacation, eh?"

Mr. Overton returned then, and Starr told him she was resigning. His face showed anger, but he spoke softly. "Think it over!" he said. "What makes you want to resign? Getting married—is that it?" He showed his teeth in a professional smile, as if it were a joke.

"No. I'm just getting more money somewhere else," she said. "I need money."

"I only hope you'll find employers as interested in your personal welfare," Mr. Overton said dubiously.

Privately Starr hoped she would not, ever again. How an employer could consider that nosing into one's private affairs was a benefit, she would never know. "I'll come show the new girl the work if you like," she said. "I start my new job Monday."

Horace Overton took note of the quality of her new suit; it was such a one as his wife might buy. His frown of holiness descended over his face. When she had gone, he told Hank that young women of today always wanted more than they could earn, and they wanted it all for vanity.

True, Mrs. Overton did not wear the suits she bought with anything like the grace of Starr Cooper. He had a good notion to tell her to reduce her waistline instead of increasing her clothes budget.

He called the employment agency instead, and told them of the position he wished to fill. "And I want a young girl," he concluded. "One that can learn the business from the ground up, beginning with a small salary." It sounded solid and reassuring, and it usually brought a pretty young girl for the smallest salary.

With her new job, a glory of confidence descended upon Starr. She did not see Jeff often, but their easy companionship was a song running through her days. He was instituting divorce proceedings, but in California it took a year, of course.

During working days, Starr sat behind a mahogany desk on which was a fresh rose in a silver bud vase every day.

Her new employer was a delight to work with. While he had sought a pretty secretary deliberately, it was part of the same urge that prompted the other accessories in his beautiful office. He was impersonal, but human. We make a good work team, Starr thought. In three months she received a raise in pay. She had paid Jeff back what she owed him.

One day when she took the day's mail to the post office, she idly scanned a notice saying that there was to be an examination for stenographers for government service. On an impulse she filed an application. It was always sensible to be qualified in as many fields as possible. She noted with interest the places where stenographers might be needed: Washington, Arizona, a desert air base—everywhere. A job there would be like a lottery.

The examination was held on a Saturday. The musty hall was full of echoes, and the seats were filled with the wildest assortment of women taking the examination. Two solemn, self-conscious men gave it, holding stop watches and ringing bells to indicate when time for answers expired. It was a game to Starr; but some of the applicants were sweating and wiping their trembling hands. When an examination meant so much, you would lose a lot from sheer anxiety, she realized, sorry for those who were tense.

After the examination, she telephoned Jeff, and he came for her. They went to his cottage, and she told him about the examination while she prepared lunch. Jeff was distracted, and finally she noticed it. She put her arms about his waist and asked, "What bothers you?"

He handed her a letter from the table. "I feel like a heel," he said. "Whichever way I turn, I fail someone who trusts me."

Starr read the letter, from Aunt Nettie. "I know how

you feel, and wonder it hasn't happened before this," she wrote. "You can't stay tied to Louise all her life, of course, and she no wife to you. No, nor support her and me. We can do on less, Jeffrey; we even can get along some way on nothing, rather than burden you.

"Louise doesn't understand about the divorce. I've told her, but at the moment she confuses you with her father. She got away last week, taking five dollars, but she came straight home with the liquor, and I found her walking the rails again, to prove she was sober."

Starr asked, "What does she mean, 'walking the rails'?"

"There's an abandoned logging road on the estate," Jeff said. "Louise has the idea that if she can balance herself and walk the rails, she cannot be drunk. I can see her walking the rails, down between the pine thicket that grew up close to the track. She wears wide skirts, and her feet are small, and her hair hangs down her back like a little girl's. You can't help being sorry for her."

"Maybe you like helpless people," Starr said. "If so—"

While the bacon burned to charcoal, he held her close. "I like people to stand on their own feet!" he said with real passion. "I like people who are brave and competent and levelheaded! I love you with a terrifying torrent, and I don't want it to destroy smaller beings who look to me. I have to be careful."

Starr discarded the burned bacon and began to cook more. Her happiness, her poise, the very choice of her wardrobe were gifts from Jeff. And in return she brought him a flock of headaches. Some of the joy had already faded out of him.

"I abandon my own family," she said. "Just when I'm able to help Mom some with the expenses. She deserves

[103]

the help, and Caro deserves the best. But I'll leave them for you. People always have to leave someone when they make a home of their own. It's not fair, but that's the way it is."

A wind had arisen, and it was tapping a branch against the window. Starr went to the door and looked to the west, and there was the dust coming, a murky cloud traveling fast and blanketing the face of the earth before it. "Dust storm," she said.

"Make it a fine meeting tonight," Jeff said. "There's an office affair, and I have to go. It's one of those things that simply isn't skipped. I might even be promoted! I'm a pretty fair man at my job."

"You're a pretty fair man, period," Starr said, trying to lighten his depression.

Jeff arose and closed all the windows and doors tight. This was a pleasant place, she thought again. When Mrs. Maple returned from her long summer trip, Starr could not come here as freely as she had in the past few weeks while summer turned to autumn. She felt as much at home here as if she had always lived here, and happiness had lived nowhere else. It felt more like home than the one that she named as her address. She started a record playing. The music would make a quiet place in the soreness of Jeff's spirits, perhaps. They sat down to a late lunch.

Looking at his face across the table, she thought it more dear than when its newness was an excitement and a wonder. It was not a handsome face, but rather a sensitive one, most alive and mobile. She could see the resolve to be gay gathering in it before he actually smiled. He was thanking her for the music, with no words.

The wind buffeted the small cottage. Then there was

another buffeting at the door, and they looked at each other with involuntary question.

Jeff opened the door and then stepped back. "Louise!" he said, and from the tone, she knew which Louise it was, in all the world. A surge of courage ran through her. The battle was joined at last.

A blonde girl stood in the door. She carried a small bag and wore a blue coat fitted to her dainty figure. Her face had the still beauty of a child's; she looked like the picture of all the fairy princesses that ever stepped from the pages of a book. She dropped the bag, and holding out her arms ran to Jeff and clasped them about his waist. "Don't be mad at me, Jeffrey!" she said, almost sobbing. "I know you didn't tell me to come, but I got a feeling you wanted me to, and ... well, here I am! I ran away from Aunt Nettie."

There was such misery in Jeff's face that Starr's heart twisted for him. Louise dropped her arms. "We have company—I'm sorry to be rude," she said, looking at Starr with a smile.

"This is my secretary, Miss Cooper," Jeff said hastily. "We were having lunch before going on with some work I had to get out this afternoon."

Starr waited for the cruel words, "My wife," but Jeff did not say them. "Please join us," she said to Louise.

"Oh, no, dear!" Louise said, beginning to peel the gloves from her white, dimpled hands. "I stopped at the airport before I found a taxi, and I had a little something for courage!" She measured an inch or two in an imaginary glass, then covered her face in mock consternation, looking at Jeff from between her fingers. One finger wore a wedding ring. "Jeffrey doesn't approve," she said to Starr. "But, darling, it was just a teensy drink, after such a long trip! It *was* a long trip!" She laughed, and the laugh had something of the quality of Caroline's gay chuckle, infectious and innocent.

"Sit down," Jeffrey said. "I have to know some things right now. Where did you get the money?"

"Money?" Louise asked vaguely. "I found it. It was in a purse."

"Where?"

"Such silly old questions, and you haven't even said you were glad I came, after all my trouble!" Louise pouted.

"Where did you find the purse?"

"On a counter in a store," Louise said, her voice thinning and her eyes anxious on Jeff's face. "I think somebody lost it."

"Somebody surely did! Did you look to see whose it had been?"

Her voice grew smaller still. "No, Jeffrey. I threw it in the woods."

"What store did you find it in?"

"Trilby's, of course! Where else do you go if you want to buy anything decent at home?"

"How much money was in the purse?"

"Oh, Jeffrey, what does it matter? I didn't count it. I don't like to count. Here!" She handed him the purse she carried. He opened it and counted two hundred dollars and some change.

"And you bought your tickets and meals and taxi fare, and it all came from the money in the purse you found?"

"Yes. Aren't I lucky?" She smiled at him.

The sandstorm beat outside. A fine dust began to infiltrate the house, and premature dusk descended. Starr turned on a table light. "I'd better finish your work another time," she said to Jeff.

"Don't go! I want to add a note to one page, anyway." He went to his typewriter and typed very quickly while she watched.

"Stand by—please stand by!" he wrote. "I *have* to go to that meeting, and someone has to watch Louise. I can't even stay here tonight—it would be a breach of divorce or something, I think. Please, can you help?"

Starr said, "Then I'll have to come back later. Would you lend me your car keys so I can run home for a while?"

Silently Jeff took the keys from his pocket. A train whistle sounded clear and close. The wind was pushing the sound this way.

"Trains! I love trains," Louise said. "I flew here, but I like train whistles, and I like the rails, all smooth and shiny!" There was no more suspicion or resentment in her lovely face than there was in Caroline's, Starr thought, and it troubled her.

She opened the door, and the dust-laden wind swooped in. "Honey," Louise said in her velvet, affectionate southern drawl, "you can't go out in all that dirt! You can't see your way!"

Jeff followed her to the door and whispered through the rush of wind, "Be so careful! I need you very much!"

Peering into the dust, inching home in Jeff's car, Starr manufactured a feasible excuse for staying away from home overnight. She would tell Cory she was going to a party given for office folk, and that she would spend the rest of the night with another office woman. She even made up a name for the woman, saying she was not certain of the address. And when she told Cory, she felt terrible.

It was almost five o'clock when she put her pajamas and robe into a paper sack and crept through the choking dust back to Jeff's cottage. The lights were all blazing.

Jeff slipped a note to her, which she read later in the bathroom.

I think things will be all right [he wrote]. I left less than five dollars in Louise's purse—do not lend her any. I have smuggled what liquor Dick had in the place into a cupboard in the garage; there's food for dinner. Try to get Louise to eat. I've wired Aunt Nettie to come take Louise home—probably tomorrow afternoon. I wouldn't leave you with this burden if I didn't *have* to attend this meeting. Now the job is important to all of us. The more so since Louise "found" the purse, of course—which Aunt Nettie will have to return some way.

Thank you, lovely Starr. If an emergency should arise, I'll be at the Hotel Stats later.

There was a stack of papers beside the typewriter. "I'll need these as soon as possible," he said. "If I don't get back before midnight, you'll know I'll be detained all night, so you stay here with Louise, will you?"

"He often gets detained," Louise said wistfully. "I'll be all right."

"I don't want Miss Cooper to risk going home in the dust again," Jeff said, "unless I can drive her. And you, Louise—don't you stick your little nose out of this house! A dust storm's dangerous. You might be run down by a car."

Louise wrinkled her pert nose at him. "I never get run down by cars," she said. "Isn't there any beer, Jeffrey? I've looked, and can't find any. I've decided never to drink anything but beer—it's only soda pop, you know—not ever again! Isn't that good of me, Jeffrey?"

"There's no beer," Jeff said easily. "It can wait until tomorrow. Miss Cooper will need dinner, though. You're bound to be hungry by this time, too!"

When he had gone, Louise said, "You'd think I was a guest in the house! You have work to do, so go ahead with it. I'll fix us some dinner." She opened the icebox and various cupboards, clicking and clucking. "Nothing much to cook," she said. "Is there a store near here?"

"Jeff doesn't want us to go out in the dust," Starr said.

"Oh, pooh! I need onions. I saw a store not three blocks from here, I know, if I could remember which direction." She was slipping into her coat, and Starr tried to devise a way to stop her. Finally she said, "I'll go along and show you. You might get lost."

Louise smiled, and when she smiled she fairly shone. "Gosh," she said, "it's lucky for me that Jeff had you to work for him, isn't it?" As they closed the door behind them, she linked her arm with Starr's.

I can't stand it, Starr thought. But she answered polite yes and no to Louise's chatter. The big grocery shone dimly through the blowing dust. Starr knew that her hair and Louise's was thick with dirt. Their noses were choked with it; it was insidiously gritty between their teeth. "How long does it last?" Louise asked.

"Blow out before midnight, probably," Starr said, glad of the impersonal question.

Louise bought one pound of onions and twelve cans of beer. Starr's heart sank at the sight. "Jeffrey just doesn't seem to understand—it's only hospitable to have a little *something* in the house to drink," Louise said reasonably.

"Daddy always gave everybody that came in a drink of *some* kind."

Beyond the small circle of street lights, the night was black and blowing dust. They groped homeward. The beer was cold through the paper sack Starr carried. She could not stumble and break it—not in cans. She remembered Bert in his sullen drunks and in his elated drunks, and how there was no managing him or reasoning with him. What would happen if she simply went home? Probably Louise would peacefully drink herself into a stupor. On the other hand, she might awaken neighbors or do something outrageous and be thrown in jail.

They had no more than set down the packages than Louise opened a beer. "Want one with me?" she asked.

"No," Starr said. "I can't drink beer and work. It tangles my fingers."

Louise quickly took a long swallow, closing her eyes. "It was a long trip," she said. "But it's a pity you have to type—even at night. You must have great need. But that's rude, isn't it? I'm sorry you have to work for your living. When you marry, you don't have to. Why don't you? You're pretty enough." She drank more, thirstily.

"Maybe I will marry someday," Starr said, "but now I must work." She made a show of typing a whole page.

"I have to get into something easy if I'm going to cook a meal," Louise was saying, almost to herself. "Who can cook in a girdle?" She began taking off her clothes, then went to open her suitcase. The latches defeated her, so Starr opened it for her. There was a tumbled disarray of beautiful, expensive garments inside. Louise stood on one bare foot in her slip before the bag. "A blouse and skirt, wouldn't you think?" she asked. Starr agreed. But Louise wandered back to the sink and opened another can of beer. She returned, set the can on the floor, and put on a deeply ruffled blouse. She was unable to locate the skirt. "Tomorrow I'll find it," she said, laughing. "Everything gets so messed up without Aunt Nettie. You don't know Aunt Nettie, do you?"

"No. But I know Jeff's fond of her."

Louise carried her beer can back to the sink. "Now," she said gravely, "a meal for our guest. A good meal, cooked by a good little wife—never drinks a thing but beer, which is soda pop, but refreshin'." She opened a third can of beer. "For you!" she said, offering it to Starr.

"Sorry—have to work," Starr said, turning back to the typewriter.

"Oh, you *told* me! Never knew stenographer before— excuse me! Drink it myself—no waste." She put it beside her own unfinished can, and placed two potatoes in a pan. "Wonder what he peels them with?" she said, rummaging. "Who's hungry, anyway?"

"I am," Starr said. "I bet you are, too. I'll fix the potatoes."

An hour later she had Louise eating a bit of solid food, but Louise was doing it only to please her guest. She held fast to her beer can with one hand. This was the fifth. Whenever she went to the bathroom, Starr set the clock's hands forward, so that Louise might think it was later and later. Perhaps that would get her to bed and to sleep with no accidents. She watched her from across the narrow table. The beauty was blurring with alcohol, but it was by no means drowned in it. There was a tiny pouchiness beneath the eyes now, not visible when Louise had entered. And when Louise walked without her girdle, still in the slip

[111]

and blouse, the soft evidence of a small pot shadowed the future. But for the present, Louise had an almost unearthly beauty and was entirely unself-conscious about it. She looked more like a dissipated young angel than a deeply troubled woman older than Starr. "You know," she said, between gulps of beer, "I wish Jeff would find some other kind of work. I think being a judge, like Daddy was, is nicer work, don't you? And you can stay home all the time. It gets so lonesome without Jeff. Sometimes I don't even remember when he was home the last time. I know he'll be back, but I never know when he can get away from work. Don't you think it's sad?"

"Yes," Starr said. "Don't let your steak get cold."

"I'm not hungry, really," Louise said. "I certainly do apologize; the steak's simply divine—but I'm excited, and scared, too. I don't think Jeff liked me to come without telling him. But it didn't cost him a thing, did it? I was just lucky!" She drank long, and continued, "I don't see why Jeffrey fusses all the time about money, the way he does. Daddy always said a person didn't need much. And he always had plenty for liquor and party dresses and— Did I tell you my daddy died?" For a moment Starr thought Louise would burst into tears.

"It was a long time ago," Starr said.

The dust was still blowing, and the wind tap-tapped the branch against the window. A train whistled again, and Louise listened as if enchanted. "I love trains," she said again. "Don't you just feel all goose-pimply when you hear them whoo-ing?"

"I haven't traveled very much," Starr said, "so perhaps I would feel quite different." The wind was slackening.

[112]

She yawned. "Aren't you sleepy? Why don't we turn in, so we'll be rested in the morning when Jeff comes back?"

"Beer rests me more," Louise said. She walked to the sink without the suggestion of a stagger, dropped a can into the sink, and opened another. "Here's to beer!" she said, holding the shining can high. "I wish it was bourbon, but it's beer!" She contemplated it gravely. "It's soda pop, you know? Just soda pop! Baby could drink it all day and all night." She brought it back and sat again at the table. Starr began to clear the table. She put beer cans in the garbage pail and washed the dishes.

Again she yawned, hanging up the dish towel. "Aren't you dying for sleep?" she asked. "I am! I can finish this typing tomorrow. Don't you think Jeff would like you to go to bed and to sleep now?" The clock said two o'clock; her watch said midnight.

"No," Louise said, slowly shaking her head. "Not sleepy! Just a pleasant time of evenin'. Maybe you think I might get drunk?" She stood very straight for a moment, then swayed. Even with her lipstick gone, she was beautiful.

"Certainly not!" Starr said brightly.

"Don't want Jeff to think I'm drunk, either," Louise said. She put down the can of beer and looked intently into Starr's eyes. Her own wide blue ones were misty. "I love Jeffrey," she said distinctly, carefully. "Some people don't think so, but I do! If I ever lose *him*, I'll die. Livin's not so much fun anyway, is it?" She finished that can of beer and set it precariously on the edge of the table. "Still sober!" she said. "Nobody can say I'm not." She went to the door and opened it. The wind and dust had died down, and a light rain was falling. Muddy rivulets ran down the leaves of dusty shrubs. Outside the rim of light from the cottage,

the world was black and still. Louise darted into that blackness, into the small cold muddy autumn rain.

Starr ran after her, calling softly. She bumped into trees,
but she could hear no footsteps. Reluctantly she returned
to the cottage and telephoned Jeff. His reply was instant;
he must have been awake. "Jeff," she said, "Louise went
out, and I can't find her. Maybe she's here on the grounds.
Where's your flashlight? She was wearing only a slip and
blouse, and no shoes."

"Did she get hold of some liquor?"

"Beer. A lot of it. I couldn't help it."

"I'll be there right away."

Starr found the flashlight and searched most of the
grounds before Jeff came. She did not enter the adjoining
brush. When Jeff came, they briefly searched the nearby
streets in the car, then Jeff parked, and they entered a small
dark wood, searching and calling. Muddy vegetation slapped
at them as they passed.

That the railroad tracks lay only five blocks from the
elegant old residential area was an unfortunate accident.
The building had stopped four blocks short of the tracks.
In this area, lawns and formal gardens gave way to tall
sand-bitten poplars infested with mistletoe, and to stands
of greasewood and wiry weeds. Children and dogs had
made a confusing pattern of narrow paths here, and one
of them ran along the edge of the irrigation canal paral-
leling the railroad tracks. Edging the concrete-paved canal,
grass rose profuse and always green, taking some moist
sustenance from the very nearness of water. Its fresh green
fringe was conspicuous in a land browned by long summer
suns.

On the path beside the canal they paused, each careful to avoid mention of the formless, stalking fear, as Jeff's flashlight beam ran down the canal's green edge. With the briefest of hesitations, the beam turned to cut probing circles of light on the water. Already the water ran more sedately; it had forgotten its summer hurry, when it ran high and swift in the steep banks, showing cords of power on its surface. Quiet or hurried, it was always there, though; and always it spoke of death to Starr.

Wordlessly they walked down the path to where the highway bridged the canal. When they had crossed over, they were almost immediately at the railroad tracks. Jeff directed his light down the tracks.

Louise was walking a rail. Jeff led her back to the car. "Nobody thought you were drunk, silly!" he said gently; and Louise burst into tears and clung to him. "Take me home, Daddy," she said indistinctly. "I'm so *tired!* It was a long trip—a long trip."

She was still limp with sleep when Starr undressed her and put the pretty nightgown on her and tucked her into Jeff's bed. She looked more than ever defenseless and like a sleeping child. She sighed deeply.

"I'll take you home now, Starr," Jeff said. His voice was tired.

Starr disregarded the fine rain; she was already muddy and dirty. So were they all. Tomorrow the paper would proclaim a "storm." She was weighted with sadness. When the car had started, she said, as if from a great distance, "You can't get away, Jeff. I see it now, as you saw it all the time."

"I must! I've already started action for the divorce. Ten months and—"

"You know perfectly well that sometime we would default. Sometime we'd need the money too badly to send it. And Louise would spend the rest of her life behind high walls—not the satin-padded kind, but the kind for the destitute—ugly and bare and hopeless. We can't do it to her! You can't, and I can't. I was wrong!" She softly beat a fist into the palm of her other hand. "I didn't understand. I wouldn't understand." Her voice shook. "There's no evil and no suspicion in her, and that's all the armor she has in the world."

"And for that I must lose my own chance at a life of my own?"

"Not just yet," Starr answered. Dear God, not just yet!

Cory said, "I thought you was going to spend the night." Starr said she had decided not to, and went immediately to bed. In the dark small room, with Ann Marie breathing easily in the bed a few feet away, Starr sat with her arms wrapping her knees tight. She turned her head from side to side to shake the tormenting tears, and made her decision. After that it hung over her like a cloud of gnats, giving her no peace.

But there was no need to share the pain with Jeff. When Louise had gone back with her Aunt Nettie, there seemed no change in their relationship. Mrs. Maple returned to the big house, and now Starr did not go to Jeff's cottage except upon rare occasions. On Sundays, Jeff painted. They would go to the hills wrapped in coats against the chill of winter. The hills were tawny then. The folds of them undulated up and up to the sky on the eastern horizon, like tan waves breaking over a reef. Starr was suddenly aware of a deep sweet familiarity with them. In whatever flat places she might find herself in time to come, she would remember these hills lifting up to mountains, flowing eastward.

Everything had this nostalgic quality. Even the desert, which she had hated forever, seemed to lie quiet and self-possessed and timeless. The small newspaper that endlessly recorded the social trivia of the Stats and Binders and Taylors, cutting the events of the whole world to their size, now commanded an affectionate, absurd interest.

Beau had a steady girl, as eager as a puppy to please him. Cory was still picking the remnants of cotton from the frost-blackened stems in the wide fields. The whole family was in better order than it had been for a long time. Ann Marie and David Bedeau were "going steady," and she was happy and content, a junior in high school. Bert complained little about his back. But then he scarcely made the pretense of work any more.

Caroline was almost seventeen months old—a jabbering, chuckling busy-footed creature, bundled in jeans and shirts, going daily to the fields with Cory. There had never been better times at 45 Angello Street than when Starr received the first notice from the Civil Service Commission. She had passed the test with exceptionally high grades. She was asked where she would prefer to work.

She put an X in the box opposite Washington, D.C., and mailed it back. It was as far removed as possible. The summers were hot, she had heard, but she had seldom known one when the thermometer had not stood stubbornly at 100 and higher. It was a city impressive with granite and marble, and in it moved the forces making tomorrow's history. Surely one girl could find a niche there

—perhaps find some sort of peace in work, since there was none to be gained elsewhere.

Three weeks dragged by before she received a telegram inquiring whether she would accept a position in Washington, D.C., giving grade, salary, and department. Her hands trembled slightly and there was an aching in her throat as she read it. Then she smoothed the paper, folded it, and put it into her purse. She telephoned Jeff.

"I'd like to see the beach again," she said. "I'd like to stay at the same motel."

His ears heard more than words. "What's wrong, Starr?" he asked.

"I didn't say anything was wrong! I just wondered if you might be free on the week end after this one. Are you tied up with anything?"

"I'm tied up with you," he answered, almost gaily, "but not as firmly as I mean to be. Swell idea, if you can manage it." She knew he was surprised. She was a bit surprised, herself.

After that she evaded him, for she did not want to tell him as yet. There were so many things to do, and her courage was at low ebb. Carefully she sorted her wardrobe until she could manage to pack all her clothing into one large bag and one small handbag for overnight needs.

"My goodness!" Cory said, looking at the two handsome pieces of luggage. "You must expect to travel a lot, to spend that much money on suitcases."

Starr put an arm about her shoulders. "I *am* going to travel," she said. "I'm going to Washington, D.C., to work, and I'm leaving in about a week. I don't want it told all around, because I don't want to answer questions about it."

Cory sat down. "Are you in any trouble, Starr?" Her face was anxious and sympathetic.

"No!" Starr was glad to see the anxiety vanish. "I just want to get around some, while I'm young. Don't you remember having an itching foot, yourself?"

"I did, for a fact," Cory said. "But I was married. I had Bert. I would've been afraid to go alone."

"I'm not afraid," Starr said. "Maybe I'll travel farther alone."

"You'll travel always the other way," Cory said. "You're leaving us for good. I purely hate to see you go, but I know you will. You've made up your mind."

Starr thought Cory's shoulders slumped a trifle. "You know what Jeff said about you once?" she asked, to distract attention from her departure. "He said you were a great lady; and I think he knows one when he sees one."

"What about Jeff?" Cory asked. "You've seemed partial to him for a long time."

"He'll drive me to Los Angeles to catch my train," Starr said. Then her voice faltered, Cory's eyes were so steadily upon her. "I'm more than partial to him, Mom! I love him very much. But he's married. His wife's—an invalid. So you see." Her hands fell to her sides.

"I see." Cory's eyes filled with tears. "I would've worried if you'd told me. Did you know it all the time?"

"Almost from the first," Starr said. "He was lonely, and I was lonely. I've even met his wife. She's very beautiful—the most beautiful girl I ever saw."

"But he loves you, Starry." It was a statement. Starr nodded. "I'm sorry for you all," Cory said softly. "But I'm *proud* of you."

Starr looked at the woman in faded, patched jeans, her hair tied in a kerchief, and saw there all the patience, generosity, and loving kindness in the world. She put her head on Cory's shoulder and sobbed.

Starr called a taxi to take her and her bags to the bus station where Jeff would pick her up. If he came to the house, he might learn that she made a farther journey than to Los Angeles.

He was gay. "I didn't want to warn you," he said, "but your wave will be iced, and beating on a beach so cold and blowy you can see it only with a coat on. But maybe we could have a storm. Now *that's* a way to see the ocean, hissing up big puffs of foam on the beach, snarling and pounding at the cliffs!"

"Oh, I'd love to see it!" Starr answered feverishly.

They came upon a light snow in Tehachapi Pass. "How beautiful!" she said, hugging Jeff's arm. "I've seen it fall, and I've seen the far mountains white on top, but I never saw it on the ground like this. Look!"

Jeff smiled. "Can't," he said. "The roads are slick now. I've seen the stuff hip deep, and it's no fun to wade around in." She was bewitched by the falling flakes, but Jeff kept his attention on the traffic. "This was a fine idea, and I'm glad you suggested it," he said, "but it doesn't seem like you. It surprised me."

"I don't see why," Starr said. "I want to go back to our own cottage again."

"Remind me to tell you that I love you every minute of every day," he said. "I'll be so proud when you really *are* Mrs. Mayfield."

"I've felt I really was," Starr said. "How else would I

have managed? Words spoken or records made wouldn't change anything at all."

"No," Jeff said. "But they would give us some assurance of all the tomorrows. Not just today, the way it is."

The words made a painful echo. Starr had been trying to avoid such words. A bleakness settled over her. Fortunately he would think she was watching the snow fall. "Let's go first to the beach," she said.

"All right. I think it has you under a spell. But it's a fine spell. I approve of it."

Ever since I bought the picture of the wave, Starr thought, it did have a pull. Perhaps she had been foolhardy to leave that picture on the wall. Once she had taken it down and packed it; then she had put it back. Its removal had left a whiter place on the stucco wall—like a scar. Actually, it was hard to leave it there. She felt that she was abandoning it; as if it knew she was abandoning it; as if it knew she was giving it up forever. But it was something of herself left for Cory.

She and Jeff were walking on the beach. The wind was cold and clean and the sky sullen. The waves came in long slow surges without sparkle. She noticed that Jeff was cold and suggested some hot soup.

Her train would leave at noon the next day. The time was coming close when she must tell Jeff. The time was coming very close when she would be in his arms for the last time—if one could imagine such an insane thing. She could not keep her glance from his face. Even when he walked away for something, she watched his back—so straight and easy and lithe. Unaccountably she thought of her father's back—bent with imagined ailments and defeats.

I shall have had more than Mom, at that, she thought, suddenly homesick for Cory, but strengthened of purpose.

Jeff carried her across the threshold of the cabin, although she protested, and the attendant who had opened the door smiled. When the door was closed, Jeff still held her in his arms and kissed her eyes and her lips. He set her on her feet and started to move her luggage.

"Feels like you brought a bag full of rocks," he said. "What in the world *did* you bring, to make it so heavy?"

"Practically everything I value, except you," she said, the words coming with a rush. Quickly she plunged a hand into her purse and brought out the telegram and a typed copy of her reply: "Will report for work in Washington as directed. Starr Cooper." She handed both quickly to Jeff. She would not watch his face as he read them. He came slowly across the room to her and forced her to look at him. She began to cry, quite silently, the tears spilling slowly down her cheeks.

"I won't let you go," he said. "I'll hold you right in my arms if I have to. Do you understand? Didn't you *know* I wouldn't let you?"

"Yes, you will." She tried a smile and abandoned the difficult project. "You knew before I did that there could be nothing but parting for us. I knew it when I saw Louise. It took time, and it took—it *takes* a lot of courage to separate us! But it has to be. You know it has to be!"

"I won't have it. Why didn't you tell me you had been brooding? Don't you remember telling *me* to be happy, that things would work out, you knew they would?"

"That was before I saw Louise," Starr said. "I wish I could be persuaded, but I can't. I've said good-by to my family, and I'm catching a train at noon tomorrow. Let's not waste the hours in argument. Maybe they're all we have together."

"No," he said. "No! But I won't argue with you—not with words." He wiped her eyes and smiled at her. "It was a bad dream," he said. "See, here you are, where you belong!"

In his arms she sighed; it was time for the end of tears. "You could think I might come back, if it would make it easier," she said.

"I don't *want* it easier; I want the whole thing stopped! What an idea! A self-administered anesthesia for loneliness!"

"There's no loneliness in here. Not right now."

"Well it casts a damned threatening shadow here," Jeff said.

"Would you rather I left right now, before my bags are opened? Would it be easier that way?"

"I wouldn't rather any such silly thing! I don't mean to let you farther than arm's length."

But he knew then, for he looked at his watch, noting the time racing away toward separation.

Afterward Starr recalled that night mostly as a depth of sorrow. She put it away in the back of her mind, deliberately remembering only the absurd feeling of security in Jeff's arms, as if she had found a little cave in which to hide from everything that troubled her. Remembering the square corner of his jawbone near his ear, when she put her hand to his face in the dark. Remembering the hands of his watch, ghostly and delicate on the table, measuring off the tormented hours and their fragments. Sometimes she would wish the hands would stop, and sometimes she wished they would hurry and deliver her from the anguished present into the empty tomorrow.

He left the train at the last possible moment, and then ran beside her window. She could see the shape of the words he spoke—the familiar curve of his lips—but could not hear them in the soundproofed glass and metal box of the train. "Hurry home," he said. "Hurry home!" How readily we grasp at straws when we have nothing else, she thought.

When he was left behind, she put her head back on the seat and closed her eyes, letting the emptiness drift like fog throughout her being. The porter came and asked her name. He handed her an armload of red roses and a note in Jeff's handwriting: "As the Spanish here used to put it, 'Go with God,' dear little Barrel of Stars."

She despaired, and she pulled courage about her many times on that journey, watching with dulled perception the ranges of mountains, the great rivers, the cities and villages and wide snowy plains flow past the train. Nights and days flowed past, too; and snow and sun, and tumbled clouds. The very knowledge of time passed and spaces spanned leached something of the fierce first pain from her. The motion of the train and the clicking of the rails were background for passage from one world to another.

She arrived two days earlier than the date for reporting for work, and in those days found the group whose business it was to help find room for a new government girl. She elected to share expenses with three others such as she, in an apartment that was undoubtedly old Mr. Perry Taylor's idea of heavenly real estate. It had the very minimum of space and comfort, and the maximum of expenses. They called it The Spenthouse.

The three women with whom she shared this intimacy born of economics were ill assorted. Iris was a pretty girl near her own age, who had come here specifically to save a thousand dollars, return home, and marry her sweetheart. "It's just as well to be away from him, because we haven't got money enough to marry now," she said. "I just hope he doesn't get away!" She was a dark-haired, petal-skinned creature, indolent seeming, yet with great driving capacities.

Emma was middle-aged, and she always made Starr think of a dumpy worker bee. She was efficient, neat, inescapably correct, probably unsexed—and incredibly dull. Like the bee, she moved in swarms of others like herself in her hours away from her filing cases.

Ona, the third woman, was a divorcee. She found Washington frustrating. She was about thirty, had a sharp tongue, and while not pretty, was engagingly smart. This she achieved with much washing and pressing of ruffles and lace for neck and wrists, and strange but simple jewelry that was neither junk nor yet quite authentic.

Starr saw these women in all stages of disarray, and often talked and ate with them. None had anything in common with the others except a bewildered loneliness for the presence of men in a world composed so largely of women.

Emma alone was not greatly disturbed by the matter; she had given up the thought of men ten years earlier, and found the bowling teams and card parties of her fellow female workers quite stimulating enough. There was never anything rough about them. Men, she had noted, were apt to be rough—even the best of them.

Iris pinched pennies enthusiastically, wrote incessant

[125]

letters home, read love pulp magazines, and went to a matinee every week. Only occasionally did she mingle in the approved fashion with her fellow workers.

Ona went out with any man who asked for a date. She went out with bald-headed men and young clerks and policemen and hairdressers. There *was* a certain triumph in it, where men were so few. But she could not deceive herself entirely. "A pipsqueak!" she said to Starr as she came home one evening. "He'd be delivering the groceries in his home town—or sweeping the pool hall. But *here* he thinks he's a gold-plated man of distinction because he has a Grade 5 rating; and he thinks his social success is due to his wit and charm instead of the law of supply and demand!"

"Ugh!" Iris said. "How do you suppose they screen them to get nothing but rejects with delusions of Robert Taylor into Washington?"

"That's only the single ones, darling," said Ona. "There are some fairly decent married ones here, probably to prove that such still exist! But pipsqueak or no, at least I had a date. And that's a distinction not shared by probably twenty-five thousand girls in this fair city tonight!"

Starr hadn't supposed that her work would be important, but she was staggered by the triviality of it. Everything was so organized that she was not even left a choice in the size of margins on the letters she typed. Her correct letters looked repulsive, and she said so to her supervisor.

The supervisor raised beautifully groomed eyebrows and said look on page thus and so of the Manual. Yea, verily, Starr thought, the Manual didn't tell how and when to breathe, but that was about all that was not covered in detail. All this bowing was to the great god Uniformity, worshiped and admired more than good sense, artistry, imagination, or anything else whatsoever. One clerk did nothing but guide newcomers, grinding into their deepest consciousness the necessity and beauty of being unable to discern who did what work except by identifying initials.

It was not beyond the capacity of the most stupid to learn these things, but Starr felt as if the Manual were a strait jacket forbidding all individual effort. It was easy, if one did not mind how ugly it looked, and how trivial its need. She was marking time for a decent interval before asking for a transfer to some other city. In some small sub-office she might hope to draw an unsupervised breath now and then. Here there were bells saying get to work; bells to take ten minutes and no more for a cup of coffee; bells by which to scamper from the office.

After a month, Ona asked her how she liked her work, and she was surprised. "Does anyone?" she asked.

"I do," Emma said primly. She was knitting something for a Christmas gift, her glasses glinting in the lamplight.

"It must be something like working in a factory—or maybe the jute mill in a jail," Starr said. "The one difference is that you can resign. What form would I use to make a requisition for a number to hang around my neck?"

An amateur psychologist at her own office had figuratively taken Starr's hand and tried to "adjust" her. Their "little chats" always were unsatisfactory to both. Starr did not care to join a joyous club of women from her home state. She did not want to bowl for the honor of her section of the office. She did not want to join a bridge club. She did not want to join a group of women strangers doing *anything*, she finally said baldly to her advisor.

"Then what hobby—" the woman began once more.

"I read," Starr said. "I read alone; I always have. And that's my only hobby."

"Then a course at the university—help in promotions. . . ." The advisor was determined to adjust this girl if it killed them both.

"I don't want to," Starr said. "I like to pick my own subjects, my own authors, and my own time." She thought that privacy of the mind was probably the only one left, and people were drilling at the crannies in it night and day. When it was permissible (according to the Manual), she asked for a transfer to San Francisco. She was told that several requests were ahead of hers, each of which would have to await a vacancy.

Starr did not smile, or even suggest that possibly some of the applicants for transfer might drop dead, be netted for asylums, or even more improbable, marry before such a transfer might go through. Solemnly she filed an application. She also began saving money once more. If the transfer did not come officially, she could resign and go anyway. She wished she could tell all these silly things to Jeff, but she never wrote to him.

He wrote her, however, having obtained her address from Cory.

Time has slowed down since you left, so that a week is about a month long [he wrote]. You wouldn't believe that a town or even a whole county could be so absolutely chuck full of places you aren't. You aren't on the tawny hill behind me and my easel, and you don't come out of the office building I call yours. You aren't even at the other end of a telephone wire when the phone rings! The other day I tried to paint you, since I have no photograph. It wasn't that I can't paint portraits—

[128]

which of course I can't—it was only that no canvas or paper would hold an adequate record of yourself. Not to me, anyway.

The divorce will be complete in August, and if you aren't back by that time, I shall come and drag you home by the hair—not harming it, of course, because it is so pretty, and feels like silk, as I remember. Starr—Starr, darling.... You know better what I would say to you than I ever could put on paper. You could at least write.

But Starr did not. She carried the letter in her purse until the folds of it were shabby, and then tore it to the correct size of bits according to the Manual, and put it in the wastebasket. Once Jeff had said that loneliness might be the natural state; probably it was. Enough loneliness ought to lay dead day on dead day until grief was buried in months and years, and the heart would be as still as if it also had died.

Starr read more than she ever had in her life. Making a living and looking after one's own domestic chores were so small a burden, after the crowded time of childhood. Of time she had more than ever before, and it was a thing of slow healing and silences. She stayed in Washington for a year, and then resigned her job.

Jeff had ceased to write or to send telegrams, which both enchanted and wounded her. She supposed that he had his divorce, but it would make no real difference in his life. Unless he should fall in love again. Starr did not even dream of him very much any more. There was only the aching hole in her life.

5.

SAN FRANCISCO was satisfyingly unlike Washington. There Starr copied a list of addresses of federal agencies and went from one to another making application. On the second day she found a job. It would be easy for her, taking up a minimum of energy. Oh, there would always be clerks with delusions of importance, which they found it necessary to burnish with petty tyranny. But they were few, and did not particularly disturb Starr. They were like little dogs, yapping, yapping, lest they be overlooked entirely in the scheme of things.

She noted that the childish look had finally fallen away from her, and there was a quality of stillness, almost a sadness in her face. Her clothes were expensive, and she had few of them. She wore them with distinction. She was twenty years old, and already knew too much about grief.

She found a small apartment and gradually bought secondhand furniture for it, beginning with nothing but a stove and a couch and some bedding. It sat on the edge of a steep hill, and although one entered the basement to get to it, the main window commanded a magnificent view of San Francisco and most of the East Bay.

In that apartment Starr first savored the true flavor of

solitude. She was free to do as she pleased, and the novelty of it delighted her, after a lifetime of being crowded. Sometimes she ate in a cafeteria, reading, then went to a movie. Sometimes she went home and cooked a meal for herself, watching the cookbook carefully. Buying food was an adventure, with all the exotic dishes of the world being prepared in San Francisco, and all the materials for them to be found for the searching.

She bathed late at night and early in the morning, for the pure joy of using the bathroom whenever she pleased, and finding it always shining, with only her own toilet things or stockings in it.

She joined the Mechanics' Library; it was a treasure in which she held a share. Public libraries had been her friends always. But at the Mechanics' one did not have to wait.

Perhaps, she thought, solitude was best for one whose ideas ran shining and shimmering and crowding each other. Certainly company that did not welcome them dimmed them.

For several months she made no effort to mingle with others. She felt as if her own self were expanding to its full width and height, having spindled up much too close to others to attain normal proportions before.

She might as well have been on the other side of the world from her family. They could obtain no nourishment from letters or convey anything to her. When a member moved out of actual reach, the family suffered a bereavement not unlike a little death. That was why, Starr thought, that particular group of the populace did not usually mind being crowded together. They had no other communication except the physical.

But not always for all of them, Starr thought without

question or bitterness. Sometimes one had a taste for reading, and the reading wedged itself between this odd one and the family, like a tangible world to the reader and an invisible barrier to the family.

"Starr's real smart," Cory used to say. "You can depend on her. She knows a lot." It was love trying to scale the strange walls of thoughts and dreams. But there was no use to try to erect a bridge for the family. They were concerned with the immediate, the tangible. All else was furrowed brows and unprofitable.

Starr still thought about Jeff sometimes. He had been right about so many things. Even prying her apart from her family. He was good for me, she thought; I hope I was as good for him, some way; and perhaps I was. We were both so lonely. He gave me myself—in a great wrench of pain, perhaps, but standing taller and not quite defeated.

It was early spring when Starr, who had been laving herself in solitude, was stirred to share her experiences. Specifically, she wished to share them with Jeff, but she put that aside. The lupine and the poppies would be starting soon in the foothills. But that was past, and there was no returning.

Lambs grazed among the sheep in Golden Gate Park, and children were busy with baseball. Daffodils were everywhere. She had no friend or acquaintance to invite to lunch, or to sit beside at a neighborhood movie. She knew a few folk at the office where she worked—an office singularly unmoved by the Regulations and Directives that each mail dropped like snow upon the suboffices from the Central Office in Washington. Except for the boss, who was happily a family man, the office offered no congenial person. They were good, honest, adequate workers, and there the matter ended. One of the young men seemed to have taken a fancy to Starr, but she had evaded him so far. She hoped to do so indefinitely, until his fancy settled elsewhere.

Every Sunday she took a trip—to the park, the beach, or even a trip across the bay. On one of these excursions, she noted that her office admirer was riding the same bus. To avoid him as he worked his way back to her seat, she arose, pushed the bell for the next stop, and prepared to leave the bus and wait for the next one. It was a nuisance, and there would be at least a thirty-minute wait, but it would be simpler. The bus stopped where El Camino Real entered Golden Gate Park. Traffic was heavy.

As she stepped to the curb, she stepped on a marble that was being chased by a small boy, and went down sprawling. She skinned her knees and tore her hose. Sitting up on the pavement, she heard a voice calling, "Starr Cooper!"

The traffic light changed, and Dash Taylor stopped at the curb while traffic behind him honked frantically. "Get in here before we get arrested for holding up traffic," he said, holding open the door of the Cad. Dazed, she obeyed him, separating herself from the sympathetic knot of people asking, "Are you hurt?"

"Doesn't it make you feel idiotic to fall down in public?" she asked, breathlessly brushing dust from her coat. "My good angel must have sent you!"

"Marvelous he did," Dash said, radiating welcome. "Do I have to take you wherever you were going, or can you include me in your plans today? I'm very much available."

Starr touched her ruined stockings with exploring fingers. "I was only going to the beach for a walk. I could go bare-legged there as well as not."

[133]

Dash parked the Cad on the Great Highway and walked with her that day. They had a surprising lot to say, considering that they had scarcely known each other previously. Starr explained that she was living here and working, and Dash said he was living here and hunting a job. "You certainly live in style!" Starr said, indicating the new, beautiful car.

Dash's mobile face was momentarily sad as he touched the car. "Cars are my enemies, and I love them," he said. "One killed Priss six months ago, did you know?"

No. Not Priss, with her flying horsetail of silken hair—Priss so alive and lithe and forever *busy*. Priss, whom Dash certainly had loved, at least to some extent. Starr cradled one hand in the other anxiously. "I'm so sorry," she said.

"The cars got my own parents, too," Dash said, his manner almost detached. "When I was a baby," he added, as if to mitigate the loss.

"Then your parents—they aren't your real parents, are they?"

"They're the only ones I've known," Dash said. "Wonderful people. I love them. Actually, he's my uncle—my own father's older brother."

He took Starr to dinner that evening, and there was a certain warmth of understanding for having attended the same school and knowing a very few of the same people. Starr tried to keep the conversation light, for now she recognized the small outward signs of sorrow. Dash still looked like Prince Charming. He still wore his courtly manners like a cloak.

She did not suppose he would ask to see her again, but on the following Sunday, without telephoning, he came in the late morning. Starr was ironing blouses and slips for the next week's work.

"Go on with your work," he said, settling into her most comfortable chair. "There's something solid and assuring about a woman pressing pretty fragile things. I used to watch the maid doing it for Mother. She used to hang them in a sort of chain of hangers, one dripping from another. I see you do that too."

"There's usually only one nail—if that," Starr said. She made an occasional minute repair with the needle, continuing to work because she felt that today he was less tense than when she last saw him.

"The maid's name was Maria," Dash said. "I loved her for years. We had conspiracies about cookies, kept a cat secretly, and when Mother and Father were away, lived a raffish life. She was a Mexican, and had a large family, which we visited at length." He smiled, almost the impish grin she had seen on him in high school.

"A big family's no novelty to me," Starr said. "Big families and not enough space are routine on Angello Street, the same as they probably are on Maria's street."

"There was something awfully nice about Maria's family," Dash said. "There were so many of them! They fought and screamed, but they laughed and loved each other, too. I used to wish I were Maria's child. She had eight of her own."

"Did I know any of them?"

"No. None of them went to high school. The boys went to work and the girls married early. It makes me feel old and sort of bachelor-uncle to see them now."

Starr folded the ironing board into the wall. "I was going to walk again today," she said, "but it's raining."

"It's not raining in the Golden Goose," Dash said. "We could drive through the rain. Maybe a hundred miles away, the sun is shining!"

"The Golden Goose?"

"My car. Because I was a goose to buy her, and she was golden in price. My dad hit the ceiling. I got an inheritance from one of my own mother's brothers—never saw the man. Had a grocery store and lived all alone. Left me everything he had. Dad wanted me to put it into the business, but I don't like the real-estate business."

"You should know all about it."

"I know too much about it! I've been sent to collect from too many people losing their miserable little homes and everything they owned. You're supposed to say you're terribly sorry, but business is business, and not to notice if they cry—then turn it over to the attorney, so you won't have to see them."

"But it *is* a business, and people who borrow know the risk—and the interest and the taxes and the plumbing that has to be fixed, and the doors that buckle and the plaster that falls off...."

"I can't *stand* it!" Dash said. "It makes me sick at my stomach. Traffic in homes is indecent! And I can't deal firmly with people crying about such things. Dad says its a weakness. Could you do it?"

"No. But I know better than you should."

"Now when real estate also happens to be oil property—then it's all fun! It's a magic—it's money that comes without hurting anyone. If we had any of *that* kind, I'd be excited about it—in fact, I'd love it! Dad's always hoping, of course, and trying to anticipate the new fields before they're proved.... But on the whole, real estate's a sad kind of business."

She knew it was absurd to feel this shadowy sorrow for a boy who had grown up with a silver spoon in his mouth— whose new Cad sat outside her door.

She joined him at the window. San Francisco swam in mist now, its buildings phantoms of changing shape with the drift of fog. "When you find work you want to do, maybe you'll feel better," she said. "I think a man needs to work."

"I don't know what work," he said. "Sometimes they don't like me, and sometimes I don't like them; sometimes I just don't feel interested. I should have been educated for something specific. And I suppose I was. Real estate."

"It isn't too late to study for what you want to do," Starr said. "Your parents would give you that easily."

"Not so long as I have a dollar of the inheritance," Dash said with a grin. "They think I'm a wastrel, and maybe I am. I despise penny pinching. For what, for what? Shall we defer breathing today to take a deep breath tomorrow?"

"Old age is a specter to the old," Starr said. "I know. They're afraid, and they have reason to be."

"Then I shan't be old! I'll die when I'm young, and I won't mind. Just so it's quick."

"Silly! We'll both be old. Nobody believes it's so, but it is. We think we'd rather die young—but if wishing made it so, no one would live to be thirty."

"How did you know that?" His gaze was steady upon her.

"To state it differently, maybe only sad things educate you," Starr said.

"You want to grow old?"

"Of course not! But very probably I shall, anyway. It

isn't growing old I fear, or lack of a job, or not having enough money. The most terrible thing would be to be caught in a backwash, where day and night, months and years, the days repeated themselves uselessly."

"That's called safety," Dash said primly, but with a twinkle.

"It might also be a prison."

Dash caught both her hands, his mood lightening. "Bundle up and let's go to a place I know for Spanish food. It has checkered tablecloths and the hottest enchiladas north of the border. I'm friends with the cook because I know a few words of her language."

It was the first of a number of interesting places Dash took her. As a sort of companionship developed between them, his spirits brightened steadily. "Are you happy being a government stenographer?" he once asked her. "You never complain."

"It's easy for me. I don't have to give it all my imagination or my thought," she said. Then venturing into foolishness she added, "Of course I don't plan to make a career of it. Within the next year or two, while I'm still young enough for a lure, I'll marry some wealthy man and have breakfast in bed the rest of my life. At least that's what's recommended by experts."

Dash grinned. "I should introduce you to Binkie," he said. "She's on a merciless man hunt of that sort. Good fun, though. Junior League and all that. Last year's debutante. Let's telephone her and get a college friend of mine that she likes very much. . . . Listen now, close to my ear, while I phone her." He dialed and asked for Bink.

"My God, Dash, is that you? Alive? I've been asking

where to send the wreaths." The full, laughing voice came over the phone clearly. "Have you got rich or anything?"

"No."

"Can't use you then. I found one prospect, but I'm still looking for three more months. Department-store heir and all that."

"Could you stop your treasure hunting and come out and make it an evening with old Ham and me and a girl?"

"You're a fiend from hell! You know perfectly well that I love Ham, and also that I have other business. How do you suppose I'll ever support my mother and worthless brother in the manner to which they're accustomed, if I don't pitch in right now and marry some money?"

"You're a woman of resource, that's how," Dash replied. "I'll see if Ham's free, and call you back."

"But I have a date tonight with Fishie," Bink wailed.

"With *who?*"

"It's a pet name," Bink said. "He has a soul of patience, a bank roll of platinum, and the face of a carp. I think I can stand everything but the thought of the children and all those teeth."

"What forethought!" Dash said admiringly.

"I know what I am," Bink said tartly, "but I'm an exclusive and expensive one!"

"I'll call you back." Dash put the receiver down. "Isn't she wonderful?" he asked.

"She's joking, of course."

"She's not joking! She and her mother and her perfectly worthless brother, as she accurately put it, are living on the last of her dad's insurance policies. He died and left them nothing else. Dear Mamma has always been accustomed to luxury, and so has sonny. About all they have to gamble on now is wardrobe and address, and these are temporary assets."

"But even so! In cold blood!"

"My friend Ham is ... I think maybe he ... Well, never mind! I guarantee we'll have fun tonight." He dialed another number, exchanged a few abuses, and found Ham available.

Bink was a tall slim girl, with trim ankles, long narrow hands, and the haughty features of a model. "Take us somewhere obscure to feed," she said breathlessly. "I'm starving to death—but not to the St. Francis, or anywhere like that." She wore a clinging red dinner dress only slightly more attention-commanding than an explosion in a room.

"What a stunning dress—it must have been made for you!" Starr said.

"I earned it modeling. Having taken one look, you're supposed to ask me where I got it, then go buy half a dozen," Bink said. "It *ought* to fit! It fits better than skin, as a matter of fact—skin *gives*, and this doesn't!" She ran her fingers up some boning in the bodice. "It's one of those dresses that you can't wear a blessed thing, not a *thing* underneath!" She laughed, looking at Ham.

Ham gave her the most fleeting of glances. "Live bait," he said.

She put her hand on his arm. "But it has built-in wolf bane for you, angel," she said. "This is bait for the big money."

"Starr has been told to pursue and marry a rich man, so I thought she ought to meet you and get some tips," Dash said to Bink.

"What have you to sell besides looks?" Bink asked. "Pioneer family, political connections, money—what?"

"I was fooling," Starr said.

"It's just as well," Bink said thoughtfully. "You'd be a rival if you weren't. And you'll have more fun being just a woman. Why, there's nothing to keep you from marrying some oaf like Ham here, and living in poverty and bliss all your life! Except that I'd strangle you with my bare hands, of course." She put an arm about Ham's waist and laughed up into his face.

"Unhand me while you can," he told her, his voice low.

"If only you had money!" Bink sighed. "I wouldn't care how dishonestly you came by it."

"I know," Ham said. "I won't be worth my salt until I'm middle aged, if then. But I'll like my job every day of the way."

It was almost as if the two were constantly a bit drunk together. Going to a restaurant, Dash and Starr joined them in follow-the-leader from where the Golden Goose was parked. They filed singly along the edge of the sidewalk, one foot on and one off. Each in order delicately touched a plate-glass window going "Ssst!" as he did so, jumping as if it burned the finger. They stepped with exaggerated high steps over the lines in the sidewalk. They attracted the attention of an officer of the law, who caught up with them and eyed them with disapproval.

Bink cast herself upon him, her arms about his neck. "Timmie!" she cried. "Come play with us as far as your beat goes!"

"My superior officer wouldn't understand," he said, disengaging her arms. "Seeing it's you, it's all right. I thought you were a party of drunks."

[141]

"Pooh. We'll invite your officer—what's his name and where is he?"

"Spare me!" said the policeman.

"Oh, all right then! Stuffy! But don't say we didn't want you."

Starr said to Dash, "Are all debutantes like this one?"

"Oh, no! This one's very special. She's Ham's girl, even if she does marry her Fishie. She's just dying, that's all— glowing and turning all colors as she does, like some strange fish brought up from the depths."

They dated often with Ham and Bink, whose names turned out to be Hamilton Inman and Berenda Colby. Always they took Bink home first. "The flesh is so weak," she explained to Ham.

"The head is so weak."

Later Starr said to Dash, "They act as if they hated each other," and Dash said better they did.

From time to time Starr thought that she might be drifting, dangerously waiting, and she remembered Jeff's warning about the things that "just happened." Dash somehow took up such a lot of her time that she never seemed to meet anyone but his friends. He worked only occasionally, and he seemed to have adequate funds, but she felt it necessary now and then to prod him toward a job of some kind. "A man just *has* to work at something—I know it!" she said.

"Don't I work and slave at pleasing and entertaining you?" he asked. "Didn't I bring you flowers to the office only last week, and create the most excitement and confusion there since the beginning of Civil Service?"

"You did, and it's a scandal," Starr said. "Don't do it again. That office is my bread and butter—maybe for all my life."

Dash turned up his coat collar and shuddered dramatically. "Don't *say* things like that! It might be unlucky."

"Much more unlucky if I had no job," she said seriously.

"Then I'd protect you!" Dash said. "I'd buy your violets in the snowstorm at the corner!"

Dash agreed that it was time they had a dinner party for Ham and Bink. He furnished the steak and red wine. She had French garlic bread, a green salad, cheese and tart apples. It was a fine party. She and Bink sat and talked while Dash and Ham washed dishes, loud with gloom and bitterness.

"Starr, my angel," Bink said, "I'm so low in my mind! Have you had any real belly laughs lately?"

"No," Starr said, filled with pity.

"There's no help, really," Bink said gaily. "Dear God! Next week Fishie and I . . . until death do us part, and no fooling any more. Three months seemed like a long time, but it wasn't."

"Are you sure you want it that way?"

"What do you suppose I worked at for a year and a half— tiddlywinks? I'm about to close a big deal. A lot of women will envy me my home, my clothes, my cars. I can repay my mother and brother for betting their shirts on me. If my father—but he's dead, he's dead!" She smoothed the shining dress over her knees. "Enough of that!" she said. "On with the mad, mad fun!"

Except that Bink drank more than her usual moderate amount, there was no further reference to the matter. She stayed closer to Starr that evening, and exchanged her customary semi-insults with Ham—if anything more outrageous tonight than ever she had been.

Going into the kitchen, she encountered Ham coming out, ran head on into him, and he put his arms about her. "Imagine meeting you here, Miss Colby," he said, the tenderness so naked in his voice that Starr moved away toward the windows.

"So charming, Mr. Inman," she managed, her voice only feathered with uncertainty.

"So horrible meeting you anywhere else," Ham said, almost in a whisper. Starr and Dash looked at each other and then at Ham. With one hand Ham motioned them toward the door. They picked up their coats without a word and started out, but they still heard sobs shake the breath out of Bink.

"Oh, damn!" she cried through her tears. "Oh, dammit to hell!"

Starr sat in the Golden Goose and squeezed her eyes tight. Dash wiped them with his soft monogrammed handkerchief. "Blow," he said. "Joy or sorrow?"

"Just let me alone, Dashell Taylor," Starr said in desolation.

"I *was* letting you alone, as well as a man could," he said reasonably. "You're a contradiction. Sure and competent and kind of— But the fact is, you're a tender sort of girl, aren't you?"

"I'm not, either!" Starr said, muffled in handkerchief, with her nose swelling. "I know perfectly well what the score is! I'm soph—sophisticated, that's what I am!"

"Undoubtedly!" Dash said, and he gathered her to his chest where she sobbed until she had finished.

A strange voice cut into the conversation. A policeman tapped at the windows. "Whatsamatter here?" he asked suspiciously. "You all right, lady?"

"Her dog died, officer," Dash said mournfully. "She can't bear to go back to her apartment quite yet."

"I was asking the *lady*," the policeman said. "You ain't got no business sitting around crying in cars."

"How can you help it?" Starr asked damply. "Maybe you never had a dog to just get sick and die."

The officer's face lengthened. "I know how it is, lady," he said gently. "The kids had an awful nice little pooch—just a puppy. . . ." He measured it with his hands. "Car run over it last week." He walked away.

"Do you suppose we might go back in, now?" Starr asked.

"Not me! I wait for somebody to come out."

Presently the door opened, and Bink did come out, her chin high, lipstick smeared. Starr ran to her. Automatically Bink smiled with her lips. "We'll take you home," Starr said.

"No," Bink said. "No company. No company ever, unless your bank account has been properly measured. I called a cab." She shivered violently, her glance moving up and down the street.

Dash put a hand on her shoulder, and she shrugged it away angrily. Her eyes glittered with new tears. "Don't touch me!" she said thickly. "It might rub off on you." Then the taxi came, and Bink was gone.

They went slowly back into the apartment. The living room was dark. Ham sat in the chair by the window. His silhouette lay black against the starry lights of the city below. His head was in his hands. He arose as they entered, and without a word walked out of the apartment.

"Maybe you better follow and take him—" Starr began.

"No. Oh, no!"

"I suppose you're right." Starr lit a couple of candles and sat down, her hands loose in her lap.

Suddenly Dash said, "Come over here by me, Starr. Sit close to keep back the cold." So she came and sat near him, without words. He took her face in his hands and examined it in the dim light, his own quizzical face near her own. "What a good, accepting person you are!" he said. "How do you manage so quietly, when things scream all around you?"

"I grew up with the screaming," Starr said. "And sometimes I cry, like tonight. Not often, but sometimes. Hardly ever where people can see me."

The next time she saw Dash, he said he was working in a furniture store, and that he liked it.

"I'd go mad with wanting," Starr said. "I never bought a piece of furniture except secondhand, and usually ugly, and it always had to be painted or nailed or something. I hate old furniture!"

"Mom dotes on it," Dash said, almost disapprovingly. "Our house is chuck full of antiques, and they get polished and rubbed as if they were made of silver and gold."

"I love the very shape of modern furniture," Starr said. "If I were furnishing a house everything would be plain and useful and clean, and I'd have it bright with color! I'd have big windows, and flowers outdoors and indoors. . . ."

Dash watched her face with some tenderness as she talked. "And what would you do about the man in the house?"

"Why . . . I know he'd like it too—and live all over it, the same as I would. His den and my den would be all of it— not any place too fine to go and play or laugh—or turn cartwheels if we felt like it."

"Wicked, wastrel Starr! Didn't anyone teach you that money is for 'taking care of,' that life should be spent in proper segments, with a large proportion set aside for meditating on ancestors (only the celebrated ones, naturally), and that love is duty?"

"No," Starr said serenely. "It's silly."

"Don't you want to live in the lushest new subdivision and have better cars than your neighbors?"

"I can't think why," Starr said. "Sounds wasteful—so much effort for practically nothing."

Dash sighed and shook his head. "Just as I feared," he said. "A savage." He brightened quickly, however. "Tell you what: Come to the store and ask me to show you the modern furniture. Pretend you're engaged, and thinking of furnishing a small home. That way we can talk when the boss turns his back."

Starr gave him a reproving glance. "It's a kind of thievery of your time," she said. "I'm surprised at you! But I do love to look at modern furniture—and even modern homes. I go into all the model homes I can find, just to look."

Two months vanished quickly. Starr decided that the time was well spent because it was full of companionship and fun. Seldom a day passed that she did not either have a phone call from Dash or see him in person. That he knew many girls and women in San Francisco she knew; she had learned that from Ham. But if Dash entertained them, it must have been rarely. "You don't have much time for the friends you had before we met here, do you?" she asked him once.

At once he was serious. "The connections were family," he said. "I wasn't much interested. Every now and then Mother writes and asks me to look up so and so, the daughter of a friend or distant relative—Money, Position, or Family—and I go and suffer through it as well as I can. But no one's so easy to be with as you, Starr." Then he was smiling again. "I'm going to have a surprise for you Sunday, so don't make any plans."

When he had gone, Starr thought about his friends who were "family" at some length. He would not want his family to know that he squired her around so much, of course. In fact, probably his mother would have a fit. She would fear an "unfortunate" marriage.

On Sunday, Dash drove elaborately around and around the hills and stopped before a cottage commanding almost the same view as Starr's apartment, but about a mile away. "You're going to see a model home," he said, "and I particularly want your opinion on its furnishings."

"Oh, is this part of your job?" Starr asked, delighted.

"You might say so," he said. "May become quite a large part."

It was a small cottage, and the garden could have stood considerable improvement. "I'd like to plant it, myself," Starr said. "I'd have a big mass of verbena there, and daffodils up both sides of the walk, and over there a flowering tree, not very big. . . ."

She went from room to room of the house ecstatically. "You've used a lot of the furniture I liked! Oh, the lovely colors and the light, and the feeling of not being hemmed in! I'd move the wastebasket from there to over there though, wouldn't you?"

"Why don't you?" He watched her solemnly change the position of the wastebasket. "Same view as you have now—and a fireplace, too," he said.

"Yes. I'm glad I don't have to buy wood for it. But wouldn't it be lovely in here with the fire going and the fog just skulking in over the bay, and candles and good company?"

Dash dropped to the seat beside her. "Repeat after me," he said. "Money is for happy spending."

"Money is for happy spending," she echoed.

"Life is for living today—not yesterday or tomorrow."

"Life is for living today."

"Love is forever."

She looked at him questioningly. "Love is forever," she said more slowly.

"I love you."

"I—what is this, Dashell Taylor, I'd like to know?"

"Say it after me: I love you."

"I love you," Starr said tentatively.

"I hoped you did," Dash said triumphantly. "Let's get married some time—in three or four days, say?" He swooped her into his arms, and she was speechless. "Don't say no, Starr! Don't say no! There's peace where you are, and I want to be there every day, all the time!"

Peace! "You mean this place. . . ?" She could hardly believe that Dash had planned this. "We've really known each other so short a time. . . ."

"But this is today, remember—not yesterday or tomorrow. Don't put it off—don't waste a week, even! Starr, I love you

[149]

so—you won't be a cautious type, will you, always busy with some other time?"

She could not answer for his kiss, and for the moment she did love him and his urgency and enthusiasm. "Sit over there," she said when she could. "Somebody has to have some wits about him." Her hands flew together, proclaiming a crisis.

"Don't think! You don't need to, right now. This is our house. These are our lives—see, I'll make you a fire in the fireplace!" He went to the back yard and brought an armload of wood. He knelt and with a pocketknife began to make kindling. "This is the slow way, of course," he said, his hands trembling slightly. "What I need is two boy scouts to rub together. But my domestic virtues are all sound, ready to be brought to flower."

Starr watched him, troubled. He was a graceful person, full of laughter and nonsense. She could not assemble words with which to question him. He had no steady occupation, she knew; his parents would be furious with him. And her mind darted to Jeff, too, uneasily, as if he were unfinished business. There had been no time of questioning between her and Jeff.

Dash was being so tactful, not touching her. "I need time to think," she said. "Marriage is forever, and we shouldn't rush into it." For a moment she considered the absurdity of having actually to ponder whether or not she would marry this much-sought-after young man. She remembered the little murmurs of feminine sighs that followed wherever he had passed.

He came quietly and put an arm about her waist, and they looked into the fire. "I'm not rushing myself," he said. "I *know*. If you loved me, you'd know, too. It doesn't take deciding. It decides itself." The laughter had gone out of him, and she could hardly bear it. It was perfectly true that one did not decide such matters.

"I'd hate never seeing you again," Starr said, fumbling. "I love being with you, being close to you. I never knew anyone who *shared* better. But how do you know that's enough?"

"I'll wait," Dash said. "But it's a shame and a loss."

Somewhere in the last few months, Dash the glamorous had been replaced in Starr's scheme of things by Dash the person—gallant, wistful, very human, and more attractive than ever. Starr turned from the fire to the window, and saw the fog blotting out buildings, rolling in from the bay across the city at their feet, to the hoarse accompaniment of foghorns. Never had it looked so lonely.

"Sooner or later, I'll have to tell you there was another man," she said, suddenly a trifle frightened. Of losing him, or of hurting him? She didn't know, but rushed on. "I was very lonely, and there was a man—a fine man, you'd like him—"

Dash followed her and put his arms about her again. "I don't give the smallest damn about the man, or any man you ever knew, or how many, or what they were to you," he said. "That was before you were in my life."

She was deeply touched. "There wouldn't be any more loneliness," she said, half to herself.

"Just togetherness and fun," Dash said. "This very week?"

"This very week," she repeated, suddenly sure it was what she wanted. But the idea did not seem real or probable. Even later, planning details for the wedding, it did not seem real. She would try to get a few days' leave, she said, and perhaps they could find some country church and a min-

[151]

ister, and get a license—maybe down the peninsula, maybe over in Marin County.

That night Starr sat before her window, with the lights out, her arms wrapped about her knees. Dash had wanted her to move into their house that very day, but she did not want to. She wanted these few days among her old belongings. She wanted to think very straight.

She thought of Jeff, and she thought of Dash, and of her parents, and of the Taylors. There had been only a slight hesitation on her part, but her agreement was not unconsidered. She would be happier married than single, certainly. And next to Jeff, Dash was surely the most endearing man in the world. He and his smoke screen of foolishness, behind which he was so tender and grave—even sad!

Most imperative was the necessity to love—more urgent than to be loved, surely. "You can't stopper it up—" Cory had been right about it, even though she spoke of a cat at the time.

She and Jeff could not sit like vultures, waiting for Louise to die. Louise was young and strong. Besides, Jeff had probably long since recovered from their almost disastrous brush with loving and being loved. She argued this calmly enough to herself—rather like touching a tooth to see if it had quit aching. It hadn't; but it was less anguish now.

Dash's parents would probably disinherit him, which would be a pity, for he had always had plenty of money. Starr was not especially interested in his possible inheritance, however. It could be that the definite lack of it would make him work and succeed better than anything else could do. Besides, she did not mind working, herself, should the need arise. No. It would be a good, serene—perhaps even a gay sort of marriage.

And as for love—obviously there were many kinds. As many kinds as the people one knew!

One thing was certain: Dash could fill to a large extent the dreadful hole in her life since she left Jeff. She had not planned it so—it had "just happened," but it would be exactly right. She did not have to measure all the details this way, like a problem in accounting. She was lucky, that was all!

There was a calmness within her, a sort of silent thanksgiving to Dash and to fate itself. She went to her couch finally, tucked the blankets about her, and went to sleep thinking about linen and blankets and silver.

But she dreamed that she had swum a very far distance and was exhausted. She found one rock and rested upon it. All about her the sea and sky were blended in color, and the water was very clear. In the water were misty coral castles and lacy fronds of seaweed, and among them moved small fish like butterflies, and the darting, filmy bright-colored creatures. And from the deeps great dark shadows moved, sometimes slowly and sometimes with flickering speed across the sand.

Starr sat naked on her rock, and the breakers came a bit higher and a bit higher in walls of blue-green breaking to lace of foam about her. She would be washed off; she must swim yet farther, and she was tired. A great wave dislodged her, and she could no longer find footing on the rock. Again she swam, this time with a dragging sense of loss, as if the rock had been her home swallowed up in gently rising breakers.

[153]

When she was very tired, she stood at last upon another rock. It was much larger—almost a small island. When she was rested somewhat, she walked about it, and it was warm to her bare feet. Then she lay in a smooth shallow hollow carved by the tides, and again she looked into the water about her. There was sand—only sand. She arose and looked down from all sides of the rock. The floor of the sea was a wet desert, riffled slightly by waves, uninhabited, safe—except at the far end, where a deep pool dropped away to shadowy depths, and within those depths moved a great fish-shaped darkness. And there were no small bright fish, no coral, no ferny places of the sea.

She left that end of the rock, and lay once more in the sun, in the depression scooped by wind and water. She drowsed to the "Shish! Shish!" of the slow carving of wave on stone.

When she arose to go to work, the rain was saying shish, shish, on the windowpane at the head of her couch, and outside the city was drowned in downpour. As she made coffee, the dream haunted her still. She could almost feel the warm place in the rock, safe, with the rippled sand below the clear water. Yes, it was a much better rock than the first one, set in safer seas. She smiled at her fancy, for she had never been in a boat on the ocean.

Much wider horizons would open for her, with Dash. There was no telling what excitement, what adventure, what strange places awaited her now. But none of them would be frightening, for she would be with Dash always, in a widening ring of peace and affection.

She reported to Dash that she had been able to obtain

a week's leave for a honeymoon. "Did you get leave from the furniture mart?" she asked.

He laughed. "Nope," he said. "It seems that it is not the policy of the company to allow personnel incessantly to take a week off for honeymoons—that it would destroy discipline or something. When I pointed out that this very likely would happen to me only once, the manager was not impressed. Must be a batch of bigamists working around there, marrying every month or so!"

"We don't have to go away, you know. Even a day off to get the license would do."

"Not for me!" Dash said with a smile. "I take a week. I always take at least a week for all my honeymoons. Sometimes a month! I told the manager so. We parted forever, without undue sorrow."

"Oh, Dash! And I thought you liked it there! Now you'll have to hunt another job."

"Not this minute," Dash said. "I'd like you to resign, too, as fast as you can. Can't you do it now? We could drive up to Montana."

"I'd have to break in a new girl," Starr said uneasily. "And surely one of us ought to have a job!"

"On the other hand! Both of us ought to be free for a while! Go phone the boss and tell him you're resigning. That ought to be quicker. I've never seen Montana, have you?"

Land of the Shining Mountains, Starr thought; but they had no more reality than the mountains of the moon. "I'll break it to him when I tell him I'm married," Starr said. For her mother's caution was stirring within her, and it said I may never be married. I may need that job very badly, such as it is. Uneasily she thought of the battered files and the unmanageable old typewriter she used, and of the stuffy, kind persons with whom she worked.

Starr packed her bags. She tranferred her small belongings to the new house and gave notice to her landlord. Dash called for her in the Golden Goose, placed the bags in the car, and they drove to the small church in Marin County. The minister looked like a comedian, in spite of his sober attire. A fat woman and a tall crow of a man, both perfect strangers, acted as witnesses, and Starr was not nervous at all. It was like taking the oath of office, or attesting to signatures on a legal document. Afterward Dash headed the car north, having refused to say where they would go.

The wooded hills swept past, the shadowed folds of mountains, the bright flash of flower gardens. They stopped for lunch at an inn nestled under a great tree. Over coffee Starr said, "I don't think you even know where you're going."

"Not where we'll be tonight," Dash said. "But we're on our way to Montana, lazing and playing. I have trout rods in the back of the car."

"But we'll have to hurry so, to get back in a week—we'll be tired to death of just driving!"

"Who said we'd be back in a week?" Dash had the suspicion of a smile about his eyes. "You're kidnaped! The Kidnaped Bride."

"But, Dash, my job! You don't understand how important—"

"I called your boss and told him all about it," Dash said. "Damned decent sort. We'll pick up the form for resignation in Oregon tomorrow, and you can do the whole thing by mail—just as neat and easy as if you fussed around!

And that makes you nothing but Mrs. Dashell Taylor—dependent, homemaker. How does it sound?"

"Like a black lie. You rush so. You hurry me too much!"

"I don't believe it either, but I'm keeping an open mind." He put a hand over hers on the table. "Starr, darling, darling! Good thing I'm not holding down a job! I'd run home every few minutes to see if you were still there; to see if you were real."

"I'd be real, all right," Starr said. "I'd push you right out the door and tell you to go earn our daily bread! You have no idea how I eat!"

"No soul!" he said sadly. "Don't think I haven't been watching the way you eat—even on a honeymoon! No telling what it will be like in everyday life. Ain't you got no sensibilities?"

"I'm happy," Starr said. "When I'm happy, I eat a lot. I'll probably get fat."

Dash shook his head. "The things I contract to do!" he said mournfully. "I'll have to beat you, to keep your figure!"

They lazed a full month. Every day Starr seemed more securely part of Dash, who knew no withholding and no secret places. They fished the streams and laughed with the road signs. One thing he never mentioned was the size of his bank account, and Starr did not ask about it. Apparently he had enough. They stayed at modest hotels and cabins; sometimes they slept under the wide skies. Within two weeks it was difficult for Starr to remember any other way of life than one with Dash beside her or certainly nearby. They exchanged bits and pieces of tales from their childhood, so that they might know and love the children who never had known each other—but who grew up within a few miles of each other. "But with an imaginary barbed-

[157]

wire fence fifteen feet high between," Starr said, and both of them thought the thing absurd.

Mrs. Perry Taylor did not think the thing absurd. Dash and Starr picked up their mail in a small town, and sat in the public square to read it. When she had finished her letters, Starr tossed them to Dash.

I hope you know what you're doin [Cora Cooper wrote]. I guess any mom is sad to think what a woman gets into when she marries. I wisht you could of come home to be married, but I know you are busy and have your own friends. I hope you and your young man can come and see us some time, but be sure and let me know so I can take the day off. I remember when Dash took you to a party. Your pa is poorly; he ain't worked five days in five months. Beau works but you know he don't bring in much, and Ann Marie spends all she makes at the dime store on clothes. But we'll make out somehow like we always done. The last few days I keep thinkin about what a pretty baby you was, and how smart, and I hope you got yourself a good man.

With this letter, she enclosed a smudged note from Ann Marie:

Dear Sis: Pa says you married well and rich, and I hope you did because we could sure use some dough in this family. I always thought Dash was absolutely glamorous and simply too neat—all the girls did—and you ought to hear what they say about you all up and down Angello Street, some nice and some not nice but everybody sayin you married well. I work in the dime store now and have a lot of fellas but I am not fixin to get married for a while and when I do somebody rich like you did.

Dash read the letters and lifted his eyebrows and looked at Starr, and again both of them laughed. But he did not

[158]

toss Starr his mother's letter. He tore it to tiny pieces, and let it drift to the grass in the baked town square. Starr turned away from the sight, embarrassed. But it was not as if she had not anticipated Mrs. Taylor's view of this marriage.

Dash pulled her close. "I never want any secrets from you," he said, "but that was a letter my mother'll be sorry she ever wrote. I've forgotten it, you've never seen it, and she'll be glad to forget it someday."

"Was she so angry?"

"Oh, she flipped her lid, of course," Dash said casually. "She does. It's a family heritage—the result of being a Binder and a pioneer."

"Something like inherited disease?" Starr was gently teasing.

Almost to himself, Dash continued, "Of course I don't have to be part Binder, thank God, but it's burden enough to be a Taylor. Someday you'll have to memorize the history and noble characters."

"Why?"

"Our children will be the only link between historic Taylor and Taylor of the future, of course," Dash said, half in mockery, his fine eyebrows raised. "Have you no sense of Family?"

"Maybe not. I might contract it, of course."

Dash did not seem to find that very amusing.

Next day they drove into a sagebrush valley, gently rolling, lightly wooded, no different from many others they had traversed, to Starr's eyes. "This is it!" Dash said, stopping the car. "I think this spot has been drawing me to it, ever since I heard about the fabulous new oil fields in

Montana. I bet there's oil right here! Doesn't it just *feel* like oil land to you?"

"No. Can you smell it? There hasn't been a derrick in miles and miles and miles—and the scenery's the better for it!"

"Why, the very shape of the hills proclaims it!" Dash began unfolding a road map, and put his finger approximately upon the spot where they were. "Haven't you watched the form of the land?" His finger retraced places through which they had lately passed. "You remember here, where there were so many wells and so much activity, and we couldn't get near them—and nobody would tell us anything about production when I asked? That was a big strike. One well there flows with more oil than a dozen at home. Now remember the look of the valley that ran through here and down here, and the shape of the hills on either side of it? It's a long way, but the same strata, approximately, were in evidence where the hills were gullied. Once this was all one inland sea. . . ." As he spoke, his vivid face was alight, and Starr watched it. She had *not* observed the strata of rock; she had *not* thought of this valley as a sea of prehistoric creatures pressed to oil by centuries, and strained through rock and crevasses underground.

Dash broke his excited discourse. "You didn't grow up with the smell of oil leading you on," he said. "It's the most exciting thing. . . ."

"No," Starr said, wrinkling her nose. "Just the smell of oil, and the black smoke from burning sumps, and the framework of the older ones standing against the flat horizon."

"*There's* a gamble!" Dash said. "It gets in your very blood. My dad has it. In all his real-estate dealings, he's never managed to get himself a well, but he has always been trying. Hasn't the news in the papers about the Montana strikes fascinated you?" Starr shook her head. "I'm not a geologist, of course. I can't come out and measure the earth with a seismograph. But I can guess at a formation when the map and the earth itself says 'Oil!' And I want to gamble. Do you mind?"

Starr saw no reason why she should mind. The money belonged to Dash. He turned the car up a winding road to a weatherworn shack, and there found the owner of thirty acres of this forsaken land. The owner, an elderly man who lived there with his massive, silent wife, seemed suspicious. When Dash offered fifteen hundred dollars, the silent woman abruptly took her husband into the back room for conference.

She wanted to haggle, but Dash would not. The couple offered chicken coops and hogs to boot, for more money; they suggested payments on time. When Dash started to walk away, they came quickly to terms.

Dash and Starr stayed in the dusty small town for several days, consulting an attorney, getting the papers in order. Then, when the legal paperwork was done, Dash gave Starr some documents. "If I should die, hang on to this," he said. "Wild Horse Valley is no place to live, and the land's no good for anything but oil. But someday there'll *be* oil! Mind a fifteen-hundred-dollar gamble?"

Starr shook her head. "Why should I?" she asked. "I never saw fifteen hundred dollars in my whole life." It sounded extravagant, however, and vaguely alarming. Perhaps it cut short their ramblings, for after that they started home. The days slid past in quietness, and the nights were peace and companionship. Holding her in his arms sometimes at night, Dash would quote a scrap from some wedding ceremony he had once heard: "With my body I thee worship; with my soul I thee adore. . . ."

Starr was sorry for the women of the world married for small reasons. For her mother, married so that her one man could protect her from the more predatory; for Binkie, married for money; for all the hoping, seeking women looking for someone to love and finding nothing but a lifelong tide of demands that sapped their strength and joy and returned them almost nothing. She was even a little sorry for all the boys who had pawed at her, most of whom never would know any more of loving than a mole knows of the stars.

Only one wedding present came. Without note or comment, Binkie sent an exquisite small figurine of a woman wearing a cape of heavenly blue. Starr held it in her hands and looked at Dash. "I never had such a pretty, useless gift in my whole life!" she said. "Even as a child, I always received something useful—mostly warm clothes." She picked a few geraniums from the border, and arranged them behind the woman in the blue cape. Afterwards she always regarded this small figure as a symbol of the richness of her life.

Sometimes Dash worked, but always he quit the job. "You need to be a specialist these days," he said. "It isn't only that the jobs I get are dull; they don't pay enough to warrant the grubby little straw bosses." Starr grew uneasy about finances, but feared if she took a job it might shake Dash's confidence in himself. She liked her role as housewife; it was like playing house. Dash was endlessly entertained and enchanted at the surprises and thoughtfulness she lavished upon him.

She was a thrifty shopper, but what she saved in the household in a month, Dash would spend on one expensive trip to Carmel, or on a beautiful lustrous housecoat for her. When she called him extravagant, he laughed. When she tentatively approached the conditions of their finances, he changed the subject.

They had been married nearly a year, and Starr was pregnant, when Dash decided that they would visit Statsville again. "It's the best time," he said. "Mother's recovering from an illness, so she won't be too severe. We have the good news of the baby. And when we get back home, I'll hunt a grindstone for my nose, and no fooling! Starr, will a baby make any difference between us? I couldn't stand anything changing you—changing us!" He was so serious! It became him.

Starr shook her head. Ever since she had found out about the baby, she had known a new energy and an abiding wonder. "Of course things will be different!" she said. "They'll be fifty per cent more fun! But more expensive, of course. We'll have to sell the furniture from the guest room, and make a nursery of it."

"We can't. It's not paid for. Maybe they'll take it back and credit it on nursery furniture." That was the first she knew of the furniture not being quite their own. It disturbed her.

And she did have to exchange the furniture at a loss. The credit manager quoted the same old thing about business being business, which, translated, meant, I am going to cheat you, and it's perfectly legal, so don't make any fuss.

She had asked Dash to pay off the loan on the furniture, simply in order to sell the unused bedroom furniture at a fair price and save a hundred dollars. He knew, however, that she was more indignant at the unfairness of the proposition offered by the furniture mart than by the loss of the hundred dollars.

"Take the loss," he said. "Pay them no attention. You can't buck customs and the law and Business is Business. Property is ever and ever so much more tenderly regarded by the law than human decency." To distract her mind he proposed that they go downtown and buy Starr some new hats and dresses. "I want you to look like a million dollars in the old home town," he said.

"But my waistline's going all to pot! I couldn't wear the dresses again for nearly a year!" Starr protested.

"Only wife in the world that turns down new clothes, I bet," Dash muttered. "Come on! This'll be fun." Thoughtfully she yielded, thinking of her in-laws.

Starr had a sense of foreboding as they neared Statsville—as if all the accumulated work and denial known by her family and herself had settled like some invisible fog about the community. She hoped to keep her family and Dash's separate, for the peace of all—and wondered if she could. She asked Dash to stop at a filling station so that she might comb her hair again and brush the dust from her dress. A small panic was invading her. The sun was blistering. Sweat bathed them, and the car itself was hot to the touch. Had she lived most of her life with this sun-made fever? The heat drove her back to the car.

Dash watched her with worship as she re-entered the car. Or could it be protectiveness? He said that anyone who didn't love her on sight had lost most of his marbles. She kissed him impulsively, then consulted her mirror to see if the lipstick was still absolutely correct.

Feeling obscurely guilty, she repeatedly banished Jeff from her mind. It was only that places made one think of people.

6.

THE TAYLOR home had once been called a mansion. Its tall rooms and carved furniture smelled of wax and Airwick. No faint scent of tobacco violated its air; no ash trays were in evidence. There was hideous wallpaper with a climbing profusion of large flowers. Living and dining rooms were done in what Starr always called Apartment-house Tan—that most dreary of all colors. Couches and chairs and chests of another day, all polished and perfect, crowded the many large rooms. It was a museum. If ever Dash as a baby had hammered at the finish or picked at the cloth of anything in this house, all record of it had been erased neatly. The small windows gave little view of the landscaped grounds; curtains were drawn on many of them.

"It's as if the house hated the outdoors," Starr said later to Dash. And he said no, it was the people of that period who hated the outdoors—the sun that faded carpets, the wind that riffled the drawn work doilies and tanned the face. The outdoors was vulgar.

Starr had seen Mr. Taylor previously, collecting payments on homes when they were overdue. He was now a large, perpetually smiling old man with a jovial voice. He kissed Starr and said he hoped they had had a fine trip, and led them to Mrs. Taylor, who arose from a couch in a darkened room. She presented a cool cheek to Starr, asked her to sit down, and rang for the maid to bring iced tea.

Wariness lay like a shield between the two women. "Make her love me!" Starr was praying. "Let her approve of me, at least, so she may forgive Dash for marrying me, and there can be peace between them."

They were scarcely settled when Dash went over to the couch and pulled Mrs. Taylor's head to his shoulder. "Just relax!" he said. "I have the most marvelous news! We're going to have a baby! You're going to be a grandmother! What do you think of that?"

"Don't get hysterical," Mrs. Taylor said dryly. "It doesn't take any brain."

Warmth rushed over Starr's face. In time she would grow accustomed to remarks of this kind. It was as near to wit as Mrs. Taylor ever came. Dash laughed quickly. "Boy, did I impress you!" he said. Then conversation languished until Mrs. Taylor said that she was giving a dinner party for them the following evening.

"But so much work for you!" Dash protested. "We were going to stay only a few days."

"Nothing is accomplished without work," Mrs. Taylor said virtuously. "When you don't do it yourself, you spend twice the time showing some Okie that doesn't know furniture polish from floor wax exactly what to do."

Again the color warmed Starr's cheeks, and almost she spoke. But she had promised herself to hold her tongue for this whole visit, if she had to tie a knot in it.

"What a peculiar name you have, my dear," Mrs. Taylor said to Starr. "Family name, I suppose?" Starr said yes,

[167]

silently adopting into her family the woman who had delivered her in the County Hospital.

"Names are a matter of family pride," Mrs. Taylor said, on a note of relief.

If Starr had said no, the name was selected because her parents thought it pretty, it would not have been acceptable. Strange! Undoubtedly somewhere in history, the Taylors had had their share of idiots and halfwits, the same as anyone else. But given the family name, all is nobility, blanket-insured, Starr thought. She longed for the evening, and time when she and Dash would be alone. She longed for the opportunity to see her own family. But the afternoon wore on with the smallest of talk—of flower culture and sewing and some antiques that Mrs. Taylor recently had acquired. They looked at the hideous carved hulk of furniture, which probably had once been a washstand, before plumbing, and Starr was glad that she did not have to give it house room.

Thankfully she heard Dash offer to go out for some ice cream, and heard his mother's gently incredulous reply: "But we *never* eat between meals, Dashell, you know!"

Finally dinner came on and came on, hot and heavy and course after course, winding up with a tremendous cake and iced tea. Starr continued to make polite, thrifty conversation, draining it of all personality and opinion so far as possible. She thought how much more congenial would have been a dinner of cold cuts and coke—so suitable for the weather. Dash not only ate cake, contrary to his normal habits, but praised it.

Mrs. Taylor was critical of it. "Ethel always makes everything too short," she said. She called all her female help Ethel.

[168]

Dash offered an after-dinner cigarette, and after a split second's hesitation, Starr accepted it. He went to the kitchen and found a saucer not reverent with age, name, and family history, and set it between them for an ash tray. Mrs. Taylor fanned the air while the smoke was carried away efficiently by the excellent air-conditioning system of the house.

"The house keeps cool enough," Dash said.

"Yes," Mrs. Taylor admitted. "That's one modern thing that *is* an improvement. Your father is always having some mad notion to move to a fine new house he has built; but I always say I like my own house, with my own things in their right places. Get into one of these squashed new houses, and you don't have anywhere to put anything. Have the whole outdoors looking in the glass walls. Bare, that's what they are—bare all over, with no place to store valuables —no reverence for the past!"

Although bedtime was early, Starr felt giddy with release when finally she and Dash were alone. The dark, heavy furniture squatted in the high room. One stained-glass window, set for no good reason near the top of the wall, cast a stained moon shadow on the bed. And such a bed! She laughed aloud, simply looking at it. She told Dash she would have to have a long-sleeved, high-necked night-gown with a ruffle, to sleep in that monstrosity. She was sure it would frown upon the frivolities of love-making, too.

With a gleam in his eye, he went and found—and actually put on—the nightshirt of an ancestor, complete with long nightcap. They went to bed holding each other, hysterical with laughter. "You need to be hysterical to sleep in this," Starr said, smothering giggles. "Either that, or in a coma. First mattress I ever felt stuffed with rocks. Corn shucks, I know—but not rocks!"

"This is a historical bed," Dash said severely.

"Oh, it is! It surely is!" Starr agreed breathlessly. "I shall tell our children, and they can tell their children about it!" She did not have time that night to say more, for Dash held her close and said she was a savage—and other charming things—and eventually they slept around and over the hard terrain of the mattress.

On the second day, they spent most of the time with Starr's family. The Cooper house had deteriorated, Starr noted, and the furniture was more shabby than ever. Bert still had not built the cabinets he had promised when first they moved in. Dash became one of them upon entering the doorway. He had a surprising knowledge of all kinds of work in which the Coopers were interested—even cotton picking. He had once earned a bicycle in the cotton fields.

Since the house was too small to accommodate all the friends and relatives who gathered to meet Starr's husband, they piled into old cars and went to the park for a picnic. Aunt Artie could not come. Her working hours prevented. No amount of good will would make Starr fit back into the Angello Street group, however.

Two spots of pure joy marked that troubled three-day trip. After the formal dinner at the Taylors on the second night, Dash took Starr out to the orange groves and parked in the fragrance and the dark. Again they had the blessed feeling of being alone and serene together, with the quiet and the strangeness.

The other occasion was when they took Aunt Artie out for cocktails at the Stats Hotel. She wore a violently flowered dress and dripped with junk jewelry. Dash loved her on sight. He kissed her, and she was appreciative. "Holy smoke!" she said to Starr. "I do believe you found yourself a man, just when I was sure they'd all died off!" She regaled Dash freely with tales garnered from the patrons and personnel of her establishment, and afterward Dash said she was a female O. Henry. He laughed almost without stopping the whole time they were with Aunt Artie, and invited her to come and visit them when she could.

On the way home, Starr assembled her opinions of her in-laws. Dash's father would make the best of whatever he had to work with. His mother was more complicated. She seemed cold and sarcastic, but perhaps it was only that she found it difficult to assimilate a new relation. Mrs. Taylor did not like movies, riding in a car, picnics, short hair, cigarettes, cokes between meals, modern literature, dogs, cats, career women, or any human being except close relatives—not including in-laws. She did like discipline, money, and, Starr suspected, power over others. She also liked antiques, which Starr abhorred. She professed an interest in gardening—though hers was done by hired help, and her flower arrangements were certainly mere bunches, even if she did show plants in the flower shows and ostentatiously used some of the Latin names of common flowers.

"What ails your mother that she's not able to get about freely?" Starr asked.

"Why," Dash said in some surprise, "she's always had delicate health. Maybe it was the babies that died at birth. Actually I don't think I ever heard."

"If it were only that, modern doctors could patch her up, you'd think," Starr said. "Wonder she hasn't had it done long ago."

"She hates doctors," Dash said.

"Then she likes her ailments better than I would," Starr said.

"That's not quite fair to her," Dash said defensively. "You have to get to know Mother to understand."

Starr was quiet. They would have to visit Statsville only occasionally. "You don't ever plan to go back to Statsville for good, do you?" she asked.

"To live?" Dash asked incredulously. "Who wants to live in a desert, except a horned toad? There's money there, and a lot of people like it there—or maybe it's just that they're used to it. But it *is* a desert, in more ways than one." He had to concentrate on the driving thereafter. A dust storm came from the west, blowing like a low tan cloud along the ground, hiding the trees and the buildings, dimming the sun, obscuring traffic and highway. "Shall we run through this, or try to stop somewhere in an air-conditioned building until it blows over?"

"Drive through it," Starr said. "You know how it gets in your food and between the sheets and between your teeth— and there's nowhere to get away from it. And we couldn't be much dirtier than we already are."

It was breathlessly hot in the car with most of the windows closed tight. In the dun light, great tumbleweeds hopped and blew against fences. Some escaped and rolled down the highway, weightless prickly skeletons. Oncoming cars carried them stuck to the radiator or dragging between front wheels like prey. Toward evening the wind grew cooler, and a sparse rain fell through the murk. "It blows breezes of dust and rains mud," Starr said. The few drops did indeed muddy the windshield. "When they suck all the water from under the valley, it'll return to the tumbleweed and sagebrush again, and all be given back to the rattlesnakes and jack rabbits."

"And centuries and centuries hence," Dash said, "man will find the bones of cars outlining the course of the ancient highway, all obscured by tumbleweed and lost. And he'll write, 'Many a car sputtered to oblivion when this route was regularly traveled by man. Our party found a green glass necklace, priceless to collectors, probably the property of some long-ago child. It was preserved in a beer tin, where it happened to fall prior to the time of the Great Dust.'"

"I think maybe this is the middle of the Great Dust," Starr said, peeling gum for both of them, for moisture in their gritty mouths.

After that trip she remembered most clearly and happily their trip at night to the orange grove. It might have existed in a mythical land that opened to them one night and vanished once more when they left. Surely it must have been a small grove; she had not known that it was there.

"I conjured it up for you," Dash said smugly. "I never told you the powers I held." He conjured up every delight of companionship. In the night Starr would awake and put out her hand to touch him, and move closer to lay her cheek against his arm. She was deeply grateful that he was there to fill the void that once existed in her life. He had even added laughter to her days.

She had not seen or had any word of Jeff in the three days that they visited Statsville. Maybe he had been transferred.

The first time her child moved within her, she ran into Dash's arms and wept. When he discovered the reason for it, his eyes were shiny, too. "How can we have so much, when there's so little in the world?" she asked.

Dash dried her eyes. "It's a magic, naturally," he said. "Would you care for an old brass lamp to rub? It's about my financial speed these days." So he was running short of money. But he was to see a man in the East Bay about a job that very day. He said he would tell her about it later.

She never knew what job he sought. The news came by phone that it might be the body of Dashell Taylor who died in the four-car pile-up on the Bay Bridge. The disembodied voice asked if she would come down and identify. . . . It grew thinner and thinner and vanished with her into revolving blackness.

She awoke in bed, weighted with the knowledge of calamity. It was no dream. Carefully she explored her body. The child was still there. She might have hurt it when she fell. How long she was on the floor before someone came, she never knew. Voices were in the living room; they seemed to belong to Ham and Binkie—those two who had gone out of her life more than a year ago.

"Just leave me alone," Binkie was saying. "I do the best I can."

"Bink, how could you? How can you?" Ham was saying, in the voice of one who repeats himself. "Look at you! You heard of Dash on the radio, and so did I, and here we came tearing at the same time. We always have the same thought, the very same ache. . . ."

Binkie's voice roughened. "Look at me!" she cried. "*Look* at the shape I'm in! Get me out of your mind, so I can get you out of mine! Go join the Foreign Legion ... so I'll never imagine the man going away down the street is you. So it never can be you to torment me. ..."

"Hush!" Ham said. "Hush for this minute! We have so few."

"At least you aren't dead," Binkie said, her voice muffled.

"No. But Dash had more than a year of loving and being loved. I envy him that. Oh, Bink ..."

Starr was too exhausted to move, and still she shrank from the voices. She could call out, if the tears would stop long enough to make her voice audible. They rolled down her face and wet her already damp pillow.

Outside was the distant bellow of foghorns, once the very essence of winter closed outside and firelight within. She would never hear a foghorn that she would not think of a fireplace, and Dash in a dark red robe singing or making up games: "Let's roast some chestnuts! I feel so English to-night. It is the *English* who roast chestnuts, isn't it?"

The first chestnuts burned up. "I don't like mine quite this well done." He had frowned, holding upon a fork a glowing coal that once was chestnut. "Do you suppose they have buckets of water to douse them with from time to time?"

Every picture of Dash that came to mind was a laughing one.

In the other room, Binkie said, "Ham, I never found a place like this to rest, in all my life. Maternity makes me tired." Then in a few more moments she spoke more briskly. "Ham of my heart," she said, "loosen up them pearly gates so I can go back to hell where I made my bed and must lie in it—all of it."

"I won't."

[175]

"But I *must* go! I want to look in on Starr before I leave."

Time vanished and returned for Starr, and Binkie was standing beside her bed, her body and her chiseled features soft with pregnancy. She put a hand on Starr's forehead lightly. "I know it's hell, and I'm sorry," she said gravely. "But at least you've had some of the fun and the glory. And it can't all quite escape." She patted the covers above Starr's midsection and smiled slightly. "I have to go. If you need anything I can furnish, I'm here." She wrote on the leaf of a tiny notebook in a golden case, tore it out, and pinned it to one of the bedroom curtains.

"Binkie, I think you're braver than I am," Starr said.

"No," Binkie answered. "I'm just worn down thinner to the bones of reality. I'm in fine fighting condition, and know the rules and penalties. I wonder who thought the stinkers up?"

Later Ham came to her bedside and said he was making a bed on the chesterfield, and would not go away. "Who do you want to come?" he asked. "I'll wire."

"Nobody." Starr closed her eyes. "I'd rather have you there than anybody. I guess you liked him best, next to me."

"I guess I did, kid. He was a hell of a swell joe." He gave Starr a glass of water and the green capsule left by the doctor, and the black fuzziness swallowed her almost immediately.

During the night Ham answered a pounding at the door, wearing a bathrobe that had belonged to Dash. A large old man was there. "I was looking for the Taylor residence—I beg your pardon," he said.

"This is it; come on in," Ham said.

The man was as tall as he, and weighed considerably more. "Where is Mrs. Taylor?" he asked.

Ham nodded toward the bedroom. "Asleep," he said. "She won't wake until morning. Who are you?"

"Perry Taylor. I've come to take her home." The man sat heavily. "Who are you?"

"Their friend. My name is Hamilton. There wasn't anyone but me to stay with Starr. I can go now."

"I need sleep," the old man said. His eyes were reddened from the long drive through the fierce heat of the valley. "Isn't there another bedroom?" So Ham showed him the other bedroom. It contained nothing but a bassinet and a chest of drawers. Perry Taylor looked at them, and one tear escaped from each of his eyes and ran into the furrows in his cheeks. He swung toward Ham with the puzzled pain of a wounded bear. "Dashell was so lively," he said. "Won't anything be the same any more."

Shock is a cushion, Starr thought later. The days pass in unreality, and so one goes through the motions. Perry Taylor was a rock on which to rest, if rest there ever would be in the world. But he was a stranger, all the same. Very old he had grown, all of a sudden. Or perhaps he was *always* old, and only now showed it clearly.

New expressions had to be learned. Mr. Taylor said that Starr "had not been left well provided for." The insurance he carried would scarcely bury him; and his bank account amounted to only a few hundred dollars. "What did he do with his legacy?" Mr. Taylor asked.

"Spent it," Starr said. "I'm glad he did—he enjoyed it."

"He never could take care of money," Perry Taylor said sadly, shaking his head. The small triangular island of hair at the top of his forehead fell forward. He was trying to

[177]

figure what assets could be saved. The car was gone; the furniture would have to go back; the house would revert to the holder of the mortgage. Starr packed her own clothing, some baby clothing, and the statue in the blue cape. "You could almost tie it up in a kerchief, like an immigrant's belongings," she said ruefully.

Perry Taylor looked at her angular face, shadowed with a peasant sadness. "There'll be another Dash Taylor," he said, obviously to cheer her, since he surely must have realized that it was an asinine statement. "Mamma wants you to come and stay with us for a few years, so that we can provide for the last of the line—and yourself, of course."

"Yes, I want to go back to Statsville for a while," Starr said. "At least I don't want to stay here. I *can't*, can I? I couldn't get a job. Of course I'll work after the baby's born."

"We can talk about it later," he said vaguely, trying not to weary her with plans. But Starr wanted to plan, for a plan was something to follow through pain and loneliness and days that were dead.

Driving back to Statsville, Perry Taylor tried to make conversation and failed. He turned on the car radio, and Starr was stricken terribly by melodies associated with Dash. They went through the lovely wooded valley in the high hills. "I'd like to build us a house here someday," Dash had said. The grasses were brittle with summer, and the creek that had brawled as they passed was now slow and quiet with the weight of summer days. If one could wipe the mind clear of memories, Starr thought in despair.

Between Pacheco Pass and Los Banos, the road made a roller coaster of itself. Here she and Dash had laughed and sung as they passed a few months previously. A roller coaster without the proper company was the saddest thing in the world. She turned her attention minutely to Perry Taylor.

He was saying that his money was very tight at the moment. He had tried twice unsuccessfully to find oil on one of his properties, and had mortgaged practically everything he owned for the venture. "It isn't that I can't pay it all off," he said, chewing a dead cigar. "It's just that money will be tight with us for a few years." Perry Taylor had a way of saying things to use the most worn-out possible phrase, and he repeated it. Hysterically Starr wondered why she had never heard anything about "loose" money—only money that was "tight." But this was nothing to share with Mr. Taylor. Again she dragged her attention back to his words. Dash had said that drilling one well cost about fifty thousand dollars. Then Perry Taylor had gambled and must pay back fifty thousand dollars. Twice fifty thousand! And his money was consequently "tight."

"I'm no burden of yours," Starr said. "I'm sure Mom can tuck the baby and me in somewhere until I'm able to go back to work."

Quickly Perry Taylor said, "Oh, I didn't mean we didn't want you and the baby! I'm sorry you were left with nothing, but young marriage is apt to be that way. Young people don't think what they're doing, any more. Mother would be heartbroken to have you anywhere else but home. Your young Junior will be the last of the Taylors, and must have the best education and so forth."

Starr did not reply. But she would return to the comfort of her mother until after the baby was born. She would not argue now; she did not have the strength for it. There was still the funeral, and perhaps she should stay with Dash's parents for a time.

Mrs. Taylor was lying down. Indeed Starr had seldom seen her not lying down—an immense inert weight with an immobile face at one end of it, and narrow feet, almost grotesque in their smallness at the other. The feet wore shoes of finest, most expensive kid.

"My dear child," said the monotonous voice from the immobile face, "you're probably tired. Go up and rest if you like." So Starr followed Mr. Taylor upstairs and contemplated the mattress that she had said was stuffed with rocks. She looked up at the carved ugliness of the headboard and prayed, Dear God, make me wise and brave and strong enough to live the rest of my life without joy or laughter, for I don't see how I can stand it, amen.

She lived in Dash's room and looked out at the tree he had known from that high, unfriendly window, in the sterile, inward-turned house. She crowded her belongings into a closet crammed with suits and dresses of an era before her time. Mrs. Taylor never thought to move them. They were "good," and one did not throw away or give away good things.

The funeral was on such a hot day that even if one were not smothering in grief, still one would fry somewhat. She and Dash once had spoken of death superstitions and had agreed that funerals were barbarous and terrifying rituals from some darker age. She had not had the strength to protest, and now he was suitably surrounded by Stats, Binders, and Taylors. Pomp and flowers exuded from every cranny. He would *hate* it, she thought. He would hoot at the idea that this was "respect to the dead." She had already been snowed under by platitudes of condolence, and more would follow. Only Bink and Ham had said anything that made an ounce of sense.

The Cooper family and Aunt Artie arrived, and Starr ran to her mother, feeling absurdly young and lost. Cory held her tight, then looked at her wordlessly. Cory had been ill. The ravages of pain were threaded across her face. The bones of her Indian ancestor were plainer now, beneath the leathery skin. But her eyes were compassionate. Why, they're a mother's eyes, Starr thought with a pang. I'll have eyes that look out at the world with that expression some-day if my child is stricken and I can do nothing. She hugged Cory, as if she would comfort her.

The music in church was splendidly selected to promote tears and self-pity. Starr sat and fiercely turned her mind from the present to the future. In a few months, she would hold this new life in her arms. She would love and protect this baby, and work for it and shield it as no baby had ever been cherished before. By Christmas she might be able to work again, and the baby . . . She would meet that problem when she came to it.

Mrs. Taylor, swathed in black veil, had tottered to the chapel supported by Perry Taylor. His face was deeply lined. Seeing they were busy with each other, perhaps Starr might rejoin her own family after the funeral.

Finding him alone for a moment after the services, she said to him, "I want to go home with my mother for a while."

He thought the girl was too tense. She had not cried at all. Once she had actually smiled! He said he would pick her up before dinnertime—would that be all right? Mom

[181]

would be prostrated by this, but she was expecting Starr for dinner, and he did not want to upset Mom. . . .

Starr agreed. But I won't always agree, she thought. I'll find myself a place back home. She climbed into the elderly car that Aunt Artie drove, and held young Caroline on her lap. How pretty the baby had grown! Perhaps my baby will be a girl, and look like this, she thought, hugging her sister close. The Taylors probably would faint. Even Dash had sworn he knew it *must* be a boy. But Caroline was a little beauty, round and gently sun-kissed, with a lovely fluff of curls and long, long dark lashes shading her blue eyes.

Even Beau had managed to attend the funeral. He looked better in work clothes than in a suit. Strange—she had not thought of how he looked in his suit, or how her father looked in his. But Jeff had made her conscious of materials and style. They seemed strangers in their "store clothes."

From time to time she questioned Cory's tired profile with a searching glance, or she came back to Ann Marie's peculiar costume. Ann Marie wore new black satin a size too small for her figure. She was *acting* bereaved.

The house has surely shrunk, Starr thought, her courage failing. The two couch beds in the living room seemed to take up most of it. Ordinarily, Ann Marie and Caroline slept on them, Beau still slept in the dining room, and Cory and Bert occupied the bedroom. Every nook of the house was bulging with occupancy. Her space at home had been taken by Caroline—a fact that she had not considered, since Caro had still slept in a crib when she had left home. There simply *was no room* for Starr to fit back into! A small panic fell upon her when she realized it.

But apparently no one else had considered it. They all

assumed that the Taylors would provide for her, being better able to do so. She sagged with defeat, and a shapeless sort of fear slithered across her mind.

The telephone rang. It reminded her that Cory was missing a day's work for the funeral. "For you, Starr," Ann Marie said with rising interest.

"Starr, this is Jeff."

As if he would have to tell her! "I know," she said beginning to tremble.

"I wanted to say that I'm sorry, and to say I'm here to help if you should need it."

It quickened the tears she had withheld all day. She spoke with difficulty. "Thank you," she said. "I don't think there *is* any help in the world! Thank you, Jeff, but make no mind!"

His voice was kind and warm. "I never thought I'd hear that phrase again," he said. "I'll go. Just remember that I'm here—same place, same job, same Jeff."

When Starr replaced the receiver, Aunt Artie said immediately that she wanted to go out for a beer. She asked Starr to come along. "You mightn't think it was respectful, but Dash'd understand, I bet!"

Starr was moved by affection for Aunt Artie. "Of course!" she said. "He'd say have one for him!" She donned the smock once more; she had been carrying it around because every thread worn was an additional source of heat. "I'll have to get *something* to wear," she said to Aunt Artie, to fill a void with words.

"We can do that, too," Aunt Artie said. "I have the day off. You got any money?" They went back to the battered car.

"Very little," Starr said, "but enough for a garment or two."

Wryly Starr considered the propriety of going shopping on the day of one's husband's funeral. The proprieties were concerned with the presumption of grief—not grief itself. Anything to keep moving, to keep doing something, helped a lot. They bought a couple of smart washable maternity slack suits.

Aunt Artie sipped her beer and turned her glass around and around in a way unlike her normal self. "Kid," she finally said, "I got to tell you something, and I hate to do it today, when you got enough hard things to think about. But we got to look after the folks that are alive, no matter who dies. You notice anything about your mom?"

"She looks so tired; maybe she's been sick," Starr said, and apprehension added a new flavor to despair within her.

"She wouldn't tell you, but she's got to have an operation right away," Aunt Artie said. "The County'll do it, but she has to wait till the right specialists can get at it. Should have it quick. It *might* be cancer." Aunt Artie's voice dropped away almost to nothing. "Don't be scared, kid," she said with more courage. "It might *not* be, too!" It must have been hope lighting up her kind face.

We spent all that money, and now I'm helpless when I ought to be helping her, Starr thought in consternation. "What can we do?" she asked Aunt Artie.

"Money to pay will make it quicker," Aunt Artie said. "Of course maybe there's no hurry, and she could wait. And maybe she can't wait any longer. I ain't got no money, naturally, but I can borrow a hundred against my salary at a loan shark's." Noting Starr's expression she added quickly,

"I done it lots of times before! I can't get but a hundred, but they know me, and I could get it real quick. But we need five hundred—maybe more."

"I have three hundred," Starr said, "but that's all. I was saving it for the baby's birth. But you can always get help at the County for that, can't you? My baby could be born the same way I was." The hateful thought caused an uprush of fresh sympathy for Cory. "I could, but probably the Taylors wouldn't let me," she said more cheerfully. "It wouldn't look well, would it?"

She put the three hundred into Aunt Artie's hands. The hands were brown and worn, but the nails wore a brave vivid nail polish. Starr then had ten dollars in her purse.

That night in bed she thought, but I still have the land in Montana, which nobody wants to buy. There would be taxes due on it soon. But she rather hoped that no one *would* buy the land—she was superstitious about it. Dash had said the taxes would be small. She turned on her finger the one ring Dash had given her. It would probably cover the taxes—and very likely she would have to sell it. She put the hand with the ring on it near her cheek, and there was a quiet sadness in her before she slept. She dreamed of the untidy small house in barren Wild Horse Valley.

Cory was not sorry for herself. The money had been raised for the operation, which would prove that there was nothing wrong with her. "Probably busted a gusset trying too hard sometime," she said. "Have to patch it up, probably."

Starr visited her family in the evenings. It was doubtful whether the change was a happy one, when she went from the cool museum at the Taylors' to the crowded disorder of her mother's home. "Dear God," she sometimes said into her pillow, "I don't feel at home anywhere at all. I must be truly a displaced person! There must be something wrong with me!" She would have liked to see a movie, attend a lecture—anything to distract her mind. She had read every book in the Taylor library—most of which were forty years out of date and both quaint and dull. She often walked the long way to the public library and sat there reading for a time.

Mrs. Taylor could not fathom this restlessness. "If you don't quit making grimaces when you talk, you'll have a wrinkled forehead," she said.

"I never thought to save my face for a rainy day," Starr said, as lightly as possible. "I have to walk. I worry about Mom."

And now that she was with her mother for an evening, she was still consumed with restlessness. Cory did not have much to say. Beau and Bert were playing cards. Ann Marie was out on a date. "Let's sit outside for a spell," Cory said.

Starr moved two chairs outside, and Cory slowly followed. The harsh light fell over the table where Bert and Beau sat holding cards. Bert was very stooped, and Beau had a petulant droop to his mouth. Neither had offered to move the chairs.

A full moon made near daylight outside the house. Children played up and down the length of Angello Street, running and shrieking and occasionally weeping. Even the nights were crowded with too many people and too much noise, Starr thought. She had not remembered how noisy it was—was it always so noisy and lacking in privacy?

Cory rocked in silence. "It was the best I could do," she said finally, as if she were reading Starr's mind.

"I know."

"I got to ask you something," Cory went on. "I ain't sure you can do it, and if you can't, I want you to say so, plain out, so's I can figure some other way." Starr waited.

"I ain't supposin' I'm gonna die with this operation," Cory continued carefully, "but there's always the off chance, of course. I got to think about Caroline. I wouldn't want Caro in no orphans' home, and I wouldn't want her taken back . . . home. You can't trust a girl baby with menfolks, and you know Ann Marie couldn't mother her—she's kind of wild and careless."

"I'll look after Caroline some way," Starr said, deeply touched. "I'll keep her until you get out of the hospital."

"Don't think I don't know how hard it'll be on you, Starr," Cory said seriously. "Likely old Mrs. Taylor doesn't remember me—she always called me 'Ethel,' anyway—but I've scrubbed her floors and washed her windows for twenty-five cents an hour, and I know what she's like. She hates children—she even hates young people, doesn't she, Starr?"

"I hoped you didn't know," Starr said, disconcerted.

"Poor old woman!" Cory said. "She doesn't love anybody but herself." She rocked gently back and forward in the moonlight. "I hate to put the burden on you, but you're the only one I can think of that could carry it. It'd be hard until your baby's born, and then it'd be easier, because you'd have something you really wanted to work for. Caro'll be a nice big sister for your baby if you let her help with it and take some care of it. She has the makings of a little mother, the same as you always did. She reminds me of you when you was little, all the time."

Cory had not been clever enough to disguise the fact that she thought she was going to die. "We won't let you die!" Starr said anxiously. "What in the world would we do?"

"If I die," Cory said, "just remember that it's part of a plan that always goes like it ought to. I never knew a person to die that somebody didn't say he couldn't be spared; and I never failed to see that in the mending, nearly everything came out all right—and sometimes better for those left. It's just that little children really need a mother. You and Beau and Ann Marie are grown. Beau and Ann Marie and your pop can make their own livings. Don't let them put upon you, Starr. They'll try!

"Bert'll be lost for a while. He'll never hold the family together. He'll probably go back to his folks. I don't know but what it'll be a kind of relief to him to go. I never liked the slowness and the dirt and the way his people or mine lived, and I *would* come out here, and I *would* stay! But it could be I was wrong for Bert—that maybe he ought to've married a girl that was more content to live his way. I couldn't say. I know you wouldn't like it there, where the pigs get more thought than the women in the house. Pigs sell for more money, you know! But if your Pa goes back to them, don't hinder him, Starr. He's lived out here among foreigners a long time, and it's been cruel hard on him."

Starr did not offer Cory a pat or a kiss, which might loosen her taut courage. "I'll do the best I can whenever I can," she said unevenly. "Don't worry about Caro. And what else have you been mulling over?"

After a brief silence, Cory's voice was shy, almost soft. "I just thought I'd tell you, Starr, that I know it ain't easy being the odd one," she said. "It's easier when you fit in to where you're born."

"I wasn't the first 'odd one,'" Starr said, looking at her mother. "You'd better be resting, if you go to the hospital tomorrow. Suppose I pack some things for Caroline and take her home with me tonight?"

Caro put off her drowsiness at the excitement of going home with Starr. Starr put cardboard boxes of clothes into the old car, and Cory reached out and hugged Caroline. She held the pretty vivid baby face between her hands and looked long at it.

That first morning, Starr dreaded to bring Caroline downstairs. She led her into the bedroom where Mrs. Taylor lay languidly reading. She had been careful in dressing herself and Caroline, and had combed their hair to its utmost simplicity. Mrs. Taylor could not bear to see one hair curling out of place. She herself was partially bald, and what hair she had was worn snugly wound on top of her head, and there secured with a heavy hair net and numerous sturdy hairpins, including two with mother-of-pearl tops. Starr never saw her hair down. She wondered if she wore it up all night.

"Good morning," Mrs. Taylor said with polite distance. "Whose child is that?"

"Mine, temporarily," Starr said as brightly as possible. "My mother has to go to the hospital, and there's nowhere to leave Caroline. She's my baby sister. Would you mind if she stayed with me for a little while?"

Mrs. Taylor resorted to a difficult silence, as if she had not heard.

"We could find somewhere else to stay, if you objected," Starr said, her face flushing. "My Aunt Artie would probably find a place for us."

[189]

"Your place is with us, dear child," Mrs. Taylor said with a sigh. "I hope the child isn't noisy. My headaches, you know."

"I'll try to keep her quiet and take her out to the park a lot," Starr said. "She's three years old."

Another awkward silence followed. Starr finally said, "I'll get Caro's breakfast," and led the child out, feeling humiliated and helpless. She hugged Caroline and went to the large old kitchen where the current "Ethel" was polishing silver.

"I'll fix us some breakfast— No, don't get up or fuss! I'll wash up after us, too. This is my baby sister. She's visiting me for a week or so."

"Ethel" dropped the silver. "It's too much!" she said, her underlip protruding. "It was bad enough with just the two of them. Then comes you, and then comes this baby to get underfoot—and in a little while, *another* baby to be waited on! No, it don't pay enough!"

Starr wanted to weep. "Oh, please!" she said. "We aren't going to make a bit more work for you! We'll hardly be around at all!"

But "Ethel" walked stiff-legged toward the front of the house. "I ain't no baby sitter besides cook and flunky," she said ominously. Her broad back was surmounted by a head of stiff, graying hair, tightly caught to her head in a hair net, neat and hideous.

Starr tried to distract Caroline while the battle of Ethel proceeded in another room. She caught an upraised voice saying, "And now that I'm leavin', I want you to know my name ain't Ethel; it's Mabel, and I don't any more like bein' called Ethel than you would! And now I'll wear my own hair like I please!" A door banged, and the ruler of the kitchen appeared scowling. She held a hair net crumpled in one hand, and her escaping gray hair was a surprisingly soft frame for her brown face. "A body can stand just so much," she said to Starr, breathing hard, "and after that they ain't no money can pay you to take no more."

"I feel guilty," Starr said. "My mother had to go to the hospital so I had to take care of my sister. Do you know my mother—Cora Cooper?"

"Cory!" exclaimed the erstwhile Ethel. "I never knowed you was Cory Cooper's girl! She's the salt of the earth! I didn't know anybody in this family had the sense to— Cory's a good woman." Heavily she sat upon a stool. "That makes things different," she said. "I'd take the baby, myself, and glad to. But I ain't enjoyed working here so much I'd change my mind about leavin'. Lots of people pay real well and give you quarters, too, and don't give you any of this high-falutin stuff about bring the china into the living room with a bowl of hot soapy water and a dish of hot clear water and a linen dish towel— Horse manure!" She glared at the wall. "I never broke any of her fancy dishes. I been washin' dishes real careful since I was a kid."

Starr ventured to pat her hand. "As an old friend of mine once said, 'Go with God.' Get the best job you can. We all do—it's the way we *should* do!"

Mabel smiled, her broad face wrinkling and a gap in her teeth becoming obvious. "Them as don't do, gets done," she quoted. "It's a hard thing to believe, but I guess it's a fact." She slowly put on her hat and walked toward the door. "If I can do anything at all for Cory, I will," she called back. "I mean it."

When she looked in upon Mrs. Taylor after breakfast, Starr found the fat old woman in a faint. She rushed to her and ascertained that there was a heartbeat; then there was a faint moan—half a sigh.

"Where's the brandy?" Starr asked frantically. Swiftly she lifted Mrs. Taylor's legs and heavy hips and stuffed cushions beneath them. Mrs. Taylor came awake. "A stimulant," she said faintly. "Some jasmine tea."

Starr made tea and brought it steaming in a silver pot. She assembled the Spode cup and saucer and the milk and sugar and rushed them to Mrs. Taylor.

"I can't use this spoon, dear child!" Mrs. Taylor whispered. "It's a kitchen spoon." Starr went and found a silver spoon.

She sat near Mrs. Taylor and asked again where she kept the brandy or whisky, and learned that no alcoholic stimulants ever violated the premises except a pint of rum every few years, to season mincemeat pies. Tea, said Mrs. Taylor, was a strong enough stimulant for anybody.

"Shan't I make an appointment with your doctor for you?" Starr next asked. But Mrs. Taylor dropped withered eyelids over her eyes and said no, in a pained tone. Starr noted that although she had preserved her face by not smiling, she had been unable to preserve her eyelids and neck for a rainy day.

"I'm sorry about Mabel going, and having to bring Caro here, and for troubling your household in the least," Starr said. "But since you do need someone to cook and clean, let me try it. It would occupy my hands and make the time pass faster, and I'd feel that I was less a burden."

"The Taylors take care of their own," Mrs. Taylor said, as if giving instruction. Perhaps it was only coincidence that she was looking straight at Caroline when she said it. "We'll try to find another servant, but it may take time. Servants aren't what they used to be, I'll tell you! Why, I had one for fifteen years. Paid her twelve dollars a month and keep. She didn't have it easy like they do these days, either. She strained milk and made butter and washed and ironed...."

The telephone rang, and Caroline ran toward it. Mrs. Taylor sat up with unexpected agility. "Don't let that child— The table's a priceless antique!" she said on a rising scale.

Caro had gone outside the door and into the hall, where she daintily lifted the receiver from its cradle. She listened. "Telfoam," she said proudly to Starr. Starr smiled at her as a reward. She looked at the priceless antique and was happy that someone else owned it. One print of Caro's starlike baby hand was registered on its high polish.

Aunt Artie's voice said over the telephone, "Now take it easy, and think about your own kid! They decided to operate on Cory right away, and she didn't live. If she had, it couldn't have been for long." Aunt Artie began with a rush, and the last words blurred with a sob.

"Thank you," Starr said stiffly, and put the receiver down. She bowed her head, and the tears began falling fast upon her extended waist. Caro came and looked into her face, her own small face concerned. She crowded to Starr's knees and smacked kisses into the air—kissing the place to make it well.

For a moment Starr stood in the door, facing Mrs. Taylor obliquely, ashamed that the immobile old eyes should see her cry. "My mother died. Excuse me, please," she said, and led Caro out to the lawn. The sun was blindingly hot, but there was a bench behind a lilac bush that offered a bit of privacy. There Starr put her head on the back of the bench and finished the weeping that was within her.

Near her feet in a barren, sandy spot, Caro brought a horned toad to bay. Three inches of armored dragon, it puffed itself and hissed, then fled, a sandy shadow across sand. But Caro pursued and caught it, and brought it to Starr in worshipfully cupped hands.

Through swollen lids Starr looked at the tiny face beneath the miniature crown of spikes. "It's so frightened," she said to Caro. "Be careful not to hurt it, and let it go safely when you've looked at it."

Caro stooped and released the tiny creature, which disappeared with the speed of a quenched light. "Go home, little horny toad," she said. She looked at the bare sand from which the small thing had vanished, then looked back to Starr. "I want to go home," she said. "Where's Mamma?"

Starr swallowed tears, unable to reply. Caro still looked at her imperatively. "Home," she said clearly.

All the ritual—all the misplaced faculty of entertainment —all the forethought that went into a Taylor dinner! Starr thought dazedly. Eating was the one luxury, the one way of measuring off the hours; it was the sum of celebration, or a stern duty in time of grief. She began a meal at four in the afternoon. I'm really a priestess, she thought. I prepare the sacred food, and as long as it appears on the table three times a day, in suitable holy vessels and silver, all will be well, amen.

She served at six, but she had already learned that she could never sit down at the table and eat a full meal in that house. She always must rise at least twice to pour out part of Mrs. Taylor's coffee and bring her fresh coffee boiling hot. And after the meal was finished, the Taylors sat and sat, when Starr would have been busy about the dishes. Gradually she looked upon each meal with dread—the most hateful times of day. But she had not yet met the monstrous Holiday Meal with Company.

"She was the best wife a man ever had," Bert Cooper said stubbornly, "and I don't aim she should have no little dinky funeral."

"But she wouldn't *want* a great expensive funeral," Starr said. "She wouldn't want all of us in debt for it! And I don't suppose any of us has any money."

"Couldn't you get some from your rich in-laws?" Beau asked.

"No," Starr said flatly. "I live on charity as it is—with Caro, what's more." In vain she begged for common sense regarding Cory's funeral. They seemed to have lost their minds. "Most of us are already in debt," she argued with the family.

"I aim to take Cory back home," Bert reiterated, his stooped figure seeming to straighten with his will. Then he came down to the heart of the matter. "We can sell this house," he said. "Cory paid on it a long time, and we ought to get something, even if it ain't paid for. A lawyer feller said so."

"It would certainly make Mom laugh to think she worked so hard so many years to pay for her own funeral!" Starr said. "She gave her very self—her hands, her head—she denied herself everything, to put something solid together for the family—for a shelter and a place we could call our own. And now you'd sell it for a funeral!"

[195]

"I aim to take her back home," Bert said again, as if he had heard not a word. He couldn't take her back alive, but dead he could.

"But she *hated* it back there—she told me so!"

Ann Marie tossed back the overcurled mane of her thick hair. "I don't want to live here," she said. "I have a promise of a job in L. A. A girl friend of mine says she can get me on, hopping cars."

"And I might as well join up before I get drafted. It's sure to come," Beau said. "I might've made a good living here, but I have to sign up."

Starr looked from one to another of them. "You'll borrow on this place to bury Mom, then you'll all be gone, and not make your payments on the notes. The loan is all you'll get from all the work and pinching that went into this place," she said accusingly. "Isn't that right? Who offers you a loan?"

"I was down at Perry Taylor's office. We still have to pay on the house, you know."

Starr began to laugh hysterically. "You know, and Mom knew, that Perry Taylor's the crookedest real-estate man in town!" she said. "And he always says he doesn't foreclose because he's mean—it's 'for his family'! And do you know where the youngest of the Taylors is this moment?" Still laughing, she beat at her distended abdomen beneath the smock. "In the name of the newest Taylor child, go forth and be robbed! Cash in what Mom built! Who cares, who cares?" She took Caroline by the hand and strode toward the door, but there she paused and looked at her family.

"Except for Caro—and I'll keep her—I really never expect to see any of you again," she said. "No telling where Beau will settle. Ann Marie will be swallowed into an army of girls as like her as so many twins, all seeking Romance in Glamour Land and finding little enough of it!"

"You'll all be my own children always," Bert said, bewildered and pathetic.

If Starr had not been near hysteria, she probably would have held her tongue, then. "No, we never were your children," she said. "We were Mom's children, and you were *your* mother's child. But Mom knew that, too."

"You're talkin' wild, Starr," her father said reproachfully. "I'd be proud to have you and Caro come home with me."

"We *have* no home!" Starr said hotly, "but we will have, some time or other. I'll work and buy us one, if it's only one room!" She stood in the door a moment, shocked at her own unkindness. Then she noticed the white scar on the wall, where the picture of her friend the wave had hung. Anger rushed over her faster than ever. She pointed at the white place on the wall. "*Where is my picture?*" she asked, almost beside herself.

"It's outside," Bert said evasively. "I was cleaning out things...."

Starr rushed through the house. Outside the back door, beside the garbage can, she found it. She wiped the painting with part of her smock, breathing very fast. It was not injured.

"Well, how was we to know you—" Bert began resentfully.

"I *know* you didn't know! I *know* you didn't know!" Starr said through hysterical tears. "I know you never *did!* Won't somebody drive Caro and me home? I'm tired."

[197]

Bert drove them back to the big house, saying nothing. Starr held to the cheap painting with one hand, and to Caro with the other.

As her first spurt of anger fell, it was replaced with sorrow. She felt that there should be something significant to say to one's father after more than two decades, but since it had been the father who would not communicate, she could find no words. "Good-by, Pop," she finally said, holding a moment to the door of his old car for the last time. Maybe they should kiss. But that would be too strange and embarrassing.

"Good-by, Starr," he said gruffly. He sat a moment in awkward silence, as if he too felt that something was missing. He drove away, then—a stranger to her, and she to him, now that the bridge of Cory had dissolved between them.

Slowly Starr led Caro into the shadows of the Taylor house. It was only October then. There was still cotton to be picked in the fields. She must live through another month somehow, until the baby was born.

On a table in the hall was a letter from Binkie. "I think you ought to know," she wrote as brutally as she always talked, "that as a brood mare for young aristocratic Fishies, I am a flop. My baby died. There will never be any more. My in-laws paid me off handsomely at the mere suggestion that I wanted out. I can dole this out to Mother; and Ham and I are going to be married. Ham should have his darling head examined. I hope to examine it myself, personally, every day of my life, beginning in a couple of months. My Nevada address is below, and Ham joins me in saying that we will do anything in our power to help you—any time, any way. Wish me luck, Starr! I've been an awful fool, but still I'm shot with good luck."

Simply reading the letter made poignant memories come brilliantly to life for Starr. She hurried upstairs, put Caro to bed, then sat by the window and wept quietly.

7.

CARO'S DRESSES were growing conspicuously short; she presented the silhouette of a wading bird. "High-water" dresses, Cory used to call them, letting out a hem or adding a flounce. But the hems of these were all let out to the last possible fragment. "Guess I'll have to put a brick on your head, so you'll stop growing for a few months," Starr said to Caro, giving her a smack on the bottom.

Caro glowed with accomplishment. She brought a brush and began to brush at Starr's hair. "I help," she said.

"My, yes!" Starr said. "You're all kinds of help. I sure am lucky that I have you."

But Caro's welcome into the household was chilly. Mr. Taylor would absently pat her head occasionally; but Mrs. Taylor was a stream of noes and don't-touch-it's. Meal-times were nightmares.

Starr learned the names and idiosyncrasies of all of the royal families of Stats, Binders, and Taylors now living—and lots of those now dead. Most of those living were old women, very large, plump, and Victorian—all daughters of pioneers who had been land hogs or the earliest of business sharpsters in the community, which constituted their sole claim to distinction. The elderly daughters now had oil, inherited acres, investments, and business advisors.

The only one who actually interested Starr very much was Mrs. Maple, who had once been a Stat, and in whose cottage Jeff lived. Wild and unfashionably wiry she had been as a youngster, and now widowed, middle-aged, and with a grown son, she was *still* wild! Even though she was wealthy—which all of them were—it was scandalous the way she spent her money. She took long trips, bought new cars, had a TV installed, and even let some young man live in Dick's cottage! She shingled her hair and incessantly bought new slim loud clothes. She gave her old ones away! And—in whispers it was said—she went out with men!

Starr could not help listening as she served tea and removed cups and saucers and silver. Every now and then she was asked politely to join the family party, and she always answered truthfully that she did not like tea—a decidedly peculiar thing, of itself! She thought it a pity that she might never learn what Mrs. Maple thought of the others, since she was an infrequent visitor. Certainly she furnished endless food for speculation and disapproval of the relatives and in-laws.

The tea parties always made Caro an extra hazard. Starr yearned to put some of the untouchables higher than Caro's questing little fingers, but this Mrs. Taylor would not permit. "The child must learn not to touch," Mrs. Taylor always said, as if it were rather vulgar of her not to have been born knowing. A tea party often involved an orgy of meddling on the part of Caro.

At table she was usually in disgrace, though cheerfully indifferent to it. She spilled some food and sometimes put her fingers in her glass. Mrs. Taylor turned her eyes away as if a pig sat at the table.

Mr. Taylor said almost nothing. He was home very little.

One saw his picture in the paper from time to time, as he undertook a new real-estate development, or made statements concerning local politics. Usually he seemed far away and wordless. When Starr met him outdoors or on the stairs—away from Mrs. Taylor—he inquired concerning her health. "I guess it's pretty dull for you," he said once, in one of those waiting times when he stood near her but obviously could not find words of comfort.

"It's lonely for me, of course," Starr said, her composure only a thin skin over raw disaster. It was no wonder he could find no words of comfort, for there were none. Only the silent scream of protest within her: Why? Why Dash, of all people? The unkind, the boors, the human vegetables lived on—and the quick smile and perceptive glance of Dash had been wiped out.

"He meant a lot to me, too," Perry Taylor said heavily. "He made this whole place different. It was different when he lived here."

Any place would have been different—would have been graced by his presence, Starr thought. Even this introspective old house full of shadows and silences.

Caring for Caro was a genuine blessing. She needed to walk, and Caro needed the freedom of the park, only a few blocks away. They went there almost every day at least once.

After a stuffy tea, she was especially thankful to escape with Caro. She sat on the end of a bench, and Caro ran to the slide to play. Starr leaned her head back against the hard bench and closed her eyes. Odd, she thought, how eagerly we reach for happiness! And when we're boiled down to the dregs of endurance, how grateful we are simply not to be harried! We would compromise almost anything for mere peace. Who would have thought it?

A man on the other end of the bench said very kindly, "You're tired, Starr."

His voice caused an instant flash back. It bruised an old wound. Hearing it was half wild joy and half bitter regret. She turned her face toward him, opening her eyes. "Yes, Jeff. I'm so tired."

She had to drop her glance, being unable to face him now. He had not changed at all—not in any way! For a moment she was alive to times past, and then she caught up with time. Things were so much messier now, and more muted with experience. But the sound of his voice was so welcome it brought tears to her eyes.

He was quickly close beside her. "My, what a face I must have developed, to make a pretty girl cry! I've come here several days after work, hoping you might come at the same time I did, once I found that you came here. I just wanted— Starr Cooper, stop crying! You want me to leave? You want passers-by to think I'm about to beat you?"

She could have wept afresh to find him so unchanged, but she wiped her eyes. "I was so lonely," she said. He was her friend once more.

"I was too! I have been, for such a long time, I almost forget when I wasn't! Some Sunday maybe we could take the easel—"

"And Caro and the baby?" Starr said. "I don't imagine it ever would work any more, Jeff."

"But I *like* children!"

"Do you, Jeff? I never found that out!" She stifled an inclination to chatter. It had been so long since she really had talked with anyone. She held her hands tight together for discipline.

Jeff took them both, separating them and holding one in each hand, smiling. "Relax, this little while," he said. "We're always parting, but when we're together, you needn't be anyone but yourself."

Her hands went limp in his, and she sighed. "What a blessed, beautiful thing to say!" she said. "Few people grant so much." Then she let a pleasant silence lie between them, comforted to have her hands in his. Presently she asked, "What of Louise now, Jeff?"

"She was in a sanitorium for a long time. She's been out for three months. Aunt Nettie says she's been very good, and maybe she's cured."

"I hope so," Starr said sincerely. "It's such a waste, otherwise." She looked at his wrist watch—that same watch with the ghostly small hands in the dark—noting that it was past time when she should have started home to prepare supper.

"I have to go," she said, and called Caro.

"Won't you meet me here another time? I suppose I couldn't come to the Taylors."

"When I come, it's usually about this time of day," Starr said hastily. "If you telephoned or I telephoned, it would all be monitored by Mrs. Taylor. The phone's in the hall near her room."

Jeff raised his eyebrows. "You know where I am, if you want to find me." He looked at Caro, coming toward them on lagging feet. "This is your baby sister, isn't it?"

Caro planted her feet firmly and looked at Jeff with interest.

"I can make a rabbit with a handkerchief," he said.

"Do it."

He made it, with his fingers in the ears to make them waggle. Caro observed it with grave interest. He whisked it back into a handkerchief once more. "Do it again," Caro said.

But he could see that Starr was anxious to go. "Next time I see you, I will," he said. "Go along with Starr. I hope you take good care of her." He sat on the bench and watched them walk away, Starr clumsy and careful, Caro still handicapped by the short legs of babyhood, and the leaves blowing about their feet in a restless tide of color.

At least every other day, Jeff met Starr in the park. She lived for those half hours. They sustained her through the intricate details and tiresome routine at the Taylor household. He seemed to sense it. To Starr it was a saving golden gift of human communication.

He wanted to call on her at home. "If I can't call, there are other means," he said darkly. "I'll send you red roses 'from an admirer'; I'll telephone you in the night. I'll come disguised as the telephone man or the building inspector, with a beard, perhaps."

Starr laughed. She did not know how very long it had been since she had last laughed. "Idiot!" she said. "You've been so good for me—much better than vitamin pills!" His face was so dear and familiar.

He cast an imaginary cloak about his shoulders and proclaimed, "Lady Starr, yon gloomy castle shall not—"

"Shush!" Starr said. "Caro repeats everything to her dolls. The old Taylors say almost nothing, but they hear everything! You could paint their portraits as a big thin shut mouth and a large pair of ears."

[205]

"With dollar signs running out the ears!" Jeff said delightedly. "I'll do that; I'll do that very thing, and send you the canvas."

"Oh, no! Don't you *dare*, Jeff Mayfield!"

He tousled his hair down over his forehead. "Inspiration burns madly," he muttered. "I can't help myself." He had made her laugh again, and it was a triumph.

A week later, the Taylor household was puzzled by the arrival of a large canvas addressed to Mrs. Dashell Taylor. The artist had not signed it. It showed a huge pair of ears exuding dollar bills, and a thin, forbidding mouth. It was titled "The Pioneer."

"How *revolting!*" Mrs. Taylor said. "How can people paint such things when there is so much beauty in the world?"

Starr murmured a meaningless nothing, running the Taylor pictures through the gallery of her mind: seven blank-faced maids in gauze, apparently kinfolk with blank eyes and floating hair. One was in peril, in dry, if insecure gauze, clinging to a cross in a considerable sea. There was also one dark brown bridge, with one end lost in browner haze—Olde English Smogge, she had termed it silently and frivolously. Then there was a man with a plumed hat—or rather half of a man, one half being lost in shadow, or perhaps it had been easier to paint shadow than the other half. Then there were three poses of overfed and underage cupids, their undeniable wings permitting the license of bare behinds in some views, all with fortuitously located leaves and modest clouds.

"But who could have sent the ugly thing?" Mrs. Taylor said.

"Maybe it's an error, and someone will call for it," Starr

said. And she thought, I could smack Jeff for this, the fiend! But it was such a rich thing to have a friend. Aunt Artie was marvelous in her own way, bless her spunky heart, but Jeff lent a feeling of reality to an alien world.

The rain and mists came early in November, and the mushrooms again sprang white in the fields. They gave Starr another reason for walking; and Caro was never tired of walking. Crawling through the fences required skill and determination, but Starr managed it, swinging from one hand a basket holding a penknife and a couple of sandwiches. Walking, she thought about her ring, and about the taxes due on the land in Montana. The bill had arrived.

But it was difficult to make decisions in the misty fields. Larks again sat on the wire fences and trilled their sweet three notes, joyous to proclaim this false spring. The earth was spongy and damp underfoot, and the mists softened the harsh land. These usually ugly fields would not warrant a second glance most of the year, but wrap a sun-bitten parched bit of one in gentle rain and blot out the rest, and it was a mysterious part of another world.

Caro quested like a puppy off the leash, running ahead and falling behind. Dash had hunted these fields. Starr felt an uprush of pity for the little boy he once had been, and a question probed toward him even in death: How did you ever live without color or music or theater—or anything but discipline all those years?

Jeff walked out of the mist. "I followed you," he said, "and for the fix you're in, you're astonishingly nimble."

"I'm a scow, and I know it," she answered, so glad to see him she could have danced. She kept an eye on Caro, running far ahead.

Jeff put an arm about her shoulders. "You'll always be beautiful to me, regardless of your figure or your age," he said. "It's not reasonable, but it's so."

"It's not reasonable, but it's lovely," Starr said. "I'll remember it when my years catch up with me." She added, "They'll probably catch up fast, because I frown and scowl and laugh out loud—and all those strenuous things—instead of preserving my face without wrinkles. Mrs. Taylor says so."

Jeff made an unflattering comment concerning Mrs. Taylor's face. Possibly, he suggested, she had also conserved the use of her body, mind, and heart quite as skillfully and consistently. Otherwise, why had Perry Taylor had a series of mistresses ever since the Year One?

"I didn't know he had," Starr said, turning over the improbable thing in her mind. "But that would account for the long, long silences when he's home. He has someone to love and to talk to, somewhere else." She laughed. "I bet Mrs. Taylor knows it and is glad of it," she said. "It saves her up for another time."

"Maybe her spirit can be pickled in alcohol when she dies," Jeff said.

"No, no!" Starr protested, half laughing, half bitter. "Jasmine tea is strong enough!"

That day she gave Jeff her ring and asked if he would try to sell it for her. He offered to lend her some money, of course, but she would not accept it. "Dash would understand about the ring," she said.

A few days later, Jeff handed her four hundred dollars as she sat on the park bench. She was surprised that it was so much. She would be able to pay the taxes on the Montana property and have some left over.

Repeatedly she dreamed of the shabby little house in Wild Horse Valley. One would need a car; one would need some money for living expenses.

The tiny sum she would receive from Social Security Benefits for Dash's child could not possibly suffice. Still, it was comforting to know that she had a house and some acres somewhere. The children could have a dog and cat if they lived there. Mrs. Taylor would tolerate neither. "What do they give you in return for care and food?" she inquired tartly.

Caroline's dresses were shabbier and shorter, and she could not squeeze into last year's coat. Starr had waited in an anguish of shyness for the Taylors to notice, hoping they might offer at least a new coat. Since they did not, Starr cut up one of her own coats and made one for Caro. Using money from the ring, she bought her a pair of shoes and several cotton dresses.

With the appearance of new clothes, which were evidence of money from somewhere, Mrs. Taylor noticed that Starr was not wearing her ring, and asked why. They were at the dinner table. Starr had steeled herself for the question, and answered simply that she had needed money and had not liked to ask for it. "You sold your ring?" Mrs. Taylor asked in shocked tones.

Starr answered that she was sorry Mrs. Taylor was shocked. Actually she was indifferent. She was learning to withdraw from the Taylors in a fashion, even before probing eyes. She sighed, but not for the ring. It seemed a thousand years since she had been eligible to seek a job.

Another "Ethel" had appeared in the kitchen early in November. "You must rest now, dear child," Mrs. Taylor told Starr, with neither inflection nor change of expression.

"Your whole consideration must be for the last of the Taylors. He will be an important link."

Interior decorators arrived and painted and refurbished a room for a nursery; it began to look like something from a fashionable picture in the Sunday supplement. Strange that the Taylors would spend money so extravagantly for the baby, and had not even appeared to see Caro's toes pushing at the ends of her tattered little slippers. Starr often pulled Caro close and kissed her with a rush of pride and protectiveness, feeling as if this child were her own. Cory had known it would be like this.

Holiday Dinner with Company was approaching, and it dominated conversation. How a woman could devote so much time to the planning of a meal, Starr could not divine. A turkey must be brought from a particular farm. Every pickle and olive was mentally assembled and reassembled beforehand. Every piece of silver was polished and inspected. Spode, coming dusty from its shelves, had to be washed on the day it was used—with ceremony and foreboding, lest one piece of it be chipped or broken. Linen had to be inspected, washed, sized, and put away to be ironed on Thanksgiving Day. Starr was sick to death of the whole project long before it had begun. She fervently hoped she would be in the hospital, safe from inanities of conversation by Taylor, Stat, and Binder on the great day of feasting. But she could iron the tablecloth beforehand. She did that much for poor new Ethel.

It was heavenly finding Jeff in the park on such days of senseless struggle. Sitting near him, she would momentarily know that insidious, familiar feeling that she had never been away from him, that all was right in the world. He had little to say, and that mostly nonsense. He had made a project of making her smile, and it was easy to smile for him.

"Did you ever get the divorce?" she asked, remembering how important that had once seemed.

Seriously he said that he had. "But we were both right, even if I wouldn't admit it," he said. "It doesn't relieve me of any obligation. Louise won't admit it, and often forgets about it—and of course the expenses are the same—sometimes larger."

"It couldn't be any other way," Starr said at length. "There are things we simply have to do. It takes a little while to learn that, doesn't it?"

"It takes a while to learn it, and maybe it takes a lifetime to get used to it," he said, tension in his voice. "Starr, I hate having the best of my life spent in small pieces on a park bench. It isn't enough for us."

It troubled her that he had momentarily lost the light touch. She had grown to rely on it. "Many and many a girl would love to go out with you," she said.

"But it's too awkward," Jeff answered. "Always I have to drag in an explanation by the tail, or make silence a half lie. It's easier alone. It's more than easy with you. I haven't gone out much with girls for nine years, now. That's a long time out of a life."

Starr touched his hand lightly, in sympathy. "Loneliness surely is the commonest ailment of all," she said. "But remember you once thought it might be the natural condition of human beings?"

"That was before I knew better."

It sent her thoughts off on a tangent. "You would have liked Dash," she said. "He would have liked you. But you're not alike."

"I know."

It startled her. "How?"

"He allowed you to remain yourself. So he must have loved you for being yourself. And we absorb some personality, you know. You have a quicker ear for nonsense now—that's probably Dash. When I love you, I must also love bits and parts of your family, of him, of Caro.... There's so much of the people we've loved in all of us."

Starr was troubled and touched. "I went down another path, Jeff," she said warningly. "I dearly love to see you now, but I mustn't burden you. You have enough to carry, as it is. I know that."

He put a hand over hers on the bench, and she trembled a little at the touch. "You loved me once," he said; and his voice compelled her attention to what she had tried to ignore.

She could not deny it. The months between dissolved into shadows when she saw Jeff. It was as if they had never been. He was as familiar and dear as if they never had parted at all. Yet their togetherness had two more wedges upon which to split now. There was Caro and the baby— and still Louise, dream-faced, gentle, and trusting. Starr could only turn her head away.

When Starr brought the special turkey for Thanksgiving, raised on the special farm, and laid it on the drainboard, "Ethel" resigned on the spot. It had to be picked, she noted simply, and she did not intend to pick any turkeys. Besides which, she did not care to work on Thanksgiving— especially without double pay.

Mrs. Taylor paid her off stoically. Starr was momentarily panicked, but she rallied and endlessly picked and plucked and tweezered pinfeathers. Under Mrs. Taylor's eye she buttered and cubed bread and made the insipid, almost seasonless stuffing. She thought of Cory's cornbread dressing, spicy with whole leaves of sage. As she lifted the prepared turkey, she was thrilled with the first forerunner of birth pains. She caught her breath, but said nothing. She smiled at the thought that she might escape a Holiday Dinner by having a baby, instead. She went early and hopefully to bed, but the one pain she had felt when lifting the turkey, vanished without repetition.

She was awakened very early by young Caro. She dressed herself and Caro quickly, wetting their hair and smoothing it down last of all, while Caro kept up a continual whimper of hunger. "Eat?" she asked for the thousandth time. "Let's eat!"

"As soon as we're dressed," Starr repeated patiently, though she herself was hungry. "We'll have company today. Try to keep clean, and try to keep out of the way of people who come visiting. Stay out of Mrs. Taylor's room. . . ." She hated all this forbidding. It was not healthy for Caro or herself. Just let me get through it somehow, dear Lord; help Caro to be as unlike a child as possible for these few hours, and then I'll let her be a child once more. . . . Starr did not know where prayer ended or began.

She went as swiftly downstairs as she dared, hoping against hope that Mrs. Taylor would still be asleep.

"Ethel?" inquired the querulous voice. "Is breakfast ready yet? What time is it? The turkey must be in the oven by nine."

"Good morning," Starr said. "I'll have your breakfast in a few minutes. Everything will be fine today."

[213]

The sun was shining outside. Starr looked through the heavily curtained windows and wished for a moment that she were free to take Aunt Artie and Caroline to the park, then somewhere for a hamburger and a soda. No cooking, no dishwashing, no fuss.... Resolutely she turned back to the kitchen. She tried to serve Caroline in the kitchen and old Mrs. Taylor in the downstairs bedroom more or less simultaneously. Caroline wailed and Mrs. Taylor beat the floor with her cane for hot coffee. Starr seized a bit of Caro's toast to munch, to avoid being sick from hunger. When she had started her own breakfast, the cane interrupted her once more.

"Would you draw the curtain over there about six inches, and open this one about a foot? And would you take these things away? I hate dirty dishes. It's just a humor, I suppose," she said amiably, "but one gets accustomed...."

Starr smiled and murmured that it was nothing. Her egg would be a cold lump.... A large thump from the kitchen was followed by a wail. She hurried back with the dishes, helped Caro from the floor, kissed the place to make it well, wiped breakfast from the small tearful face—and looked up to find Mr. Taylor in the kitchen door. He was freshly shaved and his clothes fell in immaculate creases from his sagging, shapeles old body. Starr smiled at him as she released Caro. "Breakfast for the gentleman coming up!" she said, determined to make this a cheerful day. Her own breakfast could wait.

The work schedule was tight that day. Starr hurried and was so clumsy that she grew tense. Caro was underfoot, wanting to know if they were going to the park, wanting a playmate, wanting attention while Starr fled about her tasks.

Mrs. Taylor was more underfoot than Caro. Why did she get so wrought up about a few relatives coming to dinner? Starr wondered. Guests were something to be enjoyed, normally. Finally she said to Mrs. Taylor, "Why don't you go read a magazine and relax? They're your own sisters and close kin, aren't they?"

Mrs. Taylor drew herself up. "You can't have everything for a dinner *just right* without forethought! I once served a twelve-course dinner. Started a month before, to get some of the special pickles ready, and served it right on the dot! Now Henrietta always *was* sloppy. Dinner late, sometimes, or poorly served, or a cake falls—or something every time! She simply doesn't try! On the other hand, Rosalie never makes a mistake. Of course she has a house full of servants, and always did, and I must say she has them trained." She looked at the clock. "The turkey must be basted every fifteen minutes, if it's to be properly done. I suppose potatoes can be peeled now, and put into salted water. We can leave the dining room until the turkey's almost done."

Each time Starr basted that bird, she hated it more. The cooking odors made her faint, but still she basted and followed the multitudinous instructions as well as she could. Chill the pickles. Make the radishes into rosettes. Caroline, meantime, had abandoned pleasing entirely; she whined about the kitchen.

"Can't that child *do* something?" Mrs. Taylor asked tartly.

The telephone mercifully called Starr from the kitchen. Mrs. Taylor could not hear every word—for once. "Happy Thanksgiving!" Aunt Artie said cheerfully. "How you feelin', honey?"

"Bulging," Starr said. "Harried. Thanksgiving was never

like this! What are you doing to celebrate?" She was genuinely homesick for Aunt Artie.

"A marvelous man is taking me to dinner," Aunt Artie said—maybe a cheerful lie. "But late. I thought maybe you and Caro could meet me."

"Aunt Artie, it's the loveliest thought you ever had! Maybe we can get away about four o'clock. We'll meet you in the park. If we're not there, don't wait and waste your day."

"Right, kid!"

Mrs. Taylor came out of the kitchen. "Who called?" she asked.

Starr's face was full of renewed hope. "My aunt," she said. But she did not fluster Mrs. Taylor with the fact that she meant to go out in the late afternoon.

"The turkey needed basting ten minutes ago," Mrs. Taylor said. So Starr fled to the kitchen.

Old Mr. Taylor stood behind her as she basted the turkey. "Smells good," he said. Starr wondered despairingly if they never said any unexpected thing whatsoever in that household, or if all of it were memorized and repeated in different patterns forever. Yes, she admitted it did smell good. "Don't you get tired, standing on your feet?" he asked—which did surprise her. She turned to him, wiping her forehead free of sweat. But his face told her that he hadn't meant it.

"I have no right to get tired," she said.

"These dinners do make a lot of work," he said, obviously sorry at having provoked some strong feeling. "But the girls always gave 'em."

"I understand," Starr said. "They're not for fun—they're for competition."

Mr. Taylor's old eyes widened; he sensed trouble. He retreated toward the kitchen door. "Now I wouldn't say that," he said soothingly. Then Caroline ran into him from the dining room. "Damnation!" he said, grabbing the door facing. "Don't you ever look where you're going?"

Caro burst into loud wails. She ran and clung to Starr's knees. "Go away!" she sobbed. She turned her tear-strained face up to Starr, and it held a petition. "Starry," she asked, "go home?"

Starr knelt and held the wind-blown small head to her shoulder. "It'll be a while," she said. "Meantime, maybe we can go to the park before dark. Not now, mind you, and not for a long time—but maybe just before dark!" The small arms tightened about her neck. "Be as quiet as you can. Play in the yard, why don't you?"

"No doggy," Caro said. "No kitty." She clung tightly, the tears pooling in her eyes once more.

Mr. Taylor still stood in the door, and Starr caught his eye. "I'm sorry," he said. "I'm sorry." He turned and walked away.

The turkey was swelling and gloating and hogging the whole day. Did Starr ever think she liked turkey? And gravy to be made at the last moment and *strained* lest there be some vulgar lump! The great meal shaped up. Mountains of turkey with insipid dressing and strained gravy; mountains of Spode and tons of silver and acres of damask—and for what, for *what?*

When guests came early, they did not come to the kitchen and help. They sat in the living room, after inquiring of her, "How are you, dear?" Thank heavens, the linens were already ironed!

Between bastings, she went into the garden and picked

myrtle berries for the table. Now she put into effect a mental device used previously to meet dental appointments and grave crises. In two hours it will be over, she said firmly to herself. In three hours I will have washed all the dishes, and have put them away. In four hours I will be free in the park, and this nightmare meal will be something hideous in the past.

Surely, she thought, arranging the frosty dark berries on the tablecloth—surely if Dash stood it for twenty years, I can stand it for a few months. Dear God, I must! Where are the glasses now? And let there be no fingerprint on any of them, because Aunt Henrietta never lived down one on one of her glasses fifteen years ago. . . .

Mrs. Taylor came up behind her. "The tablecloth!" she gasped. "What happened to the tablecloth!"

"Nothing," Starr said. "What's wrong with it?"

Mrs. Taylor was almost moaning. "It's wrinkled! Look at it! A banquet cloth has to be ironed just before it's put on the table—didn't you know that?"

Starr looked at the places where she had carefully, softly folded the beautiful, long piece of damask. "They're only folds," she began. But Mrs. Taylor tottered from the room holding her forehead. Starr doubted that she would faint this time—time was too precious. So the tablecloth has folds! she thought, and we'll never live it down! Why how absurd! How silly can you be?

Things rapidly became hectic. Starr basted turkey and mashed potatoes almost simultaneously. She set out the pickles and olives and crisp celery on silver and crystal. Guests arrived. The turkey came from the oven, the rolls went in; gravy was made and strained. Water was poured from the crystal pitcher. Mrs. Taylor reappeared in the kitchen, enfeebled, but able to issue orders. Caro had been banished howling upstairs. Starr snatched a moment to change her smock. When she came down, Mrs. Taylor whispered, "Are you going to wear those—trousers—for Thanksgiving dinner?"

Out of the sea of weariness, an imp of mischief raised its head in Starr's mind. "Unless you'd like me to take them off," she whispered back. "And the smock's very short. I haven't any dresses to wear."

Mrs. Taylor was plainly irritated. "In your condition, I don't see why you choose to try to look like a man," she said.

"I *never* felt more miserably female," Starr said. "And what I think I resemble is a ferryboat. I'm going to serve dinner now, then I'm going to feed Caro in the kitchen, so she won't spill on the beautiful cloth."

That mollified Mrs. Taylor somewhat. "If the child won't wait," she began.

"She can't," Starr said. Then she began putting food on the dining table.

She brought Caro to the kitchen and gave her potatoes and gravy and some peas. Carving set in hand, Mr. Taylor was wrestling with what was termed "The Bird" at the dining table, under the scrutiny of his peers. Each move he made was a ritual. Looking at him from the kitchen door, Starr met his glance, and suddenly she pitied him— he looked so caged and unhappy. All that he never said— and never could say—lay in his eyes, and for a moment Starr felt that affection for him that one condemned person feels for another.

Who wanted turkey? Starr also ate mashed potatoes, drank a cup of coffee while it was truly fresh and good, then began cleaning pans and putting them away. Something almost like serenity rose timidly within her. She could see an end to this senseless orgy.

The kitchen was clean when she gathered the dinner plates and served desert and coffee. With infinite caution she washed the dinner plates and put the beautiful loath-some things away. She was almost getting ahead of the job.

As she put the remaining turkey away and washed the last of the dishes, the guests trooped through the kitchen and told her how they had enjoyed the dinner. Mrs. Taylor was now resting. Oh, lovely that she was not asking for anything at the moment!

Starr hung up her apron and started upstairs. She could not help hearing Mrs. Taylor's raised voice. Evidently she was addressing Mr. Taylor. "You are *not* going out again today and leaving me all alone!" she said. "I overlook a lot, Perry Taylor, but a man belongs with his *family* on a holiday."

"A man belongs with the people he loves on holidays," Perry Taylor said quietly. "He's entitled to spend it like a bonus, as he pleases! He's entitled to spend it with champagne and good company. He's entitled to a joke and a cigar—"

"You needn't specify all your vulgarities," Mrs. Taylor said. "It's bad enough in private—but to make a parade of it on holidays— Well! If you don't have any consideration for me, you might at least consider your *position!*"

"I considered my position too long," Mr. Taylor said wearily. "If the depression hadn't gutted me, I probably wouldn't have. My God! I've waded through misery knee-deep for fifteen years, minding your money and 'considering my position'! And you know something, Annabelle? It wasn't worth it! I haven't bought much with my time and my self-respect. Now I'm going out, like I told you. I won't be in until late. I've made the gesture again, and it's done; and I'm going out for my own pleasure now. That's the way it is, and that's the way it's going to be! You can call it a matter of business."

"Business! Oh . . ."

Starr was hurrying, almost at the top of the stairs, but Mr. Taylor called her back. "Mrs. Taylor's fainted again," he said calmly.

Sighing with exasperation, filled with pity for him, Starr went once more to administer first aid. At his suggestion, she telephoned the family physician. He was out, so Starr telephoned for Dr. Starr—who had always appeared promptly during her whole life. There was only half an hour now in which to change to walking shoes, get a coat, and meet Aunt Artie in the park. Starr was thinking rebelliously, You can't do this to me, either, after this dreary day! I'll go out if the house falls in!

But Dr. Starr came promptly. She was thin and erect, and time had pinched her nose to a certain sharpness. Her hair was white, and her eyes were sharp as a chicken hawk's. She went directly to the bedroom.

Mrs. Taylor had now aroused. She told Dr. Starr that she had recovered. With one imperious hand the doctor pushed her back against her pillows. She thumped and she listened, and when Mrs. Taylor complained that she was quite well, Dr. Starr, with tubes in her ears, did not hear or chose not to hear.

"I didn't authorize this woman—" Mrs. Taylor began.

"Quiet!" Dr. Starr said firmly. "How can I examine you

if you *thrash?* Breathe deep. Out, in, out, in, cough!" She went on and on for some minutes.

In the hall she told Perry Taylor not to worry. To Starr, going to the door with her, she told more. "Heart?" she said. "Burden of a few years—fine muscle, well preserved. Trying to get her way about something, wasn't she?" She did not wait for an answer, but wrote rapidly on a pad. She tore a sheet out and handed it to Starr. "A castor oil by any other name would taste as sweet," she said. "Your baby's due any moment, isn't it?"

"Yes." Starr was hesitant. "I'll have to pay you later."

"Never hounded your mother about you, did I?" Dr. Starr asked crossly. "Want to see you Tuesday afternoon anyway." She glared at Starr. "You hear me?"

"I'll be there," Starr said. "But I'm vulgarly healthy."

"Health has more aspects than the physical," Dr. Starr said. "But quit wasting my time. I have appointments."

Starr gave the prescription to Perry Taylor and went back into the bedroom. Mrs. Taylor was suffering silently. She aroused herself sufficiently to say, "Women have no business being doctors."

"She says you're quite all right now," Starr said hastily. "Now Caro and I are going to the park for a while. I've been promising her all day long."

Mrs. Taylor turned her face to the wall wearily. "A little tea," she whispered. "I need a stimulant."

Starr pretended not to hear the whisper. She hurried upstairs, slipped her pumps from her feet and slid into her oxfords. She barely had time to meet Aunt Artie now. Then she discovered that she could not lace or tie her shoes. She tried desperately, turning this way and that, but it was impossible. The tears finally crowded close in her throat. She would let the laces flap, then! Caro did not yet know how to tie shoelaces.

The cane was thumping vigorously as she came downstairs. On tiptoe, holding Caro by the hand, she slipped to the back door and escaped.

The trees were half bare with winter nakedness, and the velvet nap of the lawn had worn to the threadbare roots. Still, there was a certain beauty about the lacework branches of the bare trees. The wind was chilly now, and the shadows long, and Starr walked with difficulty in her untied oxfords. She looked in vain for Aunt Artie, and thought, If she doesn't come now, I'm going to sit down and bawl.

The man sitting on the bench with his back turned was Jeff. He had delivered her from torment by being there. "What brings you here on Thanksgiving?" she asked, and he turned around.

"Oh, I was just walking in the park and thinking how swell it was that I never had to attend any of those grisly old family holiday dinners again as long as I lived. And I met your Aunt Artie and took her out for a drink. She fits better on a bar stool than a park bench, any time. And she told me to—" He suddenly became aware of the terrible tension in her face, and the nonsense fled from his voice. "Sit down," he said firmly. "What's happened?"

The fortitude Starr had cultivated all dissolved. She bowed her head and sat near Jeff on the cold bench, and he put an arm about her shoulders in the gathering dusk.

His touch released the tears. She hid her face in his shoulder. "I can't tie my shoes!" she sobbed. "It was such a long day full of cooking, and I looked forward to getting out, and I almost didn't, and then I couldn't tie my shoes! Dash ought to be tying them for me and teasing me. . . ."

Gravely Jeff said, "I'll tie them for Dash, if you like. But I'd just as soon tie them for myself, loving you and teasing you." He knelt and carefully tied both oxfords. He smiled up at her. "My darling Starr is a scow," he said.

She was trembling, but her tears stopped. "Thank you, Jeff," she said steadily enough. "I guess I'm just a baby, and sorry to be a whimperer."

"You're entitled to a whimper or two," he said easily. "Your Aunt Artie wanted me to bring you to her for a little while."

Aunt Artie was winding her two-inch hair on a hot curling iron. Her face was brown and leathery, and she laughed when Jeff and Starr came in with Caro. Caro ran to her and threw her arms about Aunt Artie's knees.

"Gwan," Aunt Artie said to Caro, "you can't sweet-talk me like you always done before." She knelt and hugged Caro. "What do you suppose? I'm going to have two little girls of my own!" She looked over Caro's head at Jeff and Starr, and she was beautiful.

"Honey," she said to Starr, "I think it's happened; it's finally happened! Jeff, here, introduced me to the finest man! He's not pretty, but he's solvent, and he has two of the sweetest little girls you *ever* saw! For them I can quit the cussin' and drinkin' and howlin' around I been doing for thirty years. Nothin' to it!" She snapped her fingers. "This time, no foolin', I got me a job I love all to pieces!"

Starr noted that the very planes and lines in her face were full of joyous giving. That had been all Aunt Artie ever wanted—just loving and giving. "I hope he *is* the nicest man in the world, and that he loves *you* all to pieces!" she said.

Aunt Artie danced a few steps, her body still lithe and firm. "No more salesmen," she chanted. "No more wolves! No more wrestling for my dinner!" She dived into a closet. "I'll be late!" she yelled, pulling the door half closed in lieu of a screen. "If he gets here before I'm ready, surround him, will you? I don't want that man out of my sight, for fear he might change his mind." There was a knock at the door. "Eek!" said Aunt Artie, like a high-school girl. "Grab him for me!"

"I wasn't goin' nowhere," the man said, opening the door. A middle-aged, partially bald man, he was laughing. Certainly he never would have been tall or handsome even in his youth. But his laugh was infectious. Jeff introduced him as Cornelius Worthington, and he said just call him Corny, because everybody else did.

"This is my niece," Aunt Artie said in muffled tones from behind the door. "The one I told you about." She emerged wearing a gray flowered dinner dress and silver earrings. Corny advanced upon her and put his arms about her and kissed her.

"Do you still love me?" he asked shamelessly.

"Yes, I do," Aunt Artie answered, a most unusual break in her voice. "I guess it's really true," she said to Starr. "I forget where you work, Corny—some ranch, wasn't it? Well, never mind! Starr's just waiting for her baby before she works in an office again." She took Caro's hand. "Corny has two little girls like you, but he didn't bring them this time," she told Caro.

When Starr and Caro and Jeff were once more in his small car, he said, "Do you suppose your Aunt Artie really doesn't know who Corny is?"

"Well, who is he?"

"Only one of the wealthiest ranchers in the whole county," Jeff said. "Pure, honest Okie, refined for the best society by the fragrance of so much money he hardly knows what he has from month to month. Mammas all over the county have been baiting traps for him ever since his wife died, a year ago. Aunt Artie can go to Europe, she can have cocktail parties and barbecue parties in the patio at the ranch; she can belong to the Cool Heights Country Club, and have her name in the paper...."

"She won't, though," Starr predicted.

"I doubt it, myself," Jeff said. "That's what makes her so attractive to Corny. He's really an uncomplicated, decent person. He's only rich by happy accident."

Caro was asleep, leaning against Starr. Jeff stopped the car. "I'll carry Caro to her bed for you," he said.

Starr had not thought about the problem of transporting a sleeping Caro. She caught her breath. "No," she said. "Oh, no! I'll say Aunt Artie brought me home." Guiltily she added, "I didn't prepare supper, or even tea or anything! They may have locked me out!" She put an arm about Caroline to lift her, then let her sag again. "*Wait* a minute!" she said breathlessly. "Wait just a minute!" She clasped her hands very tightly, then relaxed them.

Jeff looked toward her in the half dark. "What is it?" he asked sharply.

Excitement blazed within her. "I think you may take me to the hospital tonight, if you can wait a while so we can tell! It's about time, and I ..." She stopped, and her hands tightened together again. When they relaxed, she continued, "I hate to be alone. If you wouldn't mind, Jeff, could we go to your place and wait and see?"

Jeff was excited, too. "Of course, Starr. If you have to go tonight, I could take Caro to Aunt Artie. We could let her sleep in the car until we know."

Starr once again walked about Jeff's cottage. She sat in Jeff's reading chair. "I haven't felt at home anywhere, for so long," she sighed. "I had almost forgotten how this place felt and looked. I'll like going from here to the hospital. I'll like being driven by you—as if I had folks of my own." She telephoned Dr. Starr, and Dr. Starr said go straight to the hospital.

Starr stood. "This is more than I should ask of you," she said, "but I don't mind asking you for things as much as other people."

"Why should you?" Jeff asked tersely. "I want this to be my own baby. I can walk the floor for you just as well as anyone."

Caro awoke when they stopped at the hospital, and began to cry. Jeff carried her into the hospital, following Starr and reassuring Caro. "Starr has to go to the hospital now, to get the baby," he said. Caro's eyes, still wet, immediately stretched with wonder. "You can stay the rest of the night with your Aunt Artie, and then visit her for a few days, until Starr brings the baby home. Won't that be fun?"

They were a reassuring sight for Starr to see as she went down the corridor—sleepy-headed Caro and tall, somber-eyed Jeff.

It was daylight when she emerged from the delivery room—tired, chilly, and triumphant. She had a son, and he was perfect. There was no need to feel a pang of loneliness at having no one with whom to rejoice. The cart on which she lay stopped for a moment, and there was a quick hand on hers, and Jeff's cheek laid against her own. "You're a champion, darling!" Jeff said, and looked at her with a face so glowing with happiness shared that she could not help a rush of tears. "They showed him to me! He isn't as pretty as I am, but I suppose we can hope for the—"

"How ever did you know a woman likes to have someone to brag on her and gloat with her right away?" Starr asked. "I didn't know it myself!"

"I just know you, Starr," Jeff said seriously. "I just love you.... And, oh, darling, I was so scared!"

Dr. Starr had met and approved of Jeff. She said that he had gone in the night to procure Starr's bag and bring it to the hospital. He had aroused Aunt Artie and placed Caro in her charge.

In the afternoon, Aunt Artie and Corny came to see Starr and the baby. Caro and the two Worthington children were outside in the car, dying a thousand deaths of frustration, they said.

Aunt Artie lingered for a moment with Starr when Corny had gone. "It's a wonderful thing!" she whispered, her eyes shining. "I'm moving up our marriage date two weeks, so I can ask Corny to take you and Caro and the baby into our home. He can afford it, but I hate to ask him before we're...."

Starr loved her. "You can't stuff all your poor relatives down your bridegroom's throat," she said. "I wouldn't hear of it! I'll be able to work for myself in a few weeks now."

They argued fiercely in whispers for a few moments. "Pigheaded proud, just like Cory was!" Aunt Artie finally said. "But I'll find a way—see if I don't!"

[228]

"Mind your own happiness," Starr said. "It's high time you did." She waved Aunt Artie out, and sat smiling.

Jeff came happily to see her every evening. "If you stayed in the hospital all the time, I'd feel more welcome," he said. "Maybe we could break your leg next week, and you could stay on." His flowers brightened the room, and every night he observed and reported on young Dashell. Starr noted that his clothes were almost shabby.

On the second day, Perry Taylor came to see the baby. "Fine boy," he said to Starr. "Fine strong fellow to carry on the name. Fine boy." He sat gingerly on the edge of a chair. "Annabelle can't stand the smell of hospitals—makes her sick," he said apologetically, "but she'll be proud of that boy."

This rare use of Mrs. Taylor's given name sounded almost indelicate to Starr. "Thanks for the lovely room and special nurses and everything," she said awkwardly.

Perry Taylor examined his hands. "Couldn't do less," he said, clearing his throat. "Nothing. But you won't be sorry."

Payment, Starr thought. How strange! Of course she wouldn't be sorry! She loved Dashell—every squirming adorable inch of him.

Perry Taylor stood and looked at Starr uneasily. His eyes were so much more eloquent than his words! "It'll sure be fine, having a boy in the house," he said, as if to himself. And he repeated that several times.

It was not until Jeff and Caro arrived to take Starr and the baby home from the hospital that she discovered that a special nurse for infants would accompany them home. "You mean to take this infant home with another child in the car?" the nurse asked disapprovingly.

"He'll have to get used to her," Starr said. "Caro's going to help me raise him!"

The nurse clutched young Dashell to her bosom protectively. Starr opened the blanket about the baby's face so that Caro might see him. "Oh, Starry!" Caro said adoringly. "A sweetie pie!" Starr smiled. Soon she would let Caro sit in a chair and hold Dashell.

She did not know then that the nurse was going to stay, and live in the room next to the nursery.

Perhaps things would have been easier if Starr could have found a job immediately, but Dr. Starr asked her not to work for at least six weeks. Feeding time was about the only time she saw her son. At such times she cuddled and played with him. She also let Caro hold him in her arms. Caro nearly melted with love and importance. But Miss Cinch was fiercely opposed to such goings on. Miss Cinch knew that she was employed by Mrs. Perry Taylor, and to her Starr was important only as a walking milk station. She was not of a mind to have her disturb Dashell's routine in any way—especially not to the extent that Caro could intrude. She drove Caro away all day long. If Caro picked up a rattle with which to attract the baby's attention, Miss Cinch snatched it and sterilized it.

Mrs. Taylor spoke to Starr about the matter. "We pay handsomely to have Dashell properly attended," she said gently. "We can't afford to ignore what the nurse says is best. She thinks that an older child might bring germs."

Starr's temper smoldered. "Caro will grow up as Dashell's sister," she said, holding one hand in the other. "It's important that she love him and know him right now, and that she not get any idea that he's a bit more important than she is! I'll have to live with both, Mrs. Taylor."

"Of course, dear child! But while we have the nurse—"

"How long will we *have* the nurse?" Starr asked. "*I* can't afford her, and I'm strong enough to take care of Dashell now."

"I talked to a pediatrician," Mrs. Taylor said. "He said—"

Starr thought her extremely impertinent. "Excuse me," she said. "I'm going to take Caro and Dashell and go visit Aunt Artie today."

"But you can't disturb—"

"I'm *taking Dashell, too!*" Starr said, and marched from the room.

Miss Cinch objected strenuously. "If you don't pay any attention to my advice, you might as well not have me," she argued sharply.

"I'm taking the baby!" Starr said once more. "He's *my* son! *I* have to feed him. And we won't be home until time for his nap."

She found Aunt Artie knee deep in wedding plans. "Holy gee!" Aunt Artie said. "Corny's rich, I found out! We'll have a whingding of a wedding! I never had one like that before." She took Dashell into her arms and hugged him gently. She looked across him to Starr.

"I want you to stand up with me," she said, "and I'm going to have three flower girls—not just one, like common, but three!—and Caro'll be one of them. Can you get off for it?"

"I could," Starr said, "but dresses for Caro and me simply aren't possible. I can't go to work until the middle of January."

"The big wedding is so the little girls can take part in it," Aunt Artie said. "Corny and I wouldn't bother with it, just for ourselves. And as for a dress for you—kid, I'm going

[231]

to buy you the humdingingest dress you ever zipped up! I know a young man that'll be real interested. He'll be best man, seeing he introduced Corny and me."

Starr's heart beat a bit faster. As if I were still a school-girl, she thought chidingly. But she answered Aunt Artie sedately. "Then I couldn't miss it, could I?"

There was no vulgar row about Starr's having kidnaped her son for a few hours; simply a chilly avoidance of the subject. The matter was being crowded out of mind, in any event, for there was another exciting Dinner with Guests in prospect—to wit, Christmas.

Dear God, I never can live through that again, Starr prayed with real fervor. I'd rather be dead; there must be some way to avoid these ghastly festivities!

To distract attention from the dinner, she asked when they usually put up a tree, and learned that there had never been a Christmas tree in that house. "They're dirty. They shed on the floor and rugs; they're dangerous—might burn the house down—and they're common! No, we never have a tree."

And we never failed to have one, even if we had to cut it in the woods; even if it were not really a Christmas tree, Starr thought, loving the memory of Cory once more. Maybe there were no presents, some years, but there was always the tree, with a bit of elderly tinsel and a few peeling ornaments. And in that tree lay the spirit of Christmas.

"Dash and I had a tree last Christmas," Starr said. "He had such a lot of fun trimming it, and I saved all the ornaments for this year."

"What a thing to save!" Mrs. Taylor said in a rising tone.

Day by day, Dash was growing younger to Starr, as she

began to comprehend the hazards under which he grew. No music. No color. No poetry. No young friends. And now she must add to the list of his impoverishment no Christmas trees! Poor little lonely boy, cold and undernourished in all that mattered most to him! She had to turn away from Mrs. Taylor, lest her face reveal what Mrs. Taylor would never understand.

Caro came into the room and caught Starr's hand. "Come see," she said imperatively, her eyes large. "Come see!"

"Can't the child be still?" Mrs. Taylor asked. "Oh, Lord! *Presents!* I *hate* presents; I think they're stupid. You never know how much people are going to pay for them, so you can tell how much to spend. And always you have to *thank* people—I hate Christmas!"

Holding Caro's hand, Starr retreated from the room. She felt unaccountably sorry for Mrs. Taylor.

Aunt Artie solved the Christmas tree problem by inviting Starr and Caro to share a tree with "her" girls. They would have the wedding on Christmas Eve. "I don't believe it yet, and I know I ain't bein' rewarded for bein' smart," Aunt Artie said humbly. "But I never supposed Corny had so much—I really didn't! I figured on makin' dresses for the girls, and cookin' stew instead of sirloin tips. . . ." She began to laugh, and Starr laughed with her.

A sort of submerged happiness tentatively crept back into Starr's life—at least a timid belief that things did sometimes work out happily.

The very next time Mrs. Taylor mentioned Christmas dinner, Starr told her that she would be absent on Christmas. "We must attend my Aunt Artie's wedding," she said. "She's marrying Cornelius Worthington on Christmas

Eve, and we'll stay over until Christmas night. That way, Caro can have Christmas with the Worthington children."

"Cornelius Worthington!" Mrs. Taylor said, impressed. "I thought he was going to marry— Amelia will be furious! What sort of person is your Aunt Artie?"

"Tops!" Starr said. "Brave and generous. My favorite relative!"

Mrs. Taylor said, "All that money! And he came out here to pick cotton, without a good shirt to his name!"

"Wonderful, isn't it?"

But Mrs. Taylor did not smile; she muttered. Starr did not interpret the words or indeed care very much what they were. "No background and no family," said Mrs. Taylor, "and all that money!"

Starr asked if she could help with Mrs. Taylor's Christmas shopping and learned that it was done in August. "I just send subscriptions to good Christian magazines," Mrs. Taylor said. "That way there's no wrapping and fussing, and I get it over with."

So there would not even be a bit of tinsel ribbon in the house; not a spray of holly or a sprig of mistletoe—just Dinner.

Starr answered the doorbell, and Mrs. Taylor's voice was raised to ask, "Who is it?"

"Aunt Artie," Starr said, confused, not knowing whether she would be welcome.

"Bring her in here," Mrs. Taylor said. Starr made a grimace at Aunt Artie, who winked. They went into the shaded living room, where Mrs. Taylor reclined. Starr made the introductions, and Aunt Artie strode over to the couch.

"Feelin' bad today?" she inquired briskly of Mrs. Taylor. "What ails you?"

Mrs. Taylor drew back defensively. "My health is delicate," she said firmly.

"You got a good doctor?" Aunt Artie asked helpfully. "The things they can do to you these days! I got a girl friend that says she had so many operations, all she has left inside is one straight gu—intestine! Healthy as a horse now." She beamed upon Mrs. Taylor.

"I come to take Starr and Caro out to buy some clothes. I'm plumb tired of seein' Caro goin' around in high-water dresses! And I guess Starr rates a new dress as a matron of honor."

"I understand you're engaged to Mr. Worthington," Mrs. Taylor said, not so much revived as determined to satisfy her raging curiosity. Besides, Mr. Worthington was a supervisor, too, the same as Perry Taylor.

"Yes," Aunt Artie said, beaming again. "Lookit this! I always did like jewelry, and I had a lot of glittery junk. Corny says he'll change every piece I own for good jewelry!" She pulled from her coat pocket two earrings, each a web of thin gold and a splash of diamond. "Don't they shine pretty?" she asked, pleased. "I had to get holes bored in my ears to wear 'em, but for Corny I'd get holes bored in my head!"

Starr turned away to hide her smile. Mrs. Taylor's glance was transfixed, however, upon the diamonds. Aunt Artie stuffed them negligently back into her pocket. "Corny's sweet!" she said. "It's going to be hard to find anything to buy him for Christmas, though." She turned to Starr. "Maybe we could just make him some homemade candy?"

she said. "The kind Cory used to make when she had the money to buy the stuff?"

Starr nodded. "And real homemade popcorn balls with roasted peanuts all through?"

"Yes! And the girls can help make 'em—that's part of the fun. You too, Caro!" Caro came and leaned happily against Aunt Artie.

Ten minutes later Aunt Artie had whirled Starr and Caro out of the house, and Mrs. Taylor was left stunned on her couch with Aunt Artie's farewell about her like reverberations from a blow. "So long, kid!" Aunt Artie had said cheerfully, and departed.

Mrs. Taylor dragged herself up to prepare her own jasmine tea.

8.

$\mathcal{W}$HEN STARR returned, Mrs. Taylor had decided to speak to her. "I wouldn't try to advise you, but after all, you're very young, and your baby *is* the last of the Taylors. I do feel that I have some interest," she said to Starr.

Starr sat down, spilling a wealth of bundles about her, some of the brightness in her face fading once more. Mrs. Taylor continued, "While the baby's small, I don't feel that you should exert yourself socially so much. In our time, we lived in retirement for a few months. Mother's milk is such a delicate—"

Starr clasped her hands together for poise. "Dr. Starr says I'm profoundly healthy, and just built to have babies. She worries more about my state of mind, and says I must keep my spirits up—that's all—and live as normal a life as I can."

"But a wedding is so tiring! I suppose it'll be a big wedding?"

"Oh, medium! We're going to have it at Corny's ranch, and it won't be tiring—it'll be fun! The three little girls have identical dresses. Let me show you Caro's." Starr untied a box and lifted the pale blue velvet and lace concoction from it. Its full skirt stood out over a stiffened petticoat. "Won't she be a darling?" Starr asked.

Mrs. Taylor replied indirectly. "Wash frocks are suitable for children," she said. After a struggle in which curiosity won she asked, "And you?"

Starr unfastened another box and took out a gold lamé blouse and a heavenly blue velvet skirt. Mrs. Taylor looked upon it without expression. "Mourning?" she murmured.

"I assure you no special dress is needed for that," Starr said, more sharply than she had intended to do. She gathered her packages and went upstairs. There she laid both dresses on a sewing table, where she looked at them to feast her eyes and her spirit. Dash, she thought to the little boy who once lived in this room, look what pretty things have come to your house! She tried to remember Dash as her husband and the father of her child, but she could only think of him as a very sad, thin little boy, lost in a sea of grayness and touch-not's—very quiet in a silent, gloomy house where love had never lived.

She went quickly into the nursery and looked at young Dashell, making minute adjustments in his blankets.

The telephone rang, and she went downstairs to answer it. After she had identified herself to Western Union, she listened to a telegram from Montana offering two thousand dollars for her land in Wild Horse Valley. She had a strong, exciting hunch. Speaking softly she said, "Reply to the address given: 'No longer for sale.'" Furtively she cradled the receiver.

"Who was that?" Mrs. Taylor called. "Who were you talking to?"

"Wrong number," Starr lied cheerfully. Smiling slightly she added, "Somebody named Sadie." Sadie had been a

[238]

Cooper gremlin blamed for all inexplicable accidents for all her life.

"That's the trouble with telephones," Mrs. Taylor said restlessly. "No privacy. And we hardly ever use it—just costs money every month. I've often said I would have it taken out."

The next day Starr suggested that the Taylors go out for Christmas dinner, for fear of having no cook again.

"We *never* eat dinner out," Mrs. Taylor said regally. "But we might have dinner with Henrietta."

The nights were crisp and chill and lonely now. Starr looked out of her window, from which she had removed the heavy draperies. So Mary had probably looked at the stars before the first Christmas, she thought; and she brought Caro out of bed in her sleepers and let her look also. She told her part of the story of Christmas, and Caro said, "Ah, sweet little baby!"

When Caro had been returned to bed, Starr went back to the window once more. Oh, Dash! she thought, her eyes smarting. All the years, all the years when you were small, and no Christmas tree—just Dinners! Now I know why your face was sad when it relaxed, and your smile flashed and your wit turned and glittered like a sequined thing away from home. It was escape from loneliness. And you never acknowledged it, even to yourself! It would have been a rudeness, wouldn't it? But it'll be different for young Dashell, I promise you!

A week before Christmas, Starr received Christmas cards from her father, from Ann Marie, and from Beau, all in one mail. Her father's card came from his old home town, and contained nothing but the oversweet verse, signed formally with his name. Beau's card had a small note on it, saying that he liked the Navy training, and this was the life for him. Ann Marie had written all over both sides of her card, telling about the real keen young man she was going to marry.

Starr carried them in her pocket that afternoon, going to meet Jeff in the park. The family's settling, she thought; they're going to find their own separate ways of life. Jeff would be glad to know it.

But she did not mention it to him at all, as it turned out. He had no smile or joke for her that day. Almost at once he said, "There won't be many more of these meetings. I'm being transferred the first of the year."

Starr's heart leaped like a hunted thing. "Where?" she asked, curling her fingers into her palms.

"Away up north somewhere, I think. Too far to commute. Starr, won't you join me?" He did not touch her, but his eyes were full of hope and tenderness.

The temptation was enormous. "Maybe we can come later," she said carefully. Then her restraint broke somewhat. "Oh, Jeff! You know how easy it would be to say yes! And you know you can't afford all three of us, and Louise and her aunt too! We'd all be a burden, and things would be so hard, and maybe we might quarrel! I know what a burden Louise has been to you. You see, I noticed that you hadn't had a new suit for—how many years, Jeff?"

"You don't really care about the suit, Starr."

Starr unfastened her coat at the throat; she felt as if she were smothering. "It's too hard to give you up again!" she said, beginning to tremble with the loss, but trying to maintain composure. "But maybe it just wasn't to be. I know you can't fail anyone depending on you, and you know the same of me. And we have too much responsibility already. We simply can't afford each other, and you know it!"

He came very close, but still did not touch her; his voice was low. "We could try! Maybe we'd be lucky. We deserve some luck. Maybe we wouldn't need as much as we think. Darling, I *can't* wait forever! I've waited too long now."

"I know." Starr touched his cheek in quick affection, then put her hands into her coat pockets distractedly. "We still have two weeks."

Anger rose in his voice. "We always measure time in hours!" he said. "Probably better not to see each other at all!"

Walking home that night, Starr did not know whether she could bear this final wrench. There had been too much pain and loss, and she was tired. She could neither live in peace with the Taylors, nor go with Jeff as a burden. She certainly could not abandon the babies—and no more could Jeff abandon Louise to public charity. We're simply stuck, she thought hopelessly. At least I have the babies to love, but Jeff has nothing at all.

She would wake at night during that time, to find her hands tightly clasped; and although it was winter, she would be sweating at the recurring tormenting dream that she toiled up an endless hill. We'll never in this world be given a third chance, she thought. Never.

But she was slowly winning an undeclared war with Miss Cinch. Almost every afternoon she took young Dashell for a stroll in his magnificent buggy—a positive Cad among buggies. Caro loved to push it. A few days before Christmas, they walked downtown so that Caro could see the decorations—perhaps even see Santa Claus in a store window.

[241]

Dashell would sleep the whole time, she knew, but he should not be excluded from such great occasions.

It was a long trip, but rewarding. Caro was all eyes and shouts of delight. But as they passed the bus depot, Starr's casual glance rested on a sad-faced woman standing at the entrance. She slowed her pace. She had really walked past before her troubled senses identified the woman—eyes blue as twilight skies, soft fair face, and silken blonde hair. Louise Mayfield! And Jeff was out of town on a field trip. He would not return before midnight!

For the sake of peace, she must walk on—that was her first thought. She had the children. But her feet slowed, and finally she doggedly turned back. "Aren't you Louise Mayfield?" she asked.

Louise smiled uncertainly, drying her eyes on a handkerchief of cobweb lace. "Yes," she said. "Did Mr. Mayfield send you?" She stared at Starr in bewilderment.

"No," Starr said. "I'm Starr Cooper—don't you remember me? I met you once when you were out here, and I was doing some work for Jeff."

Louise's pretty face smoothed with relief. "You're lucky for me!" she said. "I just don't know what to do, but you'll know." Starr fancied that there was an aura of disaster about her. But Louise looked at the baby with angelic tenderness.

"I married, you see," Starr said to Louise, trying to steady herself.

Louise put a hand on the buggy and continued her rapturous gaze at young Dashell. "So little and so sweet!" she said, in the same tone of wonder Caro used—looking but not daring to touch. "Maybe some time when he isn't asleep you'd let me hold him a minute?"

Caro examined Louise with intensity.

"And where in the world did such a doll of a little girl come from?" Louise asked, beguiled anew. She knelt beside Caro. "Who are you?" she asked.

"Starr's girl," Caro answered, surprisingly; and Starr was unexpectedly touched. "Let's all go have a soda!" she said. Mentally she counted the few coins in her purse. Well, if she took only a coke, perhaps. Or water, if the sodas were expensive.

"A cocktail!" Louise said, beaming.

"Not with Caro and the baby," Starr answered, the premonition of trouble thickening about her.

"Honey, of course not! Let's do have a soda. I'm hungry." Louise fell into step beside Starr, and Caro pushed the buggy with great importance. Starr thought perhaps Louise had already had a drink or two, but it was hard to guess, and her perfume prevented the possibility of smelling. . . .

"I'm in such a mess, Starr," Louise said over her soda. "Aunt Nettie got sick and they took her to the hospital, and it was so *lonely* in the house! I looked until I found some money—but not very much. I had to come by bus, and I'm all tired and dirty, and Jeffrey's not at home, and his office says he's out of town! You know they lie to a wife— office people do, you know. I've tried to telephone him before, and they always say he's out of town, or they can't find him. Isn't it a silly old office?" She wore a warm light coat of softest gray blue, and her face was as innocent as Caro's. Caro herself was completely occupied by the unexpected, marvelous soda.

"Did you ask Mrs. Maple to let you in—the woman from whom Jeff rents?" Starr asked.

"Honey, she's not home! The big house is all dusty and locked up. And I don't have any money."

There was only Aunt Artie to help. Starr went to a public phone and tried to reach her, but there was no answer. "Please!" Starr said silently over and over, listening to the buzz of the phone ringing and ringing. Slowly she put the receiver back on the hook. Surely she would be able to reach Aunt Artie before dark. Meantime, she must start home. It was a long walk. She returned to the booth where Caro and Louise were still enjoying their sodas.

"You better come with me," she said. "We have to walk home, because I don't have taxi fare, either." She looked at the graceful spike heels on Louise's small feet. It could not be helped.

They took one overnight bag from the bus depot, and left the others there for the time being.

All the way home Starr's mind raced around the coming crisis. Of course she would not have been involved if she had not happened to pass the bus station. It was no business of hers. It would be simply impossible to explain Louise to the Taylors—who hated company at best and unexpected company bitterly. And drink of every sort—even sodas.

"Honey," Louise said halfway home, "my feet hurt something terrible! Would it be too awful if I took off these shoes and put on my slippers? They're kind of fussy, but so comfortable—if it wouldn't embarrass you?"

"It wouldn't embarrass me," Starr said gently. "I have to explain to you now that my husband died. I live in the house with his mother and father. I can't even ask you to spend the night. I have very little money. But you could come and visit for a few hours, while I try to telephone my

Aunt Artie. She'll take you in, sight unseen, if I can only reach her."

"You mean you can't have guests where you live?" Louise asked incredulously. She was wriggling her toes in her blue feathered house shoes, and as she looked up, a strand of shining hair fell across her forehead. "I didn't know anybody that *was* anybody ever acted that way!"

"It isn't that they've told me not to," Starr said conscientiously. "It's only that they're old, and company upsets them. And Louise, there's never a drink stronger than tea served in that house!" Starr fervently hoped that the statement would sink deep.

"My goodness!" Louise said. "Are they preachers, honey?"

"No, only Puritans," Starr said, smiling at the thought. "Mr. Taylor's in real estate, and I wouldn't be surprised if he had all his cocktails somewhere else."

Louise nodded. "Aunt Nettie has a cousin like that—all about temperance and the devil, you know! Her husband goes on tears, and she won't let him in the house, so he comes and sleeps it off at The Willows."

"Is that your place—The Willows?"

"It's really Aunt Nettie's place," Louise said. "But she lets me stay there all the time. You don't know Aunt Nettie, do you? She's so sick they took her away. They've taken *me* away lots of times, but not Aunt Nettie. The sink got all full of dirty dishes. I want Jeffrey to do something about getting Aunt Nettie home. I know he can if he will. My husband travels a lot, but nobody can say he doesn't *do* things!"

Starr decided to tell the Taylors that she had run across an old acquaintance who would visit for a few hours. She must feed Dashell and bathe Caro. And somehow she must get hold of Aunt Artie. She would call the ranch and ask where Corny was. With the wedding less than a week away, probably they were somewhere together.

Louise made a very pretty appearance at the Taylors' except for her house shoes. Her soft southern voice was shy and respectful when she was introduced. Mrs. Taylor's immobile face showed no change—neither welcome nor rejection. She barely said how do you do.

"Come help me bathe Caro," Starr said. "This is a time of day when all mothers belong to the I-wish-I-had-four-hands Club." She took Louise upstairs and gave her a stuffy magazine to read while she fed young Dashell and handed him over to authority in the nursery. She bathed and hugged Caro and put her into pajamas. "Now we'll all go downstairs for dinner," she said, leading Caro into the bedroom.

Louise was putting a flask back into her overnight bag. She lifted it out again and said, "Don't you want an appetizer before dinner? I always do."

Starr shook her head. "In this house we *can't*," she said, panicky. "It simply isn't done!"

Louise smiled radiantly. "I can't imagine such a thing!" she said. "When we have a guest, the house is *his*, as long as he stays!"

"Come on down to dinner," Starr said, remembering that other dinner when Louise would not eat. She swung Caro up into her arms. "You weigh as much as an *elephant!*" she said to Caro, butting foreheads with her.

Caro laughed and put dimpled arms about her neck. "I *love* you, Starry!" she said, hugging inexpertly.

Starr set her down and said, "Downstairs with you! Scamper, before I catch you!"

She excused herself from the table to try again to reach Aunt Artie. At the Worthington ranch they informed her that Corny and Aunt Artie were out dancing, and probably wouldn't be in until nobody knew when—bless them! She had enough money to put Louise up at a hotel, but dared not send her there alone. After Dashell's ten o'clock feeding they could taxi to Jeff's, and maybe she could find a key, if he still kept an extra one hidden in the same place. Then they would wait there until he got home. There was nothing else to do. She must keep Louise here for four more hours, and Louise had the flask.

After dinner Starr took her immediately upstairs. What Louise had said while she was out of the room, she could not know, but her tongue was certainly loose enough. Louise reached immediately for her bag. "Something for my spirits," she said. "I feel so *sad!* Mrs. Taylor doesn't like me. I'll have to go now." She closed the bag once more and picked it up.

"Wait until after the ten o'clock feeding, and I'll go with you," Starr said. "Mrs. Taylor isn't unkind, really. They've fed and housed the children and me for more than four months."

Louise nodded her head dreamily. "I know," she said. "I've been in any number of these places—sometimes for several months. But I can leave this one." Apprehensively she added, "I *can* leave, can't I? You aren't a nurse now, are you?"

"No," Starr said gently. "I'm not a nurse; I'm your friend."

"They say that, and then they don't let you go," Louise said suspiciously. She backed toward the door, her eyes watchful.

"Wait until I get Caro into bed, and I'll go with you!" Starr said impulsively. So perhaps she would have to come home, and then go back again, and it would cost. But it seemed the only way.

She telephoned for a taxi, knowing that old Mrs. Taylor was listening. Then she went into her room. "I'm going out for a few hours," she said. "I'll be home in time to feed the baby."

Mrs. Taylor's eyes slanted obliquely at her. "Don't *forget*," she said. "Dashell depends on you for milk."

Both tone and inference were quietly insulting, but Starr pretended not to notice. The taxi came promptly, and she went outside with Louise. Louise said intensely, "Honey, I wouldn't go back at all if I were you. Next time they may not let you out!"

Having no flashlight, Starr groped in the garage for the nail where once Jeff had kept an extra key to his apartment. The taxi waited, a lighted blur purring in the darkness under the trees. She could have wept with relief when her hand finally closed over the key. She paid the taxi driver and led Louise into Jeff's place with a sense of great accomplishment. Now she must beguile Louise for hours, and she prayed that Jeff might return before ten o'clock, but it was not to be expected.

Unobtrusively she checked the liquor cabinet and found it locked. This was a lucky break, for she never could have found a way to move the liquor. It belonged to Dick, and Jeff never touched it.

Starr began making coffee and straightening the room. She washed a few dishes left in the sink, and dusted a surface here and there, glad the familiar place was a bit untidy, so that she might make it pleasanter.

She suffered a small shock when Louise came out of the bathroom wearing Jeff's bathrobe. Louise had discarded her coat and suit in a heap on the floor. Automatically Starr picked them up and looked for a place to hang them.

Louise was having another drink. There was not much left in the bottle, and she viewed it with an anxious glance, as if there must have been some error. She sat on the couch, and as she did so the robe parted to reveal her figure. Definitely she had bulges. A sharp pity flashed in Starr, looking at her. It was true that she herself was gaunt with strain and effort, which was not becoming. But the neglect of Louise's silken body was like the neglect of a work of art.

Louise held the bottle to the light and said, "It *can't* just go away! It *has* to last through the night, with something left over for morning! I can't face Jeffrey without something. . . . He may be mad at me again. But I haven't done anything to him but love him—I never did anything. . . ."

"You're so tired—why don't you take a nap before he comes home?"

"The best dreams come in bottles," Louise said. "Never sad, and never lonesome, and always plenty of money and pretty clothes and beaux—where else can you find all that?"

"A job, maybe! It might be fun for you."

"Did you find it fun, honey?" Louise asked. "Daddy raised me not to work at all. I never so much as washed out

[249]

a hankie for myself before he died. Did you know my daddy died?"

"Yes," Starr said. "But if you never tried working, how do you know you wouldn't like it?"

"I'd rather be supported by my husband," Louise said, "like my mother and her mother were."

"Would you like me to read aloud?" Starr asked, later in the evening, hoping she might lull Louise to sleep before ten o'clock.

"It would be soothin'," Louise said, her face as still as a flower. "Read poetry." So Starr put a record to work with gentle music, and thumbed through a book of poems. They're all about love, she thought despairingly. Jeff and I have made them all ours. Then she noted that Louise was curling up with her flask and thought, Just so it has rhythm. Probably the music and the rhythm will be all she hears. Louise looked at her, gently expectant, and pulled Jeff's robe about herself. Desperately Starr began to read "Annabelle Lee" for its music, trying to give the words as little inflection as possible. After two verses she stopped, however. Louise was weeping, her pretty hands clenching and unclenching.

"I'm *sorry!*" Louise said. "It's too sad; I can't stand it! Everything's too sad, and I don't even have enough bourbon to last until morning. How in the world do you get along without it?"

"I couldn't afford it if I needed it," Starr said. She desperately wished Louise would go to sleep, with ten o'clock racing closer, when she would have to hurry home.

"My mother and her mother danced all night and slept half the day and had a hundred beaux," Louise said. "Their mothers and their maids fixed them pretty, and made lovely ball gowns for them. They got everything they wanted in the world just for being pretty and well bred. And I'm just as pretty as my mother was—but it didn't happen that way for me. You know the nasty old war? And simply nobody left at home when it was time for me to have my parties and my beaux. Just some young men from the military. Not that I minded entertaining 'em—but you see how it was? And then Daddy died, and Jeffrey came. Nobody but Jeffrey! I love him! But all the fun, the flowers, the parties? Maybe our mothers used them all up? Maybe they went out of the world, like Mummie and Daddy." Louise hugged her arms to her breast, and the tears ran steadily from the clenched eyelids—down the pretty, flower-like face and past the moist full lips, now innocent of lipstick.

Starr moved close beside the couch. "You aren't alone," she said. "Lots of people miss *all* the parties! I went to just one ball in my whole life. There are so many really sad things—people starving, and unjustly imprisoned, and right now men fighting battles and bleeding and dying. . . ."

"Honey," Louise whispered, "you talk like a man—like my daddy—but I'm a woman, and I wanted parties and pretty gowns and jewelry and a maid—things *nice!* And now I haven't even got Aunt Nettie!" She pushed her bright hair back. The long, childish eyelashes almost covered the faintly purple, slightly swollen smudges beneath the eyes. Starr was quiet, hoping she might drift into sleep. After a few moments, she tiptoed to the telephone to call the taxi. As she did so, Louise sat up. Her eyes were haunted. "Don't leave me, Starr!" Her voice was pleading. "Stay with me at least until Jeffrey comes home! I'm *afraid* of something. Did you ever feel the dark somethings coming close, and not know what they were? Please, Starr!"

"I'll be gone only a little, *little* while," Starr said, as to a child. "I have to go feed the baby, and I'll come right back." She did not like leaving her alone. But if she brought her back to the Taylors, more mess of some sort would surely ensue. She told herself that Louise was only on a crying jag. She tried to close her mind to the helpless sobbing as she left.

A light was on in the downstairs bedroom. Mrs. Taylor was up and watching. Why did she watch, watch, watch? Because she had no life of her own, of course, Starr answered her own question. She was the victim of her own starvation, and Starr was caught in the cruel meagerness of it.

"Oh, there you are, Starr!" she said with relief in her voice. "Would you lock up before you go upstairs? Burglars have been here before."

Starr checked windows and bolted doors. She would have to unbolt one when she left directly. The baby was crying, and she ran upstairs.

Miss Cinch said, "He's such a good baby, aren't you, Precious?" She stood watching Starr as she prepared to feed young Dashell. "He never cries when his meals are on time."

She *watches*, too, Starr thought distractedly. She took the baby and nursed him, and still Miss Cinch watched intently. She held Dashell against her shoulder and patted him, forgetting Miss Cinch, momentarily forgetting everything in the world but this beloved small person.

"I about decided you weren't coming," Miss Cinch said.

"I haven't missed a meal yet, have I?" Starr asked, irritated. In the back of her mind she could again hear Louise crying. She must hurry back. Dashell was almost asleep as she put him back in his crib.

Quickly she went to look at Caro. Tousled Caro slept with one plump arm above her head. Starr brushed her hair back from her face, filled with the special rush of love engendered by sleeping babies.

Now she must get out of the house. If it took a scene, then she must be steeled for it. The light was off in the downstairs bedroom, but that did not mean that Mrs. Taylor was asleep. She went to the phone in the hall. When her hand was on the second numeral of the dial, Mrs. Taylor stood in the door to the hall, her face stern in the dim glow of the night light. Her presence was as quiet and hostile as a tiger's. "What are you doing?" she asked.

Starr continued to dial, fighting the sense of menace. "Calling another taxi," she said. "I have to go back to Mrs. Mayfield. She's ill."

Mrs. Taylor put one hand upon the cradle of the phone and disconnected it. "I don't wish to be rude," she said, "but you *must* consider what you're doing!" Her face did not change, but her voice was adamant.

"Please!" Starr said sharply. "I *must* phone; then we can talk until the taxi gets here."

The old hand did not release the phone. "Mrs. Mayfield is very peculiar," Mrs. Taylor said. "I think she has been drinking."

Starr was getting more frantic by the moment. "Even if she took dope, I still have to get back to her," she said. "Please, she needs help, and there isn't anyone but me to help her! I would have her here if this were my home."

"You *must* realize your position, my dear!" Mrs. Mayfield said, fiercely firm. "I don't like having to interfere, but now that you have a child—"

"The children are safe, and fed, and asleep, and watched!" Starr cried. "I must go, even if I walk! There are things I must do, right now!"

"And one of them is to discriminate among people," Mrs. Taylor said, tenacious and thin-lipped. "This girl obviously has no breeding—"

It was so hard to waste all this time with words; Starr was almost in tears. "She can match ancestors with most," she said, "but right now none of them can help her. I can. I don't know when I'll be back—but before next feeding time." She hurried from the telephone and unbolted the door.

"Don't you see we can't leave the door unlatched all night?"

"Then I ought to have a key!" Starr said. "You bolt it after me if you like. I can walk around all night until you get up in the morning! I'll be on the doorstep before six— how's that?" She opened the door, and Mrs. Taylor followed her.

"I just can't bear these scenes," Mrs. Taylor said faintly. "You know there's no extra key! It's dangerous for a woman alone—"

"All living is dangerous!" Starr said. She rushed outdoors. They might have given me a key long ago, as a simple courtesy, she thought. You'd think I was breaking jail— and maybe I am!

Ten thirty was not so late, but everything was closed. She could not hope for a cruising taxi in a residential neighborhood. Street lights made a large shapeless shadow before her as she walked out of each pool of dubious light and into the dark.

All the houses were snugged behind dark hedges, and most seemed as deserted as if all life had fled. Her own footsteps sounded loud and hurried on the slumbering streets. Finally she saw a liquor store disguised as a Spanish villa, with the most discreet of pastel green neon signs proclaiming its sin of commerce. It was open, and she hurried inside and called for a taxi. She had walked a mile, and used up precious time.

The lights were blazing from Jeff's cottage and the radio was high. Louise had broken into the liquor cabinet, and she had helped herself. "All this lovely stuff was locked up!" she said. "Fix you a highball, a pink lady, anything you want! Got all the stuff now!" She held to the sink, her eyes big in her dazed face. "Jus' a little drinkie to keep up your spirits, and to keep the dark some . . . shom . . . some-things away outside!"

"Sit down. I'll help myself," Starr said. She poured seltzer water into a glass and sipped it. Louise would not notice what went into the glass.

"Ever live in a big house all by yourself?" Louise asked, steering an uncertain course to the couch. "Lonesome. Mighty lonesome! Nothin' to do but think. Pretty wife shouldn't think; husband sh'd think for her, wouldn't you say? But he's not there. Simple—go where he is, I say, wouldn't you shay?" She waved her glass vaguely, and some of the contents spilled on the floor. Her blouse was partially unfastened; Jeff's robe fell away from it and from her bare legs. Again Starr thought of a dissolute angel.

"Lie back and rest; you've had a hard day," she said.

"I'm not drunk," Louise said, with suddenly acute perception. "A little bourbon doesn't make me drunk, like it does some people that don't know how to drink." She spoke slowly and distinctly. "In our family, we can drink like ladies and gentlemen. Daddy always said so. But I think maybe men have changed. He said not ever to do anything for a man if he could do it for himself, and not to do anything for myself that a man ought to love to do for me. He said look pretty and be entertainin', and I do. But does it really work? Does it work for you, Starr?"

"It might be the only way. I never had time to try it," Starr said gently.

"My husband loves me, even if he does travel," Louise said regally. "Did your husband love you?"

"I think so. We had a fine time together, any way."

"But he left you without even a home."

"He didn't plan to die that day."

"I want to die before I get old and ugly," Louise said. "What else does a woman have?"

"Something, surely! Think of all the girls living happy lives even if they aren't pretty." Starr was trying to soothe Louise. Dash had wanted to die young, too. This repetition of the wish chilled her. Surely she would hear Jeff's car soon. Before six o'clock, she prayed. She was sleepy, herself, being used to hours suitable for cows and chickens. She opened the door a crack, and let in some cold air that set her shivering. Still she was sleepy. Louise began to doze. She would arouse with haunted eyes, ascertain that Starr was there, then relax again. She was asleep when Jeff's car drove in.

Starr went outside to him, closing the door softly behind herself. She was shivering. The lights would have warned him of company. "Jeff," she said, and put out her hand.

"You're cold," he said, his smile a welcome, and no questions asked. He opened his overcoat and folded her partially inside with him, and for a moment Starr could not speak, but clung to him in the only truly warm safe place in the world.

"Louise came; she's inside," Starr said finally. "I watched over her as well as I could for you. Her Aunt Nettie's in the hospital. I'm in the doghouse with the Taylors. I may be locked out."

She dumped it all on him so confidently. He only held her closer. "Starr Cooper—Barrel of Stars," he said quietly, "I love you so! It never has been anything but trouble to you, but at least I love you! Thanks for your help again."

Starr leaned her head against him. "You know I always loved you, don't you? Even when I ran away. It wasn't any use."

They held each other quietly, and then the telephone began to ring in the cottage. It would wake Louise. Jeff ran inside to answer it, and Starr slowly followed.

Louise slept on, her silken hair loose on the pillow, her whole exquisite body melted with sleep. Jeff's face was deeply serious as he listened and answered at the phone. When he finished, he put a hand to his forehead as if his head hurt. "Aunt Nettie died," he said. Then he straightened up. "It needn't trouble you. Louise looks like she'll sleep where she is until I can get you home. No use keeping you up longer than need be."

The Taylor house was dark. "Wait to see if I can get in," Starr said.

The knob did not turn under her hand. She herself had latched all the windows. For a moment anger and humiliation filled her throat. Caro and young Dashell both were inside, and they belonged to her—but she could not make a noise or demand to go to them. Slowly she turned from the door and went back to Jeff's car. "They've locked the door," she said. "I don't want to sit on the steps in the cold all night."

"I can damned well wake them up in a hurry," Jeff said, opening the door of the car. "I woke them up once before, when you went to the hospital. Mrs. Taylor acted as if she thought you had deliberately chosen to have a baby at night to inconvenience them."

Starr put a hand on his arm. "Make no mind—let them sleep," she said. "They have to let me in to feed the baby at six. I can wait at your place until then, can't I?"

"You can wait at my place," he said, pushing the car into gear. "You can marry me and bring Caro and the baby, and live at my place, wherever it is, all your life! You don't have to live in a tomb!"

Starr looked straight into the darkness ahead. "We'll see," she said steadily. "Right now there's Louise. Hurry, hurry! There's something so wild and sad about her. She came to ask you to get Aunt Nettie out, confident that you could do it."

"She's like a child," Jeff said. "Such a pretty, good child —with no malice in her. But one that will never grow up."

He stopped the car in front of the cottage, and they sat in the chill black shadows and talked softly. "It was the Judge who telephoned tonight," he said. "He was Aunt Nettie's cousin. He says The Willows is left to me. That would be to help pay expenses for Louise. But it's probably not worth much, it's so run down—and it'll take time to realize anything at all on it."

Starr touched his hand. "You'll find a way. And I don't

[258]

want you worrying about us until you do—do you understand?"

"There are no other close relatives," Jeff said. "And the
institutions are so ghastly—except the terribly expensive
ones!"

Starr interrupted his troubled train of thought. "We have
to have some sleep—we must go in," she said. "My day
begins at six in the morning, and there's no putting it off for
ten minutes."

As they started for the cottage, Starr tried to remember
about the lights. The cottage was dark now, and a sharp
fear tugged at her. She had a strong urge to hold Jeff back,
but he went inside and turned on a table lamp. Both of
them looked immediately to the couch which was now
empty. Quickly Jeff stepped to the bedroom door, then
looked at Starr and shook his head.

Without words, they began to run toward the car. "She
may have been partially awake and heard about Aunt Nettie," Starr said breathlessly. "The railroad tracks first this
time—there's a train soon. I've heard it in the night, lying
awake and trying to get to sleep. . . ."

"I know." Jeff turned the car sharply; its wheels spun in
the half-dead grass. They covered the five blocks swiftly,
but before they stopped the car they heard the hoarse honk-
ing of the streamliner. It was lessening speed as it entered
town, but still was very fast. Jumping from the car, they
looked up the tracks toward the swinging eye of the approaching train. It was possibly a mile away, and Louise
was less than half a city block. She was walking toward
them, a careful silhouette balancing on the rail. The one eye
of the engine swung around and around, as if seeking some
other route; as if it were trying not to see the childish,

[259]

bright-haired figure balancing there. Jeff's robe slid along the rail behind her, like the train of some royal garment, and her bare small feet set themselves precisely on the rail, one in front of the other.

They both raced toward her, and Jeff dragged her from the tracks with time to spare. "I'm not drunk!" she said through the roar of passing wheels, as the alternate light and shadow of the train's windows raced over them. Jeff still held fast to her hand, and Starr had abruptly sat down on the top of the steep embankment, a deathly sickness rushing over her in waves.

"Maybe you're not drunk," Jeff said sharply, "but you certainly were close to being dead! Good Lord, Louise! Couldn't you hear the train? Didn't you see the light?"

Louise burst into sobs. "You're mad at me again!" she said in a voice choked with despair. "You could see I walked the rail, and you're still mad at me!" She took her hands from Jeff's and stood on the narrow path at the ends of the cross ties. "Don't speak to me, Jeffrey Mayfield," she said, her voice breaking.

Gently Jeff put an arm about her shoulders. "Let's go," he said. "You need some sleep, Louise." She drew away, but when Starr led, she followed her, and Jeff came last, single file.

Driving back to Jeff's cottage, they were quiet with exhaustion. Once inside, Louise headed straight for the liquor cabinet.

Jeff blocked her way. "Don't you think you've had enough?" he asked gently. "Your daddy wouldn't want you to get drunk, you know."

"Jeffrey," Louise said quietly, apparently quite sober, "you know I always drink like a lady. You know I never do a single thing to bother anybody, or make a lot of noise—or anything! I'm sorry you're mad at me, but I do need a drink."

Still Jeff stood before the cabinet. "This isn't my liquor, Louise," he said. "You mustn't drink it—it's rude!"

Louise cast herself upon the couch and covered her face with her hands. "Nobody lets me do anything!" she said in a sort of anguish. "Whether I go home or run away—nobody lets me do anything! If Daddy had lived, people would look sharp to please me! If Daddy had lived, I wouldn't be scolded—I'd have parties and pretty dresses and handsome beaux...."

Jeff let the speech run down. "Starr's spending the night," he finally said. "One of you can sleep on the couch, and one on the bed, and I'll stay here in the big chair. Which would you rather have, Louise?"

Louise looked at him in a puzzled fashion. "Aren't you going to bed?" she asked. "We could sleep on the bed, and Starr on the couch."

A moment of taut silence ensued. Then Jeff said gently, "That's a fine idea. You go ahead, and I'll come later." He settled back into the chair, and Louise went into the bedroom. After a few moments he arose and found a pillow for Starr, and a blanket with which to cover her.

"I'll tuck you in," he told her, and she realized that she was unbelievably tired. She put the pillow beneath her head and Jeff spread the blanket over her and patted her gently. "Sleep now," he said. "I can stand watch the rest of the night." He went back to the chair. Vaguely Starr thought that one of them should be sure that Louise actually was in bed, but sleep was already loosening her will. She could see that Jeff, in the chair, was succumbing to a like condition, and tenderness and sympathy for him moved drowsily within her. She remembered turning the table lamp to its lowest—then she slept deeply.

In scarcely more than thirty minutes, she started awake. Alarm quickened within her before she realized where she was, or what might have awakened her. Jeff was carefully closing the door, going outside. Starr slipped her feet into her shoes swiftly and ran to the bedroom door. Louise was gone, too. Running to the door, she saw Jeff's back disappearing into the trees, a darkness above the disk of light on the ground. "Wait!" she called softly, and he stopped.

The flashlight beam showed the delicate prints of Louise's bare feet. They followed them through the grounds, over the fence and into the wood. They lost them and found them again. "She didn't have more than a minute's lead," Jeff said. "I heard the door of the liquor cabinet open, and it woke me; but it took a minute to realize—and then she was out of the house, with a bottle in her hand."

Louise must be running ahead of them, through the cold wood, in the faint star shine, barefooted. Straight through the wood the little prints led, and presently the beam of the flashlight discovered her sitting on the bank of the irrigation canal. She darted to her feet, her eyes a flash of terror in the brief beam of the light. "I'm not drunk," she said breathlessly. "I'll show you! I can walk a rail as well—"

She stepped quickly backward—and disappeared over the edge of the canal. There was almost no noise—neither the sound of her soft body falling against the sloping concrete wall, nor any perceptible splash into the water running in the bottom of it.

Dropping the flashlight, Jeff was almost instantly over the edge. Starr recovered the flashlight and directed its beam toward the swift-flowing water. Jeff might have stood in it except for the current. His hair glistened dark and strange as he groped and probed in the water, hampered by cold and his inability to keep his footing. Floundering, he searched, but there was no sign of Louise.

For the first few minutes, Starr felt certain that Louise would come to the surface any moment; then the uncertainty pushed and expanded. Finally a frantic sense of calamity gripped her. She continued to follow Jeff's floundering, groping, stumbling figure with the light, but as she followed down the bank she felt the tears quietly rise and run down her cheeks. No one could stay under water so long and live.

"Maybe she got to the other side," she said to Jeff, steadying her voice.

"She couldn't have climbed out easily—and I think I saw her once in the water. We'll have to work downstream. Maybe she can hold on to something and keep her head above water. She doesn't swim." His teeth were chattering. He zigzagged from side to side of the water, sometimes wading waist deep, sometimes swimming when he lost his footing.

Starr walked slowly along the bank, holding the beam steadily on Jeff, while his words ran like the click of rails under a train, over and over through her mind: She doesn't swim, she doesn't swim....

Abruptly the bridge was at hand. A car crossed on it, swiftly whispering tires and flash of lights, and then the road was uninhabited, and only the water gurgled under the bridge in the stillness. Jeff stopped for breath. "Flag a car," he said, conserving his energy. "Have them call the fire department—drowning equipment." His lips were blue.

His clothes stuck to his thin body, and Starr held him in the light a moment before he went under the bridge, into the narrow dark place. She then stepped to the middle of the empty road and prayed for a car from either direction. Finally one came, and she stood in the road and waved the dimming flashlight, willing the car to stop with a fierce concentration. The driver did stop, and quickly agreed to help. He was gone in a moment and she ran to the other side of the bridge.

Jeff was under the bridge; the beam did not find him. His voice came out in echoes. "She's here," he said. He did not say "She's safe." So Starr knew then. Jeff floundered from under the bridge toward the side of the canal, holding Louise, keeping her head above water. The tall, rounded concrete wall offered no handhold. Frantically Starr flashed the light about, seeking a board or a log—anything! Sand, sand, and tiny wiry bushes met her frantic glance.

"There's no way to get you out!" she cried, "But the fire truck's coming." She cast herself on the ground and reached her hands down. Jeff could have reached them somehow— but not while holding Louise, who lay limp and helpless. The swift current carried both of them relentlessly downstream, Jeff keeping to the side of the canal and trying to brake their progress with his feet.

The scream of the fire truck's siren was the most beautiful sound Starr ever heard. Following Jeff along the bank she called down, "Hear the sirens? They'll be here in just a minute!"

"Now listen, Starr," Jeff said with difficulty. "Go back. Go back home! Get out of the whole mess right now. We'll be all right."

She ran toward the truck, its lights pulsing red in the early morning dark, She flicked her flashlight off and on to draw attention as she ran. "Ladder," she said. "This way." She ran before them down the bank. An ambulance screeched to a stop beside the fire truck, and more men came from it. A ladder went down into the canal—and only then did Starr sit down in the sand in the dark, and the great sobs shook her.

Presently a young man stood before her and asked if she were Mrs. Taylor. Mr. Mayfield was calling for her. Starr arose to find him, and was dismayed to see the crowd that had collected at the sight of ambulance and fire truck— photographers, firemen, newsmen, curious passers-by. Jeff came toward her, wearing a blanket someone had placed about him. He was shaking off the hands trying to detain him. "I won't go anywhere in an ambulance," he was insisting. "I'm all right."

Louise was a round shape under a sheet, and men in white carried the dripping stretcher on which she lay. Pity welled in Starr for the waste—pity for the baby who had once been tended and loved and fed, and over whose drowsy golden head some woman had sung lullabies in the scented southern nights. Pity for the beautiful young girl, behind the eyes of twilight blue, looking into yesterday and finding no chart for today. Starr's hands were tight together when Jeff reached her side. "Come away now," he said. "We've done all we could." The high white light of a flashbulb lay over them for a moment.

They were not to get away easily. There were the police and the reporters. She learned that Louise's head had struck the concrete wall as she fell. So that accounted for her silence. Shivering, Jeff did most of the talking, protecting her as well as he could.

At six o'clock Miss Cinch opened to Starr's knock and found her on the front steps, her eyes swollen. "Were you locked out, Mrs. Taylor?" she asked, clicking and clucking again. "It won't be good for the milk, being upset and no sleep. . . ."

Even the downy early morning charms of young Dashell failed to intrigue Starr's attention. Caro was sitting up drowsily in bed. When she saw Starr's face, she ran to her and clasped her arms about her knees. "Hurt yourself, Starry?" she asked, patting gently, her upturned face bright with sympathy.

Tears again scarred Starr's tired eyes. "I did hurt myself, for a fact," she said unsteadily. "But make no mind. It's better now. Let's wash faces and hunt some breakfast." She could hardly hold her eyes open as Caro dressed, but she went doggedly to the kitchen later.

Mrs. Taylor was there already. "What on earth happened to you?" she asked. "I stayed awake until two, and still you didn't come in, so I had to lock up."

"It's all right," Starr said, her wits dull with shock and sleepiness. "I was sitting with a very sick friend."

"I trust she's better," Mrs. Taylor said drily.

"Yes. She's dead." Starr put water to boil for oatmeal. "She needed more care than I could give her."

Startled, Mrs. Taylor said, "I'm sorry. What happened to her?"

"I can't go through it again," Starr said, looking directly at Mrs. Taylor. "It was horrible! You can read about it in the papers, probably. I'm going to feed Caro, and then I'm going to sleep until ten o'clock. I don't think any reporters will come, but if they do, I don't want to be awakened." She turned to Caro. "Would you watch over Starry while she sleeps, and play quietly in the room?"

"*Reporters!*" Mrs. Taylor said with real horror. "Not a *scandal?*"

"It depends on what you call a scandal," Starr said. "But I'm so tired. . . ."

"If only you hadn't gone out again!" Mrs. Taylor wailed. "If only you had tried to understand our position. . . ."

Starr shook her head, trying to clear it of sleepiness for a few moments longer. "Make no mind," she said to Mrs. Taylor. "I had to go. *You* didn't have to go. I should have brought her home with me and kept her here. But I didn't." She went upstairs then, and Caro followed.

Even the Taylors and Stats and Binders had to grow small in the paper to allow room for the violent death of Mrs. Louise Mayfield, ex-wife of local geologist. Starr's sleep was disturbed by the phone ringing repeatedly with the shocked condolences of Stats, Binders, and Taylors for the unfortunate publicity. From time to time she struggled awake from nightmare, calling to Louise; but she sank into the dark coils of sleep again and again.

When she awoke, she took the paper Miss Cinch had been reading, and steeled herself to read it. The house was a frozen silence. There was a poor flashbulb picture of herself and Jeff, faces a blur of shock. Mrs. Dashell Taylor was a witness to the early morning tragedy, the paper stated. Mrs. Taylor was the young widow of the late Dashell Taylor, son of Perry Taylor, prominent real-estate dealer and civic leader. She and Mr. Mayfield had seen the beautiful young Mrs. Mayfield fall into the canal, and had attempted to save her. Mrs. Mayfield had lately been in poor health, and had arrived in Statsville only the day before.

Starr held the paper and hated to go downstairs. It was like living in a dragon's lair, she thought. Then she reminded herself to be grateful. She read aloud to Caro, and she fed young Dashell. But eventually she had to go downstairs again. On an impulse, she rummaged in the boxes in the closet and brought out the picture of the wave. Caro patted the familiar picture, and Starr set it on a dresser; but it was no comfort, being alien there.

Well, it was only a few days until Christmas. That would allow her to escape for one day. Jeff might not want to be in the wedding party now, but he would be there, and that would make everything in the world all right for a few hours.

She took Caro's hand and went downstairs. Mrs. Taylor was prostrated, naturally. She called to Starr, who went to her.

"I didn't know you were already involved with a man," Mrs. Taylor said coldly. "The same one that woke us up when the baby was born."

"I've known Mr. Mayfield for several years," Starr said. "I had met Louise. I knew someone had to watch over her until he returned home."

"The paper says they were divorced."

"I believe so. But that didn't end his responsibility."

"Then why a divorce?" Mrs. Taylor asked. "What good was the publicity and legal action?"

"It's none of my business," Starr said pointedly.

"Then, dear child, why did you take it on yourself?" Mrs. Taylor asked, almost wildly. "With your name and picture in the paper, a scandal to us all. Everyone will presume an affair between you and this man...."

Starr caught one hand in the other to quiet them. "I apologize for your embarrassment," she said. "But even if I'd known what she would do, I still would have had to try to help her. I felt sorry for her." She stood up, agitated unbearably. She could see again the swift dark water and the round concrete trough. She could see the dark place under the bridge, where Jeff went ... where Louise went. ...

Mrs. Taylor went relentlessly on. "Surely you must realize—"

"It's done!" Starr said, her voice on edge. "No amount of talking can change it—it's done! She's dead! We couldn't help her. There are things you have to do—at least things I have to do! But I'll try to pay you back for what you've spent on us. I'll find a job tomorrow or the next day, no matter what the doctor says!"

She dreaded going to the table, but she was a nursing mother and must eat. She went, looking weary and thin but now composed.

Silence usually lay thick and almost visible at the table; but tonight Mrs. Taylor still pursued with questions. "You said something about a job?" she asked.

Mr. Taylor's lowered lids raised in question, but he said nothing.

"As soon as possible," Starr said.

"I suppose Dashell could remain comfortably where he is? You wouldn't owe us anything for him."

"He'll go where Caro and I go, of course," Starr said, bracing herself. "We're a family."

"For his sake, you might let us care for him! You have your little sister," Mrs. Taylor said. She even smiled. The unaccustomed smile was more terrifying than if she had made a dreadful face.

Starr spoke distinctly and slowly. "I shan't give up either Caro or Dashell," she said. "They're mine."

"But as the last of the Taylors, Dashell is entitled to—"

"What his mother can provide for him," Starr said, painfully, consciously polite. "Exactly the same as Caro."

"Are you being fair to the child? Don't you suppose he'll resent it some day?"

Starr put down her fork. She was no longer hungry. "No," she said. "Will you excuse me?" Going upstairs, she trembled all over with anger. Caro, following her wordlessly, stumbled on the stairs, and skinned a knee. She wept loudly, and Starr picked her up to comfort her.

"That child!" Mrs. Taylor said to Mr. Taylor. "So much noise!"

The next morning Starr went downtown and carefully looked for a job. In two hours she came back with a wry triumph. "I found a job," she told Mrs. Taylor, "but it doesn't begin until the first of the year. If you can wait another week, we can be out of your way then."

"Where will you go?" Mrs. Taylor asked, her old eyes hooded.

"I think I can afford a room and kitchenette somewhere, and a woman to mind the children," Starr said. "I'll be a long time paying you back—but I will, someday. Thank you for keeping us for so long."

"You're being a little hysterical and foolish, don't you think? Why leave this safe place? We haven't asked you to go."

Starr was silent for a while, trying to assemble tactful words, while being resentful of the question itself. "It has been kind of you not to ask," she finally said. "We won't wait until you do."

That left a frozen silence in the house once more, until the evening of the following day. A car's headlights turned into the driveway then, and the cane beat upon the floor downstairs. Starr buttoned the last button on Caro's sleepers and told her she would be back in a few moments.

"Now who can come bothering us at this time of night?" Mrs. Taylor was fretting. "Never, never any peace!"

Starr's heart lurched as she opened the door. Outside stood Jeff, Aunt Artie, Corny, and both of the Worthington children. They were burdened with bundles tied with bright ribbon. They shouted Merry Christmas, and Corny came inside carrying a small, fully decorated Christmas tree.

Jeff looked infinitely tired, but he came straight to Starr and kissed her. Her heart thudded with involuntary fear of being seen, and at the same time rejoiced at the sight of him.

Aunt Artie sailed past into the living room, where Mrs. Taylor reclined in disapproving silence. "We brought you some things," she said. She beckoned to Corny, who came in followed by his two small daughters. He set the Christmas tree down in what seemed a suitable corner, and turned and smiled at Mrs. Taylor.

"Oh, not so near the whatnot with that thing!" Mrs. Taylor said, rising slightly. "What *is* all this—who are these—"

"You remember my Aunt Artie," Starr said. "Mr. Worthington, his two daughters and my friend Jeff Mayfield."

Aunt Artie said, friendliness in every pore, "We thought how lonesome for you it would be on Christmas morning, waking up with your children all at our house, so we brought you some presents!"

[271]

Mrs. Taylor struggled wordlessly to her feet, studiously avoiding the glance of anyone in the room. She turned and walked out, down the hall, and closed the door of her bedroom behind her.

A painful silence lay in the living room. The guests stood awkwardly, holding the packages in their arms, and Starr's face flamed with embarrassment. "I'm sorry!" she said, her voice faltering. "I'm so sorry!"

Jeff was quickly at her side, one arm about her shoulders. "*You* needn't apologize!" he said fiercely. "It's probably a good thing! Go right now and get your things together. There *are* places where you're not only welcome—you're wanted!"

Still Starr stood there, shocked and ashamed. She noted that Perry Taylor was standing in the door to the hall. How long he had been there she could not guess. Perhaps he had seen it all. His face was serious beneath the triangle of his front hair, and his eyes were as sad as a spaniel's. "I'm the one to apologize," he said. "I'd go with them, if I were you. A person's entitled to some courtesy—to some consideration as a human being."

Starr went over and took his dry old hand in hers, and they stood silent a moment, remembering Dash; knowing that her going would take out of this home the little boy who might have made it endurable once more. "*You* take the presents," she said to Mr. Taylor.

He thanked her. It was no substitute for the boy; but he had great dignity at the moment. "I'll always be here," he said wryly. "You needn't ever want."

Jeff came to Starr's side. "We'll all help you pack and move, right now," he said. So she led toward the stairs.

"There won't be much packing," she said distractedly. "We never had closet space. Everything's still in boxes. Even the wave and the blue woman. . . ."

All the party carried boxes downstairs, and very quickly there was nothing left except the two children. Corny took the drowsy Caro, and Starr went to the splendid new nursery to get Dashell.

Miss Cinch stood between her and the crib. "You can't take this baby at this time of night, when he's sleeping."

Standing in the door, Jeff said, "Stand back, nurse, unless you'd like me to hold you back." He spoke quietly.

Miss Cinch ran to the top of the stairs. "Mr. Taylor!" she screamed down the stair well. "They're kidnaping the baby!"

Mr. Taylor's tired voice came very clearly upstairs. "It's her baby," he said. "I don't blame her a bit!"

Miss Cinch continued to guard the chest of drawers containing most of young Dashell's clothing, while Starr bundled him into the blankets from his crib and put him into Jeff's arms. Then she turned to Miss Cinch. "You better go look after Mrs. Taylor," she told her. "You might have a steady job there. She *needs* care."

Starr finally returned to the hall. She knocked on the door to the downstairs bedroom, but there was no reply. She turned to Mr. Taylor and told him good-by, once more holding his hand. Slow tears rose and stood in his eyes; he drew her to his chest and patted her. "It's all for the best, honey," he said. "It's all for the best for you and the baby."

She started for the door. She could hear Mr. Taylor instructing Miss Cinch to sit by the door to the bedroom until she was admitted. "I'm going out," he told her. "You just

[273]

sympathize with Mrs. Taylor and bring her jasmine tea—it'll be all she wants."

"When may I expect you back?" Miss Cinch asked.

"Not until you see me coming," Perry Taylor said. "I don't expect to meet any deadlines here, ever again."

Starr glanced back once more at the dark hall, the stairs climbing into shadows—at the sad house, the locked door. Aunt Artie stood at the front door. She went outside with her.

In the car, Jeff said, "My God, how did you live with that dragon?"

"How did I get away?" Starr asked, beginning to weep. "I felt like something caught in a soft web. Oh, Jeff! The poor old woman!"

Many hands made the cottage ready for Starr and Caro and the baby. Laughing and hospitable, Corny's relatives moved out to move Starr in, and were tactfully gone in a matter of minutes. They would double up, and make pallets in the big house if need be. The warmth of the family enfolded Starr. She began to put the baby to bed while Jeff was left to care for sleepy Caro. He drew her into his lap, and she looked up at him with trustful eyes and heavy lids.

"Do you suppose I could help you and Starr take care of the baby?" he asked Caro.

Caro nodded, going more limp every moment. Jeff smoothed the shining hair back from her face. He looked up and saw Starr in the door, and she motioned him to bring Caro to bed.

When Caro had been tucked in for the night, he followed Starr on tiptoe back to the living room. "When they're asleep, they surely get you where you live, don't they?" he asked, touched.

"You're not supposed to tiptoe," Starr said. She pulled what dignity she could muster about herself, determined to be fair and impersonal if she choked in the attempt. "When they're asleep, they always remind you of music and angels, and they melt your heart. But awake, they can be trying. Be sure before you commit yourself." She stood apart from him, straight, thin, and very serious.

He drew her quickly close. "I was committed a long time ago," he said. "I was committed on a hill covered with lupine, in a range of blue-shadowed mountains. There never was any turning back."

"Where do we go from here?" Starr asked, suddenly relaxed, leaning her head against him in blissful indifference.

"Tomorrow we get a license, so we can be married on Christmas Eve with Aunt Artie and Corny. Then we'll have a few days before I must leave for the new job. When I find a house, you can come."

Starr discovered a lump in one of his pockets. He took it out—a small box—and opened it. In it was the ring Dash had given her.

She remembered poignantly his worn suits and many small economies—and the beautiful clothes Louise had worn. Probably he hadn't even eaten enough for months. "You couldn't afford it!" she said.

"I thought probably the little guy would want it, someday. I got you another one." He brought a carved golden wedding ring from another pocket and put it on her finger. "Finally, finally!" he said, and she felt the long cold sweep of loneliness in the words. Looking into her face, he kissed the ring and the hand that wore it.

[275]

"You could do better," she said, putting her arms quickly around his neck. And he could; he did!

Presently they sat close beside each other and talked more intelligibly. "Where did you say we were going?" she asked. "Not that I care!"

"I'll work at a place in the wilds of Montana," he said. "We've been keeping the strike hushed up, but now that the news is out, it'll be hard to find a place to live. Oil, oil, and more oil, in a brushy canyon where it snows chin deep to a giraffe! Can you take snow?"

"We can if you can."

"Sounds like something from the wild, woolly west," Jeff said. "Place called Coyote Canyon."

"Would that be anywhere near Wild Horse Valley?"

"Do you know Wild Horse Valley?" he asked, surprised. "It's about twenty miles away, I think. I've been through it."

"Then you can commute. Oh, Jeff! We already have a place there! Just a little shack, but we can all go home together! I gave up Dash's ring to pay taxes there. He bought it to gamble on its future value. At first I couldn't find a buyer, and then I came to feel that it was a secret place to keep in case we had nowhere else to go . . . and I needed to know there was such a place, Jeff."

Jeff drew her closer. "Of course you did!" he said. "But Dash's judgment wasn't far wrong at that—if it was wrong at all! Still, all I can think of is the fact that there needn't be even one more parting for us! I admit I couldn't stand the thought of it!"

"Perhaps," Starr said slowly, "it wouldn't look right for us to marry so quickly after—"

"To hell with the looks of it!" Jeff said, laughing. "We've bent the knee to that old thing once too often! Life's for the loving, Starr—not for cowards or the dead."

He had more potent arguments than words; Starr ardently agreed with all of them. She moved in his arms and put her hands to his face, loving the very shape of it.

"Now what do you say?" he asked.

"That I love you—just the same old thing as always."

"You can think up variations on that for the next fifty years or so," he said approvingly. "The main idea's so absolutely sound!"